An Earlier Heaven

D.W. MARCHWELL

Dreamspinner Press

Published by
Dreamspinner Press
4760 Preston Road
Suite 244-149
Frisco, TX 75034
http://www.dreamspinnerpress.com/

An Earlier Heaven
Copyright © 2010 by D.W. Marchwell

Cover Design by Catt Ford

ISBN: 978-1-61581-639-2

Printed in the United States of America
First Edition
November, 2010

eBook edition available
eBook ISBN: 978-1-61581-640-8

To Candace, for her unwavering support and encouragement.

Chapter 1

WILLIAM BALDWIN MCKENZIE sat on the bottom step of the stairs outside of his new school waiting for David to come and pick him up. Soccer practice had been over for almost fifteen minutes, but David had still not arrived by the time William got tired of standing at the curb. *David's never late*, he told himself as he checked his watch, a digital watch, a birthday gift that his dad and David had given him. William looked up and down the street once more as his fingers played absentmindedly with the heavy-duty rubber strap of his new watch. *Not really that new anymore*, William thought; it was hard to believe that it had been three months already since the best birthday he'd ever had and almost a whole year since he'd arrived at the ranch.

He couldn't help but wonder what kind of adventures the three of them would have during spring break; it was only two weeks away. Even if they didn't do anything as special as what they'd done at Christmas, William would be happy to spend the days in the barn helping his dad or in the house helping David. He'd come home after his last day of school before Christmas break to the surprise that David and Jerry had planned for months, a trip to Switzerland. Not only had they been able to spend Christmas in Europe—which had always been William's favorite time of year when he'd been a student in Switzerland—but they'd also been able to stay until January 2, so they could all celebrate his eleventh birthday. And not just by themselves. He remembered how excited he'd been when Jerry and David had driven him to a beautiful house in Fribourg, a typical Swiss house with white stucco and wooden beams. William couldn't remember ever having been to Fribourg in all of his years at the boarding school in Lausanne, so he had no idea what his dad and David had planned. His curiosity grew even more when they insisted that he ring the bell while they waited a few feet behind him. He did as he was instructed, and when the door opened, he almost forgot to breathe.

Frau Zimmerman stood there, an apron around her ample waist and smelling like she'd been baking all day. He turned to look briefly at his dad and David, and seeing their smiling faces, launched himself into Frau Zimmerman's arms and tried not to cry as he heard her voice and felt the kisses to the top of his head for the first time in almost a year. How many times he'd thought about her and about when he could—or would—ever see her again. Even though they communicated sometimes via e-mail, William had lain awake so many nights wondering if she missed him as much as he missed her. But then Jerry wanted to be his dad, wanted to adopt him, and William found he didn't think of her quite so often. When he did, he would find himself smiling.

The rest of the evening seemed to pass in a blur, but he was quite sure that he'd heard Frau Zimmerman thank David, in German, over and over for having called her to arrange the visit. *I was so worried about William*, she explained in English when David pointed out that William's dad didn't speak German. William was so excited to see Frau Zimmerman again—never having expected it—that he'd found himself speaking German to her, only to hear David translating for Jerry. *This is your day, cowboy.* Jerry would smile whenever William apologized for rambling on in German. *You go ahead and speak German if you want.* William felt like his heart would burst, it was so full—a new dad, two new dads, who loved him enough to bring him back to see a woman who had always been so kind and loving toward him. William had fallen asleep that night convinced that he was the luckiest boy in the world. Within a few months he'd gone from being alone, not wanted by anyone, to having two dads who wanted him more than anything else.

A noise off in the distance brought him back to the present. He stood up as he saw a car coming down the road, his hands finding their way to his side to grab his bag, his heart racing at the memory of eating Schweinsbraten, Weinzenbier, and knodel, foods William had never thought he would eat again when he left Switzerland for Canada. But then he had no idea that he would meet David, let alone that David would become one of his two dads. As the car approached, he sat back down on the step; the car was red, but wasn't David's.

"Hey, Billiam!"

William jumped a little, having thought he was all alone out here, and turned at the sound of the nickname that only one person used. "Hi, Cory." William scooted over on the step, his smile broad and sincere. He liked Cory, a high school boy who was volunteering as the soccer coach's assistant. Even though William was only in sixth grade, Cory—who was in the tenth grade—always found time to talk to him and the other members of the soccer team. William hadn't been all that confident that he would make the team, but Cory had been really patient with him, showing him some tips and tricks to compensate for his small size. It had been Cory, in fact, who had shown William that being smaller than some of the other boys could be used to the team's advantage. It may have been only a month or so since William had made the team, but he could still depend on Cory to stay a few extra minutes after practice to help him improve his skills.

"Parents forget you?"

"I don't know." William looked at his watch again. "David's never this late."

"You call your dad *David*?" Cory finally took the seat beside William. "My dad would kill me if I called him by his first name."

"David's not my real dad," William started.

"Oh, I get it." Cory nodded as if he understood. "Stepdad, huh?"

"No." William looked over and smiled. Jerry and David had explained to him that not everyone would understand, but he was pretty sure that Cory would be okay with his having two dads. "David's married to my dad, Jerry. Jerry adopted me after my parents died." William saw Cory's head turn and study his expression for a moment.

"I'm sorry about your parents, Billiam, but it's cool that you've got two dads," Cory offered after a brief smile. "I have a cousin who's a lesbian. She lives in Ireland, I think."

"Cool," William echoed. He looked both ways down the street, checking to see if he recognized any of the cars that might be approaching. When he saw nothing, he turned to Cory. "What about you? Are you waiting to be picked up?"

"Me? No." Cory shook his head to emphasize the point. "I usually hang out here and kick the ball around for a little while before I bike home, or I go over to my mom's work and wait for her to finish so I can walk home with her."

"Where does she work?"

"She works over at the grocery store, just over there." Cory pointed to the other side of the main thoroughfare that separated the middle school and the large outdoor mall complex that housed a large supermarket and a few lesser-known retail outlets. "I'm going over there to meet her in about twenty minutes."

William nodded. "Hey, thanks for showing me those new tricks today." He pointed off to the large field beside the school. "I would never have made the team without your help."

"Anytime, sport." Cory draped an arm over William's shoulders and offered a sincere smile. "You may not be able to tell now, but I used to be smaller too."

"Really?" William's eyes widened in disbelief. "But you're so tall now."

"No lie, man." Cory nodded for emphasis. "You'll see. One day you'll wake up and you'll wonder why the ground looks so far away."

"I don't know. My dad says that I may not get to be very tall."

"Maybe, maybe not." Cory shrugged and looked down the road and back at William. Cory pointed to the pickup truck coming down the road. "Is that your ride?"

William looked, studied the pickup, and recognized his dad's beat-up two-toned truck. "Yeah, that's my dad." He pushed himself off the stairs and waited until the truck neared the curb. Cory followed suit and stood with William until the truck stopped parallel to where they were standing.

4

"HEY, chief," Jerry yelled as he came around to the passenger side of his truck. "Sorry I'm late, but David just told me…" Jerry turned to look at Cory. "Jerry McKenzie, William's father. Thank you for waiting with William. I'm sorry if you missed anything while you waited for me."

"I'm Cory." Jerry noticed the firm handshake and that Cory was only about two or three inches shorter than he was. "It was no bother, really. William's a great kid."

"Cory?" Jerry let go of the young man's hand and looked over at his son. "Cory who's been helping William, who helped him make the team? That Cory?" Jerry looked from the young man to William, who was beaming from ear to ear. Jerry smiled at the slight blush that crept across Cory's face. "Man, I can't thank you enough for working with him like that. He hasn't stopped talking about you for weeks. Do you need a ride?"

"No," William answered. "He has his bike and his mom works just over there." He turned to indicate the supermarket across from the school. "He showed me some more moves today." William stepped closer to his dad, his hand reaching out to grasp the tail of Jerry's denim shirt. "Hey, can we have Cory over to ride the horses sometime?"

Jerry pondered this for a moment. *We're hardly ever home anymore*, he thought before nodding. "Sure," he said with a smile at his son. "We can do it this Friday, if that's okay with you, Cory?" Jerry stole a glance at his son, delighting in the big smile and the happy, but anxious way his son was studying this young man.

"I, uh," Cory stammered. "This Friday's not really good. My mom will be working, and I have to be home when my dad gets home from work when she's not there, and…."

"No problem," Jerry said and put a big hand on his son's shoulder. He guided William to the truck. "If we can't find a good time, maybe we'll just have to have you and your parents over." Jerry laughed at his own joke, but stopped when he was caught off guard by Cory's reaction.

"*No!*" Cory put out his hand, as if he knew he were about to fall into a hole from which he would never possibly escape. "I mean, they don't like to socialize much. And they're real tired by the end of the week and all." Cory took a deep breath and stuffed his hands in his pockets. Taking one out quickly, he turned to William and offered a closed fist. "I'll see you soon, right, Billiam?"

"Right." William smiled and bumped his fist against Cory's. "Bye, Cory."

Jerry was pretty sure there was more to this story, but he told Cory he understood and got into the truck, looking over quickly to make sure William was buckled up properly. When he had the truck in gear and moving toward the intersection, he turned to study his son. "So, Billiam?"

"It's what Cory calls me. He asked me if anyone ever called me anything other than William." He shrugged when he looked up at his dad. "He told me I was like a forty-year-old in a kid's body because I'm always so serious all the time."

"Well, Cory seems really nice. And he obviously thinks you're the greatest thing since sliced bread."

William laughed a little nervously. "That's such a weird expression."

"Better than 'He thinks you're the bee's knees'."

William laughed a little louder this time. "Bees don't have knees."

"How do you know?" Jerry reached over and gently squeezed his son's knee. "And I can see how much you admire him, partner. I'm happy there was someone who could help you make the team."

"Yeah," William agreed with a little sigh. "Dad?"

"Yeah?"

"When people lie to you, are they doing it because they don't like you enough to tell you the truth?"

"Uh, not always." Jerry rubbed his two-day growth of beard as he looked over at his son. William was looking out the window, his face a study of indecision. "Why? Is someone lying to you?"

"I don't know." William looked over at him. "I think Cory's hiding something."

"What makes you say that, chief?" Jerry glanced at his watch. David's instructions had been very clear: pick up William and stall for at least thirty minutes. "Hmm," Jerry said thoughtfully as they approached the Dutch Maid. "I don't know about you, but I always think better when I'm eating ice cream."

"You'll spoil your dinner."

"So we'll get small cones." Jerry smiled and looked over at his son; William looked as if he were working all of this out in his head and arriving at an unhappy realization. Jerry wanted to stop the truck and hug him, hoping he would never grow up and have to face some of the disappointing facts of life. There will be people that lie to you, treat you badly, and some might even try to hurt you on purpose just because of who you are or what you believe.

"No," William urged, "David won't like that."

"Nah," Jerry muttered as he shook his head. "Not if we bring him one."

"Vanilla!" William wrinkled his nose. Neither of David's men understood how he could possibly like plain vanilla ice cream. No sprinkles, no chocolate sauce, nothing but vanilla ice cream. They'd both managed to turn David on to ice cream sandwiches, but that was about as daring as he'd ever gotten.

"I know," Jerry sighed, as if it was an answer that father and son had shared enough times to negate the need for any further explanation. "Come on, sport, let's see how many sprinkles you can pile on today." Jerry pushed open the door and let his hand rest on William's head as they passed through the second set of doors and into the cool, sweet air of the ice cream shop.

William announced his usual to the petite blonde girl behind the counter and turned to look up at his father, smiling when he felt the big hand come to rest on his shoulder. Jerry ordered a small cone with a single scoop of chocolate ice cream and chocolate sauce and looked down at William, offering a knowing smile. Jerry had almost gotten accustomed to the ribbing that William and David gave him about his inability to stay away from anything chocolate, and he was getting better at resisting the urge to indulge that particular vice. Of course, it was easy to resist when David always promised him something better when their son was fast asleep in his own room. Who would be fool enough to choose chocolate over that?

"Okay, partner, you go find us a table, and I'll bring the cones." Jerry smoothed his hand over his son's soft blond hair, his chest tightening a little when he saw William smile and nod. He continued to watch, partly out of fascination with where his life was now as compared to a year ago and partly because he still found himself worrying about William. Not just the height and the small, too-slim frame, but that he still seemed to have only a few friends, and part-time friends it would seem. Jerry couldn't really remember the last time William had been to someone's birthday party—one that hadn't involved some of David's colleagues or Lenore's twins. He'd thought that by this point in middle school, William would have been able to make more friends.

He'd hesitated to say too much, especially in front of David, after he'd made the mistake of wondering—out loud, late one evening—if William was still suffering the effects of the Bennett Brigade's efforts to dictate everyone else's morality. Sometimes when Jerry thought of how Bennett Thiry had taken it upon himself to try to have David removed from his position as a teacher, he still felt the panic at having almost lost the family he now cherished more than anything. David had almost let Bennett and his brigade win, but in the end, he couldn't bring himself to acquiesce to the intimidation. Jerry felt the raw emotion of that night when he learned David had not given up fighting after all, the night when he'd vowed never to be without David or William again. Perhaps this was one of the reasons he was so concerned now; after all, it was his responsibility to keep his family happy, wasn't it?

There was no doubt in Jerry's mind that William was full of love and compassion, and he probably had Frau Zimmerman to thank for that. Jerry was sure that his son would grow to be the smartest, bravest man of any he'd met in his life. But there was still this annoying voice in the back of Jerry's brain that told him that he wasn't doing enough for his son.

He turned when the petite blonde girl announced that his orders were ready, and he took the cardboard tray from her. After asking for a small empty cup, he stood at the little counter with sprinkles, scooped some into the cup, and headed to sit with his son.

"Okay," he sighed as he lowered himself onto the chair. "So what makes you think that Cory is hiding something?"

William thanked his father for the ice cream and studied the spoon and the cup of sprinkles for a moment, finally deciding to invert the cone into the sprinkles. "He always seems to be alone."

"What do you mean?"

"Like tonight," William said through a mouthful of sprinkles and ice cream. "Even Mr. Lapis, the soccer coach, was gone, but Cory was still there. Why didn't he go home? Or meet up with some of his friends afterwards?"

"Maybe he doesn't have a lot of friends."

"Maybe," William said as he shrugged. "I never hear him talk about his friends or even himself." William licked some of the sprinkles from his ice cream and wiped at his chin when some of them managed to escape. "All the other kids around his age, like the grade eight kids at my school, all they talk about is themselves and what they're doing and how they go out and drink and party—"

"You mean...." Jerry gasped and then took a breath before looking around the almost empty Dutch Maid. "There are kids in grade eight who are drinking and... stuff?"

"Sure," William said as he licked his lips.

"Sure?" Jerry suddenly lost his appetite and couldn't help the growing ball of tension in his stomach at how easily his son seemed to accept the fact that twelve-year-olds were drinking and partying and doing who knew what else. "Do... have you... I mean, have any—"

"Relax, Dad," William interrupted and took a bite of his cone. "That's not what I want. I'd rather ride my horse and help you and David on the ranch."

"I wasn't worried," Jerry protested, but knew from the look on his son's face that he'd been caught. He looked at his watch. Forty-five minutes and a near-coronary. *That should be enough time for David to have done everything he needs to do*, Jerry thought as he thanked William for collecting the trash.

He made a mental note, as he followed his boy out to the truck, to speak to David about this drinking and partying thing; surely David would know more about it. *Maybe I'll ask him if there is any more stuff like this I should know about.*

Chapter 2

DAVID sat back in the chair, which was far too small for him, and stared at the screen. Jerry had left only ten minutes ago and the installation was almost complete. *At this rate*, he thought somewhat smugly, *I'll have William's surprise set up and dinner finished with enough time left over to get Jerry's surprise ready for later tonight.* When the little bell chimed on the iMac screen, David found himself wondering why he'd never made this switch from PCs sooner and how much time he'd actually wasted struggling with those annoying machines. He'd never really found himself thinking about the Apple versus PC debate except for those moments when he would lose documents or his PC at work had to undergo yet another update to prevent malware or spyware or whatever-ware. Or those moments when he would be kicked out of a program with that annoying pop-up message asking if he wanted to report the error.

He'd only thought seriously about it when William came home to report that he had made the soccer team, and then again when he and Jerry had attended the first game of the season only to see him score two goals. *Is it called a goal in soccer, or is there a special name, like touchdowns in football?* David frowned as he hooked up the modem with the cable line that Jerry had had to run up from his office downstairs a couple of days ago while David kept William busy in the barn. He clicked on the Safari icon and watched the screen come to life. It was later that night, after William's first goals, that David had suggested that they get William his own computer. William had never fussed about having to share the one in Jerry's office, but David also knew that he would need one of his own very soon. Middle school and then high school after that would definitely mean that William would be inundated with the need to do research, type papers, learn spreadsheets, and even learn about multimedia presentations. And David also knew that William was more accustomed to working on Macs, so the decision had been a relatively easy one. And David was glad that he'd had the chance to do all of the setup, because he would be replacing Jerry's office computer with another one of these very soon.

After another couple of clicks here and there—everything seemed quite intuitive—David had the photos uploaded from the memory card and, after another few clicks, had the screen saver set to random, and sat back to watch the parade of photos that he and Jerry and William had taken during their extended Christmas vacation in Switzerland. There were photos of William, his face covered in flour, as he tried to help Frau Zimmerman with the cookies and cakes that Jerry hadn't been able to get enough of. There were photos of William sitting beside a very happy Frau Zimmerman as she opened the Kitchen Aid mixer that he'd picked out especially for her. Of course, he'd been under the assumption then that they would be sending it to her through the mail or through a courier service. He'd never dreamed that Jerry and David had been planning to bring it with them all along. Neither Jerry nor David had been terribly certain that she would be happy with kitchen appliances, but William assured them both that she'd mentioned wanting one for as long as he could remember, and here was the proof on the new computer screen.

It wasn't hard for David to fall in love with Frau Zimmerman during their short visit; she was so kind and caring. He cringed many times when William kept on providing her the details of how he'd come to end up with two dads instead of just Jerry, but to her credit, she never once said anything that wasn't supportive. *I'm just so happy that William finally has people who care as much about him as I do*, she would say over and over again in German.

They'd spent almost an entire day with her, and David understood how William could be so sad when they had to leave; he hadn't wanted to leave either. In many ways, Frau Zimmerman reminded David of his grandmother, the one he'd spent so much time with before she passed away, leaving him with no one and no family. But with promises to return—maybe during summer vacation—Jerry had carried an exhausted little boy to the rental car, and David had found himself hesitating at the door. He'd wanted so badly to ask her if they could bring her to Canada, but he knew that that would have been inappropriate; she had a life, her own family, there in Switzerland.

When the screen went black, the computer having gone to sleep, David sighed with the happy memories and ran down to the kitchen to ensure that dinner would be ready for his men when they arrived home. He checked the Wienerschnitzel, the carrots, the potatoes, and finally the bread, which was taking a little longer to bake than he'd anticipated. He turned the knob on the oven up a couple of degrees, and then checked the Sachertorte in the fridge. *Perfect*, he thought with a smile, *everything is perfect*. And it was.

He was half-way up the stairs when he heard the familiar crunch of gravel beneath the tires of Jerry's old pickup truck. Glancing at his watch, he wondered how he'd lost track of time so easily. Indecision kept him glued to the middle step for a few seconds before he realized that he would have to ready Jerry's surprise later; perhaps while the two of them ate dessert he could sneak away.

He waited just inside the door, prepared to give his men a warm welcome home, but when they came through the door, David could tell by the look on Jerry's face that something was off. Jerry didn't get that look very often, but when he did, it usually had something to do with William. He wondered if perhaps William had had another bad practice, more frustrations over his small size. If that was the case again, David would have to raise the issue of pulling William off the team until he grew a little bit more.

Despair creeped in a little bit, and David wanted to ask right away what the problem was. Instead, he took William's sports bag. "How was practice?"

"Great," William announced with a bright smile. "Cory showed me some more moves. I scored two goals during practice." *Goals! No, no special word*, David thought, wondering why basic sports

13

information went through his brain faster than water through a sieve. "And Dad took me for some ice cream." David turned to Jerry, his eyebrow raised.

"It was a small one." Jerry shrugged and leaned in for a kiss.

"With how many sprinkles?" David mumbled after he obliged his husband with a quick kiss.

"Not that many." Jerry reached into the breast pocket of his work shirt and pulled out an ice cream sandwich. "This is for you." Jerry offered his best smile, and David couldn't help but chuckle. "You might want to put it in the freezer for a few hours."

"No way," David laughed and sneaked up behind William, tickling him under the arms for a few seconds. "I still remember what happened the last time you two brought me ice cream and I put it in the freezer."

"That was his idea." William giggled and backed up against the fridge door to get away from any more tickling.

"Turncoat!" Jerry reached out a hand and placed it—claw-like—on William's head. "Can't believe you'd throw me under the wheels like that."

"It was!" William insisted and then disappeared into the downstairs bathroom to wash his hands.

"So," David turned to lean into his lover once William was out of sight. "What was that look for when you were coming through the door? Practice not go well?"

"No, nothing like that. Even met Cory." Jerry turned around to check that he was alone with David. "William said something about grade eight kids drinking and partying and doing other stuff. Is that true?"

David sighed and brought his hand up to smooth the worry away from his husband's face. "I'm afraid so," David sighed again, "and it seems to be getting worse each year."

"Grade eight?"

"That's nothing." David pulled away from Jerry's warm body and grabbed the oven mitts. "I've heard from some of the other teachers at the elementary that some of the students there are beginning to smoke and drink as young as grade four."

"Jesus!" Jerry's voice was hushed, but both he and David looked toward the entrance anyway.

"You don't think that William…?" David turned to look at Jerry and had to fight the urge to laugh out loud. David wondered if Jerry honestly thought William would do that. "Listen, baby, William is not that kind of kid. He's got both of us, and I know we're not going to let anything like that happen."

"I wonder how many parents of addicts said the same thing."

David put the hot dish on the trivet in the center of the kitchen table and reached in for the baked potatoes. "And how many of them had frank discussions with their kids like we do with William… about everything?" David pulled out the last potato and let it fall out of his covered hand onto the plate alongside the other potatoes. "Besides, you've heard him talk about how he wants to be a veterinarian and work with horses." David tossed the gloves onto the counter and sidled up to his husband. "Call it intuition, but I don't think William would do anything to prevent his being around those horses he loves so much."

"Funny," Jerry smiled and stole another kiss. "But William said something like that too."

David pulled back a little, trying not to look concerned. "What exactly did you ask him?"

"If he'd ever… you know…."

"There, you see!" David rubbed at Jerry's muscular chest. "You're already doing the right thing."

"I am?"

David wrapped his arms around Jerry's waist and let his lips trace a path up the strong neck to his lover's mouth. "I love you. And for what it's worth, I think you're an incredible father."

"I love you, too, baby." Jerry brought his hands up to cradle David's face as he stole another kiss. "And thank you. But I still think there's a lot for me to learn."

"I can help you with that." David let his hands fall to Jerry's butt, his fingers working their way into the back pockets. "I'm available later on this evening for some private tutoring." David noticed Jerry open his mouth, but then close it, as they both heard the footsteps approach the kitchen.

"What's for dinner?" William pulled out his chair and sat down.

"Well, let's see." David pulled the lids off several dishes and let William peer inside. "There's Wienerschnitzel, carrots, baked potatoes with butter just the way you like them, and even Brussels sprouts. And for dessert, Sachertorte."

"Those are all my favorites!" William announced, as if neither of the men knew. "But it's not my birthday." William looked from David to Jerry.

"We know that," Jerry laughed, delighted that he and David had pulled off the surprise. "We just wanted to do something special for you in honor of your making the soccer team and for being such a good boy… young man, I mean."

"We're very proud of you, William."

William looked again from David to his father. "I didn't do anything special. It was Cory who helped me make the team."

"Just the same, we love you, cowboy, and we're very proud of you." Jerry and David sat at the same time. "Maybe we can do the same for Cory someday, you know, as a way to say thanks?"

"And I could show him the horses?"

"Sure thing, partner."

"Maybe I could call his parents and invite them all over?" David raised himself out of his chair and retrieved the basket of bread from the microwave. "Do you know Cory's last name?"

"I think it starts with an F," William offered as he started loading his plate with some carrots. "But I do know that his mom works at Sobey's across the street from my school."

"Okay, then," David announced as he accepted the carrots from William. "You leave it to me, and I'll see what I can find out."

"Oh," William interjected when Jerry placed one of the breaded veal cutlets on his son's plate. "And I love you both too."

DAVID stood outside William's room, the door closed, and waited for William and Jerry to finish loading the dishwasher. He'd not had a chance to sneak away and prepare Jerry's surprise, but that would just have to wait for another day. He couldn't wait to see the look on William's face when the little guy saw his very own computer. He was positively vibrating with excitement when he heard his two men coming up the stairs. David made a mental note to surprise Jerry tomorrow night, when William was fast asleep.

"We have one more surprise for you, cowboy."

David smiled and stepped away from the door. "I hope you don't mind, but I had to go in your room to set it up." He motioned toward the door. "Go on in and see for yourself."

"A dog?" William's eyes got very wide as he twisted the handle on his bedroom door. "You're finally going to let me have a dog?"

"Uh… well, no, it's not a dog," Jerry offered, as he looked over at the equally confused expression on his husband's face. "But now that we know that's on the list, we'll see what we can do."

"Dad," William sighed, his tone full of exasperation. "I've only asked you for a dog like… a million times."

"That many, huh?" David smiled at Jerry and then turned back to William. "If you don't open that door, I'm going to."

David watched as William finally pushed open the door. He wasn't sure if William had noticed the new computer at first, but then the little guy's head swiveled toward his father and then toward David, his mouth agog and his eyes almost as brilliant and wide as the computer screen.

"So you like it?" Jerry laughed as William's arms wrapped—or tried to wrap around—his father's waist. David noticed that William was definitely getting taller, his head coming to rest at least two inches above Jerry's navel.

"I love you, Dad," William gushed after a few moments. Then, turning to hug David, "And you, too, David." William let go of David's waist and turned to the computer, his words slow and soft. "My very own computer."

"All yours," David confirmed and moved closer to the computer. "Why don't you come over here and hit a key." He watched as William took a seat at his desk and hit the space key, the images of Frau Zimmerman and the day they'd spent with her coming to life in a slow slideshow.

"It was David's idea." David heard Jerry's voice behind him and felt his hands come to rest on his shoulders.

"Thank you, thank you, so much, David." William was out of his chair and hugging David again.

"You're very welcome, William." He let go of the little body again and leaned back against his husband. "Now you won't have to worry about me or your dad hogging the one downstairs."

"It even has a built-in cam." William sat down in his chair again and his hands came out to trace over the screen. "I'm going to send Frau Zimmerman an e-mail right away and maybe send her a picture of my new computer."

"I sent her copies of the photos from our trip already," David explained, "and told her about your new present. She sent me a message explaining that she would get her son to help her set up a camera so you two can talk and see each other at the same time."

"Then I'm going to send Opa Niels an e-mail with a picture."

David glanced at Jerry for a moment, knowing that Jerry might not be particularly fond of the idea. Jerry had made his feelings about

David's father quite clear on more than one occasion. It was one of the few things that David and Jerry argued about from time to time. Jerry still didn't trust Niels, even though he'd never been given any cause for concern.

"I think he'd like that, cowboy."

In the end, Jerry and David had always been able to agree that whatever their differences, they weren't about to deprive William of a grandfather. It was difficult enough having to explain why Niels visited but not any other member of David's family. David's heart fairly broke sometimes when he thought of William having cousins that he'd probably never meet.

"May I stay up past my bedtime? Just this once, I mean?"

"I think that would be okay, but we'll check with your dad first." David turned to Jerry who nodded.

"One hour past your bedtime, then it's lights out." Jerry backed up toward the door, pulling David along with him. "And I don't want you filling up the hard drive with those violent video games. You play those downstairs on the TV like usual, okay?"

David noted that William's attention was fully on the screen now, his little hands working the keyboard and the mouse frantically, as if he'd been without a computer for far too long. Jerry repeated himself, and William turned and nodded, insisting that he'd heard his dad the first time.

David and Jerry now found themselves on the other side of the half-open door. "You realize, of course, that we're going to get the 'just five more minutes' thing again, just as we did with the cell phone. You know that, right?" Jerry's voice was a mere whisper, but still filled with a weary anticipation of things to come.

"I'll take that bet." David led Jerry to their bedroom. "And if I win, I know what my prize will be."

"Sometimes I think I take these bets just so I can be the loser." Jerry slapped David's ass as they quickened their pace and closed the door behind them.

Chapter 3

"I WIN again." Jerry held up the game controller in his hand and imitated the roar of a crowd while he bowed his head over and over.

"I like playing with David better; he doesn't cheat." William jabbed his father in the ribs and tried to run away, but Jerry caught him by the tail of his pajama shirt and pulled him onto his lap.

"What was that?" Jerry let his big hand hover over his son's belly, ready to unleash the tickle monster. "Did you just call me a cheater?"

"No," William giggled and clasped both of his hands around his father's wrist in a vain attempt to forestall the inevitable. "I think you need to have your ears checked."

"Oh, no," Jerry whispered while he looked at his hovering hand. "Now you've upset it. You know it doesn't like it when you say things like that."

"I'm sorry, I'm sorry," William pleaded as he pushed as hard as he could on the hand that was descending toward his stomach.

Jerry felt the hands on his shoulders and tried to stay sitting cross-legged, but before he knew what was happening, he was flat on his back watching David and William trying to hold him down, both of them giggling as if they thought they'd gotten the better of him.

"Should we show him what happens to cheaters?" David asked as he looked over at William.

"Not the mark of the cheater!" Jerry pretended to be afraid.

"Yeah," William squealed in delight, pushing Jerry's T-shirt up a few inches so that he could place a couple of quick slaps against the skin of his father's stomach. "The mark of the cheater!"

"Oh, please, kind sirs, I promise never to cheat again." Jerry wriggled and pleaded, but to no avail.

"Dad, your tummy's getting jiggly like J-ELLO."

"What?" Jerry lifted his head and craned his neck to see the red palm prints. "I'm not fat!"

"That's what happens when you eat two desserts every night." David clucked his tongue and held up two fingers.

"Whose side are you on?" When he was free, Jerry sat up, then stood, lifting his T-shirt and trying his best not to look as if he was sucking in his gut. "See? Must have just been because I was lying down."

"I don't know," David sighed and looked over at William. "What do you think William? Do you think your dad eats too many desserts?"

"Not enough exercise." William stated matter-of-factly as he walked over and hugged his dad. "We still love you."

"Thank you, William." Jerry brushed his hand over William's blond buzz cut. "Okay, so are you ready to get some sleep? We've got a big day tomorrow cleaning the barn and fixing some of those fence posts." He narrowed his eyes and looked at David. "And apparently I've got some exercising to do." Jerry watched, only slightly amused, as David threw up his hands as if to say, *What did I do?*

"And then we can go for a picnic by the lake?" William asked as he climbed the stairs ahead of David and Jerry.

"Maybe for dinner," Jerry responded. "I don't know that we'll be done with everything by noon. Maybe by two or three in the afternoon."

"And if not tomorrow, we'll be sure to go on Sunday," David said and turned to Jerry. "I'll check to make sure everything's locked up."

Jerry glowered at David, delighting in the confused expression on his lover's face. "I'm not speaking to you."

David's laughter filled the stairwell. "Big baby," he muttered and headed to check the windows and doors.

Jerry followed William into his bedroom and waited for his son to crawl into bed. As he pulled the covers up to William's chin, he nodded toward the computer. "Did you get a chance to send off the e-mails you wanted?"

"Uh huh," William grunted as he pulled his arms out and let them fall by his sides, on top of the duvet. "It took me a while to remember how to do the German accents, but I figured it out." William squinted at Jerry and then asked, "How many hours ahead in Switzerland?"

"If memory serves, cowboy, they're eight hours ahead of us."

"So then maybe I'll have an e-mail when I wake up." William turned on his side and pulled his little fists up under his chin.

"Maybe." Jerry leaned down and kissed his son's forehead. "Sweet dreams, cowboy. I love you."

"I love you, too, Dad."

"And I love both of you." David braced himself with one hand on Jerry's knee as he leaned down and kissed William's forehead. "Sweet dreams, William."

"G'night." William's eyes closed as he let go of a big yawn. "Hey, Dad?"

"What is it, chief?" Jerry turned to see William's sleepy eyes looking at him.

"Do you think that I could invite Cory out after practice sometime next week?"

"Of course you can." Jerry offered a smile and turned toward the door, almost reaching it before turning back to look at William. "Do you know if he can ride?"

"Dunno. I'll ask him on Monday."

"Don't let the bedbugs bite." Jerry flipped the light switch and stepped through the door, leaning against it once it was closed.

Jerry was still smiling when he reached the bedroom that he shared with David, his mind still not quite able to grasp sometimes that William would be in his life—and David would be in his life—forever.

It was all a little overwhelming sometimes when he realized that he still had so much to learn. Like today's discovery that William was around kids who would be tempting him with alcohol and drugs. *How do parents do this when they have three or four kids?*

He found David in the bathroom, already in the shower. He stripped quickly, letting his jeans and T-shirt fall in a pile beside the laundry hamper and reached out for the shower curtain, noticing his profile in the mirror. He squared his shoulders and brought his hands to his belly, wondering if he'd actually put on that much weight. *My clothes still fit; they're not getting tight or anything.*

He laughed at how silly he was being. His hairline was receding, and he was noticing that his arms weren't long enough to read the paper anymore, but neither of those bothered him as much as the thought that he might not be as trim and fit as he used to be. As he pulled back the shower curtain, he decided to start fixing this particular problem tomorrow. David was keeping trim and fit and sexy as hell, so the least he could do was keep up with his husband.

He reached out with his hands and caressed the soft skin of David's back, smiling mischievously as he brought his hands around to the smaller man's chest and stomach and pulled their bodies together, his cock already filling in anticipation.

"I thought you weren't speaking to me." David turned himself around in Jerry's arms, his hands moving slowly to the cleft of his husband's ass.

"Who said anything about talking?" Jerry waggled his eyebrows and brought their mouths together. He kissed David gently at first, his tongue darting out to tease and lick at the delicate skin of those full lips. He brought one hand up to cradle the back of his lover's skull as his tongue went further into David's mouth, his senses assaulted by the heat from the water and from their two tongues moving against each other.

He moaned and broke the kiss when he felt David take hold of both of their cocks and stroke them gently from root to tip. His head fell back as David's long, slender fingers pinched and rolled his foreskin ever so gently. "Oh, David, yeah," Jerry whispered, his eyes closed and his head reeling from the sensation. He felt their bodies slide together as David moved to his knees, taking the foreskin between his teeth and biting gently. Jerry had learned over the past several months that he never needed to ask for anything. David always seemed to know exactly what he wanted.

"Oh, sweet Jesus," Jerry grunted as he felt David's fingers slide between his cheeks and tap playfully at his hole. "Need to stop, baby. Wanna make love to you. In bed."

Jerry felt their bodies sliding against one another again as David stood slowly. He wrapped his arms around the smaller man and took his time kissing and tasting his lover's mouth. He squeezed David's body against his own for a moment while his tongue traced a lazy trail from the pouty mouth to an ear. He'd never experienced anything like the feeling he got when he kissed and licked at David's ears; he felt like some sort of god, an all-powerful god who could reduce his beautiful husband to incoherent grunts and moans just by sucking on an earlobe or whispering nonsense into these ears.

So incredibly aroused by the sight of his panting and flushed lover, Jerry pulled away and turned off the water. Pulling back the shower curtain, he led David to the bed, their bodies still dripping. Jerry sat on the edge of the bed and brought David to his lap. Sparing a moment to reach and open the drawer of the nightstand in order to have the lube handy, Jerry then wrapped both of his arms around his lover's trim waist and lowered both of their bodies to the mattress. With David still pressed against his chest and stomach, Jerry pushed David's hips up and forward, his engorged cock finding its target right away.

David moaned and Jerry did it again and again, slowly, knowing that it would drive David crazy. After a few moments of teasing his lover's entrance, Jerry reached for the lube and slicked himself, then breached David with first one finger and then two. "Like that?" Jerry asked through a knowing smile as he pushed his fingers farther and farther into his lover. "Nothing better than how you look when I fuck you, mountain lion."

"Oh, Jerry, baby, I'm ready."

Jerry let go and watched as David raised himself to a sitting position and lowered himself onto Jerry's engorged cock. It had been only a month or so since they'd stopped using condoms, both of them having had negative test results for everything they could think of, but Jerry was still enraptured by the thought that nothing separated them anymore; it was skin against skin now, nothing in the way. Jerry shut his eyes and let his hands rest on David's thighs as the contractions pulled and caressed his dick. "So fucking amazing, baby."

"Oh, Jerry, baby," David panted as his hands came to rest on either side of Jerry's head. "Kiss me."

Jerry did as he was told, knowing how much David loved to kiss as he was being fucked. As David leaned forward, the wet locks of hair dripping moisture, Jerry brought his feet up and braced them on the edge of the bed. Then, with his hands kneading and massaging his lover's cheeks, Jerry began to increase his rhythm, his buttocks clenching as he pushed up and into David's heat. He let his mouth and tongue match the intensity of his husband's kisses, and soon they were both panting and writhing and moaning the other's name.

When his thighs started to ache, Jerry slowed down and holding one hand at the small of David's back, moved their bodies so that David was now on his back and Jerry was braced above him. He reached behind him and took hold of his lover's ankles, bringing first one and then the other to rest on his shoulders. As he straightened his legs out behind him, Jerry heard David gasp and felt his lover's hands squeeze his triceps. Jerry knew full well what this meant; this was the position they'd discovered only a few months ago that allowed Jerry to hit David's prostate with every thrust. It was also one of the few positions that they'd tried where Jerry was able to make David come without either of them touching his dick.

"You ready, baby?" Jerry waited for the familiar panting and the breathless pleading, but all he could see was David rolling his head from side to side. His body prone as if he were about to do push ups,

Jerry began slowly, his movements eliciting more panting and begging from the flushed man underneath him.

"Yes, right there," David panted. "I'm gonna come, baby."

Jerry felt the vise-like contraction and then heard the sharp intake of breath. "So beautiful, baby, so fucking unbelievable." Jerry continued to thrust slowly, his own orgasm building quickly as he watched the waves of David's orgasm. Jerry increased his speed slightly, knowing that he would not be able to last much longer. And when David reached up and began to massage his balls, Jerry drew in a sharp breath of his own and let go completely, grunting almost soundlessly as he emptied himself into his lover.

"Never get tired of that." David reached up and stroked the sides of his husband's face as Jerry lowered himself to lie beside the satiated body of his lover.

"Not too bad for a fat man, huh?" Jerry wrapped his arms around David and pulled him closer.

David let out a muted snort. "You're not fat, baby." David turned onto his side so that he was face to face with Jerry. "You're absolutely perfect, just the way you are."

"But?"

"No buts," David said as he pressed his lips to Jerry's. "Did it bother you what William said?"

"A little," Jerry admitted truthfully. "But not because of the fat. I don't want you losing interest in me, that's all."

David raised himself up on one elbow and looked down at his lover. "Seriously? You think I'd lose interest in you if you gained weight?"

"Wouldn't you?"

"Jerry!" David pushed Jerry onto his back and then crawled on top of him. "When we're making love, I'm not thinking about your body or how thin or fat it is." He shook his head and stole a kiss. "You could be a whale, and I'd still be just as much in love with you." David put a hand on Jerry's chest. "It's what's in here that I'm making love to. The way you are with William, the way you've helped him grow and thrive. How attentive you are to me." David shook his head and stole another kiss. "I fell in love with you because you're the sweetest, kindest, most… everything I've ever met."

"Good," Jerry said as he accepted another kiss from David. "Because I love you too…, and the extra weight will be gone by the end of the month."

Chapter 4

THE only thing William didn't like about weekends was the end. He swung his legs over the side of his bed and wiggled his feet into his slippers, before rubbing his eyes and stretching his arms up as if he were a cat. He flexed and stretched his fingers and his toes, his legs going rigid as he fell back onto the mattress, feeling a little less sore, but still very tired. He hadn't realized until this morning how much work he'd actually done on Saturday morning. Jerry and David had both had to come in several times each on Saturday morning to get William out of bed. It wasn't that he wasn't willing to help; in fact, he was always excited about spending time with Jerry and David. William especially loved the play fighting and how his dad and David would tease each other.

"William?"

"I'm up!" William rolled onto his side and pushed himself up into a sitting position. He wasn't surprised when he heard footsteps growing louder as they approached his room; he usually yelled back that he was awake, but both David and Jerry had quickly figured out that he wasn't actually up, just awake—sort of.

"Up as in vertical, or up as in awake?" David knocked at his door and waited until William granted permission for him to enter. If there was one thing both his dad and David insisted on, it was that everyone have manners both inside and outside the house.

"You can come in." William cupped his hand over his mouth as another yawn sneaked up on him. "My stomach is sore… and my arms and my legs."

"Do you feel sick?" David's hand was on his forehead before he could answer. The only good thing about being sick was David. He would sit with William and watch movies with him, make him soup and give him ginger ale so that he could burp, out loud; the burping always made William feel better.

"No, not pukey sick, more like achey sick."

"Maybe you just worked too hard on Saturday." David rubbed William's upper arm between his hands and then did the same for his legs. "I'll tell you what. You go hop into a nice hot shower, and I'll see if your dad will let you stay home today. But just today."

"But what about soccer practice?"

"Well, how about if you just stay home this morning until you're not so achey?" David smiled as he smoothed his hand over William's blond buzz cut.

"Nah, I can handle it." William made his way to the bathroom, with David close behind. "If I get tired, I'll call you from practice, and then I'll come home and go to bed early. Okay?" At this last word, William stopped and turned to look up at David.

"Yessir," David teased and offered a salute. "But if you feel sick or tired or achey, call your dad, and if he doesn't answer, call me, and I'll come and take you home."

"'Kay."

"Now, you've got fifteen minutes to get ready if you want waffles. If it takes you longer than that... I'll still make you waffles, but you'll have to eat them in the car."

William let a small chuckle escape. "Where's Dad?"

"Your father is in the barn trying to finish those last two pieces for his exhibition in Edmonton this weekend." David turned and started down the stairs toward the kitchen, but then stopped suddenly. "Do you still want to come, or do you think you might like spending the weekend at Lenore's better?"

"No," William said through another yawn. "I want to come with you two."

"Good," David answered with a big smile. "He's very excited about you coming along." David pointed to the bathroom. "Now you only have twelve minutes."

"Wait," William protested, "you can't count that. You were talking to me." He turned and pushed through the partially open door, and grabbed for his toothbrush while trying to undo the buttons of his pajama shirt at the same time.

WILLIAM had managed to get through a day filled with an experiment in Science class, a surprise quiz in Math, and one of the most boring short stories he'd ever read for English class. He wasn't sure now that he should have ignored David's offer of a morning at home; he was beginning to feel sick to his stomach as he bent over and tied up his soccer cleats. *Figures*, he thought, feeling a little cheated. *I manage to make it through all the so-so stuff, and then feel sick when I get to the good stuff.*

He sat up and saw double for a few seconds until Cory's approaching smile came clearly into focus. "Hey, Billiam, you okay? You don't look so hot." Cory sat down beside William and immediately reached out a hand to touch his forehead.

"My dads and I did some work around the ranch on Saturday, and then went riding on the horses out in the sun. David says I probably just overdid it a bit."

"Smart dad," Cory said as he reached for his cell phone. "What's his number? I think you need to go home."

"No, I don't want to go home." William tried to make himself look better, happier. "I want to play soccer."

"I know, buddy, but you're way too hot on the forehead." Cory opened up his phone and waited. William finally relented and dictated the seven digits to him. As Cory dialed, William opened his bag and began pulling out his sweat pants and his hooded fleece jacket. Cory handed him the phone.

"Hi, David. Can you come and get me?" William nodded a few more times before saying goodbye and handing the phone back to Cory. "He said he'll be here in a couple of minutes."

"I hope you feel better soon, buddy."

"Thanks," William said, feeling a little bit more deflated. "See ya." He liked that David would be looking after him and making him soup and all that, but he didn't want to miss the practice today. Cory had told him many times that he would have to practice these various moves in order to get better. It was why he spent an hour outside practicing with David or Jerry—or both of them—at least four times a week. And he could tell he was getting better; even Cory had noticed the improvement.

He made his way over to the curb, knowing that David would be faster than ever to pick him up; nothing worried David more than when William was feeling sick. He'd barely sat down on the curb when he realized that he'd forgotten to ask Cory if he wanted to come to the ranch this coming weekend. But it was too late to go back. He raised himself off the curb when he saw the familiar shape and color of David's car coming down the street.

William was safely inside the red car and buckled up by the time he saw Cory running toward him with something in his hands. He did a quick inventory, but couldn't figure out what he was missing. He was home and in a hot bath before David asked him what he'd done with his cleats. *That's why Cory was running for the car.* And he'd had a story and some flat ginger ale by the time he heard the doorbell.

AS HE headed for the door, David wondered again where Jerry was; he should have been home from Edmonton already. He was relieved that William was a little too sick to ask where his dad was; David didn't like giving William platitudes or pat answers, especially when he knew that William was bright enough to know better. He pulled open the door.

"Uh, hi," the young man said before David could say anything. After another fraction of a second, David noticed that there was a light drizzle outside. "My name is Cory. I help with William's soccer team, and he forgot his cleats at the field today."

David noticed the cleats being offered and took them, then moved aside to let Cory pass. "Please, come in. How did you get here?" He asked when he didn't see a car. He closed the door and turned to put the cleats on the mat beside the door.

"Uh, bike," Cory said. David noticed that Cory seemed a little nervous. "Is William feeling better?" Cory shuffled from one foot to the other. "Coach cancelled practice on account of the sudden rain, so could you tell him that he didn't miss anything." Cory stuffed his hands in his pockets. "He was kinda bummed about having to miss practice."

"I'll tell you what," David began, "you can tell him yourself, if you'd like. And thank you for calling me. If I'd left it up to him, he would have played until he threw up." David motioned to the stairs. "While you're up there visiting, perhaps I can fix you something hot to eat and drink. You must be cold riding in the rain like that."

"Oh, no, it's okay, really. It didn't start raining until I hit the end of the driveway." Cory followed David up the stairs. "I can only stay for a minute, and then I have to get home."

When David pushed open the door to William's room, he saw the little guy sitting up already with his eyes wide and a big smile on his face. "Well, I guess you know who's here to see you."

"Cory!"

David stifled a laugh at the obvious hero worship that William had developed and walked over to put a hand on the little guy's forehead. "Looks like you're feeling a little better. Better enough for a visit with Cory?"

"Can Cory stay for dinner?"

"I think he needs to leave soon, but maybe some other time?" David responded while looking at Cory. When Cory nodded his head, David turned back to William. "Maybe you can get a video game in before Cory has to leave?"

Without even waiting for any kind of objection from Cory, William slid out of bed, stuck his feet into his slippers, and headed for the stairs, signaling for Cory to follow. David worried for a moment that William might overdo it again and start to feel worse, but then rationalized that as soon as Cory left, he could have William in bed and asleep within a half-hour—maybe sooner if William didn't want another story.

As David headed into the kitchen, leaving the two boys in the living room, he remembered and called back to William, "Did you thank Cory for bringing your cleats home?" He heard William talking excitedly and opened the fridge to get some of the ingredients for the stew he'd planned to make tonight. As he stood, fridge door open, wondering if he should even bother to prepare something since he wasn't sure if William and Jerry would be there to eat it, he felt the vibration of his phone in his right-hand back pocket. He looked at the call display and a knowing smile came to his lips.

"I thought I told you never to call me, or my boyfriend might suspect something."

"What, I'm late for one dinner, and I've been demoted to boyfriend?" Jerry laughed into his phone, and David felt that familiar thrill at the sound of the deep, bass voice. "How's our boy doing? I got your message."

"He's in the living room. Cory brought back the cleats that our son forgot at the field because he was too intent on playing today."

"Is he sick or just overtired from too much excitement on the weekend?"

"Maybe a little of both." David hadn't asked if Jerry was close to home, but he decided to make some dinner anyway, even if it would only be William and David eating it. "That flu that I thought we'd all luckily escaped may have not missed all of us after all." David pulled a few pots and pans out of the cupboard. "By the way, you wouldn't happen to know what Cory's last name is, would you?"

"Don't think I was ever told. Why?"

"No reason, he just seems awfully familiar to me."

"Were... teach... elementary... Lenore?" Jerry's voice was cutting in and out due to the storm that was settling over the area.

"You're cutting in and out. Where are you?"

"I said, 'Were you his teacher in elementary? If not, ask Lenore.'" Jerry was speaking as if David was in the advanced stages of hearing loss. "I'm about twenty minutes from home. Listen, it's really starting to come down out here, so I'm gonna hang up, and I'll see you soon."

"Okay, I love you."

"... Love... family."

David heard the dial tone, shoved his phone back into his back pocket, and headed for the living room. "William, your dad's about twenty minutes away—"

"I should get going then," Cory interrupted and stood.

"Wait," William called, "if you can't stay tonight, will you come on Friday? When it's nicer? We can go riding on the horses?"

"I can't promise, but I'll try."

David admired how Cory was able to handle William's request; he was quite sure that a young man Cory's age probably had better things to do than to hang around someone as young as William. David also admired how devoted Cory seemed to be to William—to come all this way just to drop off William's cleats? A strange thought suddenly hit David, a realization of why Cory looked so familiar. He pushed it aside and turned to Cory. "Are you sure you won't stay? At least until the rain lets up a little. You're more than welcome to stick around."

"No," Cory said as he smiled and shook his head. "My mother's probably wondering where I am right now."

34

"Well, I tell you what then." David moved aside so that the boys could go into the kitchen. "Why don't I fix you something warm to eat, and when Jerry gets home, he can drive you. It'll be a lot faster than you trying to ride that bike in the rain." He could see the protest forming and decided to cut it off. "Please? It's the least we can do to thank you for all you've done for William." David noticed Cory glance down at William, and he understood what Cory must be feeling. *It took me forever to learn how to say "no" to that face.*

"Okay," Cory conceded, "maybe just a few more minutes won't hurt."

David wasn't sure he'd ever seen William move so quickly because he had Cory's hand in his and had both of them heading for the living room before David could even open his mouth to ask if Cory had any favorite foods. So, David made another trip to the living room, found out that William and Cory both liked grilled cheese sandwiches, and headed back to the kitchen.

He was just finishing the cleanup while both boys ate at the kitchen table—David having been very glad he made several sandwiches when he saw how hungry Cory actually was—when the front door opened and the sound of water and wind was soon replaced with the familiar bass voice.

"Holy Dinah," Jerry whooped, "I haven't seen a storm like that in quite some time."

David turned around, expecting William to run over to his dad for a hug, but William just sat beside Cory and tried to finish his sandwich. "Have you already met Cory, Jerry?"

"Sure have." Jerry removed his damp suit jacket and stood beside the table, his hand reaching out reflexively to ruffle his son's hair. "Hey, partner," Jerry said to William, "David tells me you're not feeling so hot."

"I think I just overdid it on the weekend," William explained as he got off of his chair and wrapped his arms around Jerry's waist.

35

"Cory said he might come over for dinner this Friday." William took his seat again and looked over at Cory, who just smiled.

"Hey, that sounds like fun." Jerry sat down in his own chair, and David placed a plate of grilled cheese sandwiches and french fries in front of him. "Thanks, baby."

"Listen," David said as he walked to the front entrance, "Cory needs to get home, so I'm going to use your pickup, so we can put his bike in the back." David reappeared a few seconds later with a slicker over his arm and a set of keys in his hand. "Cory? Ready?" Cory smiled and stood up from the table, plate in hand. "William? Can you put Cory's plate in the dishwasher for me? And I want you to be in bed by the time I get home, okay? We don't want you getting worse."

"I promise." William took the plate and had it in the dishwasher and was running back for the door before Cory had a chance to completely disappear. "Thank you, Cory. I hope you can make it on Friday."

"I'll do my best, Billiam."

Chapter 5

DAVID walked through the door, excited that he'd finally made the connection, finally figured out why Cory looked so familiar. He deposited his keys on the foyer table beside his cell phone, which he'd forgotten to take with him, and searched the kitchen for Jerry. Nothing. Living room? No, not there either. He wondered if something was wrong with William and headed for the stairs, but saw that the light was on in the study.

"Jerry?" David wasn't sure if William was asleep or just on the computer, so he kept his voice low. He pushed open the door, cringing at the familiar creak of the bottom hinge, to see Jerry with the phone to his ear.

"I don't see the problem." Jerry turned to offer a smile and then to roll his eyes playfully. *Kitty*, David thought. "So I change a few of the pieces; it's no big deal, Kitty." He waited patiently, hoping the phone call would end soon. He wasn't exactly sure why figuring out who Cory was would be of any interest to Jerry, but considering that the young man had become a very important part of William's life, David decided to err on the side of caution. "I thought the objective was to get people into the gallery and then to actually buy the paintings." Jerry nodded at something David couldn't hear. "Right, my point exactly, so why include paintings that aren't for sale." *Not for sale?* David thought as he looked at his lover and shrugged his shoulders. "I know they might be some of my best work, but they're not for sale, so why show them?" Jerry slumped into a chair, as if to signal that he was done with this particular conversation. "I won't budge on this, Kitty." Jerry wiped his hand over his face, a sign David recognized as Jerry being only moments away from swearing and raising his voice. "Okay, well, you do that then, and I'll talk to you tomorrow... right, okay... bye, Kitty."

"Do you want to go first or should I go first?" David walked over and leaned against the beautiful mahogany desk that Jerry had inherited from his parents. Jerry sighed, reached out, grabbed David by the waist, and pulled him onto his lap. "Okay, well, I couldn't help this feeling that I knew Cory from before. I knew he wasn't an ex-student because I always remember those faces, but... is William okay? Did he throw up or have trouble getting to sleep?"

"Out like a light when his head hit the pillow."

"Poor little guy." David snuggled closer when he felt Jerry's arms squeeze a little tighter. "I wonder if he's getting that flu finally?"

"We'll wait and see what he feels like tomorrow." Jerry pulled David's shirt from his jeans and ran his big hands up and down the soft skin. "Cory?"

"Oh, right!" David shook his head as if it would help him ignore the sensations of being so close to Jerry. "Anyway, Cory Flett is the student that Lenore and I nominated for the citizenship award five years ago." After taking a quick breath, he looked at his husband wide-eyed and fanned his fingers in front of him. "*Big* controversy because Bennett was hoping that his daughter would win that year, since she was a crossing guard and had been instrumental in raising the money for new fluorescent vests—"

"Has anyone ever told you that you put way too much detail in your stories?" Jerry pushed his hand below the waistband of David's jeans. "Because as soon as you're finished with this story, I was planning on taking you upstairs to have my way with you."

"Cory didn't win and neither did Bennett's daughter. The end."

"Very funny," Jerry chuckled and gave a squeeze to David's behind. "So neither of them won. Where's the controversy?"

"Well, Lenore and I were really hoping to have Cory win because he was new to the school that year, and his mother had passed away, which was why his father had decided to move—"

"What?"

"What what?"

"His mother passed away?"

"Yes, cancer, very sad."

"But...." Jerry shook his head. "Maybe it's his stepmother."

"Okay, I'd like the record to show that you're the one slowing this story down."

"Smart ass!" Jerry gave David's ass another little squeeze. "It's just that William said that Cory's mother worked across the street at the supermarket."

"Maybe William meant stepmother? Although I would find that hard to believe. Do you know he ate four grilled cheese sandwiches? The poor kid. I don't think he's eating very well... regardless of how many parents he has."

Jerry pushed David gently off his lap and stood. "Come on, we can figure all this out tomorrow. If there's anything to figure out." David moved ahead of Jerry to the stairs. "So what did Cory do to get you and Lenore so gung-ho for him to win?"

"Well, there was this little boy in grade four—Lane, I think his name was—who was always being picked on by some of the grade five boys because he liked to play with dolls and do skip-rope with the girls during recess." David waited at the foot of the stairs while Jerry double-checked the front door and turned off the lights in the kitchen and hallway. "Cory came to Lane's rescue so many times throughout that year, and *always* without violence or throwing even one punch or muttering one threat, that Lenore and I thought he was more than deserving of some kind of recognition. And he's so kind and patient with William. I hope William doesn't get too attached to Cory."

"Why's that?"

"Don't get me wrong, I'm glad for William, but I worry about him sometimes. You know, that he doesn't have enough friends."

39

"Yeah, I know, I've worried about that a time or two myself, but…." Jerry steered David away from William's door. "He's fine, just—"

"I know," David whispered, putting up no resistance to being pushed toward the master bedroom, "but I just wanted to see for myself."

"Liar," Jerry whispered against his ear. "You just want to make sure that I didn't dent him or let him go hungry." David turned to protest, but Jerry had him through the bedroom door and on the bed within seconds. "So, William tells me that he's excited about coming to the art exhibition in Edmonton."

"I was going to tell you," David said as he felt the flush of color rise to his cheeks. "It was actually going to be a surprise, and I was going to tell you last night, but I got distracted."

"Thought we agreed he was too young."

"I know, but hear me out." David removed his shirt and threw it toward the hamper by the bathroom. "I thought I'd get a hotel room and William and I could put in an appearance just so he could see what it is you do and hear how much some people love your pieces, and then I could take him back to the hotel room, and then you'd be free to schmooze, and you wouldn't have to worry about anything but—"

"You think I'd think you two were in the way?"

"Uh, no, I didn't mean—"

"Relax," Jerry chuckled and pulled David so that he was on top. "It's a great surprise, and I can't wait to show off my family."

"But I overstepped?"

"No, not at all." Jerry kissed him tenderly. "But I don't want to force things on him. My parents did that with me all the time, especially with sports, and I hated it when they did that. I don't want him to grow up hating me."

"Hate you?" David pulled his head back, his face a study in confusion. "He'd never hate you; he loves you." David accepted

40

another quick kiss from Jerry and then asked, "And you didn't hate your parents, did you?" Jerry shook his head slowly. "Good, so one hour, I promise, and then we'll leave... sooner if he doesn't like it."

Jerry gave a grin and with one hand on the back of David's neck, pulled his lover in for a lingering kiss. David responded to the kiss and to the stroking of those hands over his back, wishing he could crawl inside of this man forever.

WHEN David awoke the next morning, he could already smell the coffee brewing in the kitchen and hear voices, taking a few moments to recognize Jerry's and then Kitty's. He glanced over at the clock, wondering what Kitty was doing here so early. *I thought she was in Edmonton preparing for the show.*

He threw off the duvet and headed for the bathroom to shave and shower. He did some quick mental math in his head; William would have another hour to sleep before David would go check to see if he was any better today. And if he wasn't any better, David would have plenty of time to call the middle school to warn them of William's absence.

His mind was occupied, flitting from one thing to another, as he shaved and then lingered under the hot water of the shower for fifteen minutes, hoping that he wasn't going to get sick with whatever had William under the weather. It wasn't the being sick that bothered him so much as having to go in and teach while he was sick. He knew he should probably stay home, but preparing for a substitute teacher was so much work that he always found it less stressful to just go in himself.

It was only Tuesday, but he threw on a pair of chinos and a polo shirt and his loafers, and then headed to William's room. He didn't knock this time and turned the knob very slowly so as not to wake the little guy. Where William should have been was a mass of blankets and pillows. *Must be feeling better*, David thought and headed for the stairs.

Once he was in the kitchen, he saw William sitting at the table munching on some toast, an empty bowl pushed off to the side. *Definitely feeling better, then.*

"Good morning." David took the seat beside William, smiling at the sight of the flushed cheeks fresh from sleep and the little legs dangling over the side of the chair. "Feeling better, William?"

"Uh huh," William said as he chewed on his toast. He took a big gulp of orange juice and turned to look at David. "I heard voices, and I wasn't sleepy anymore, so I came downstairs."

"Two bowls of cereal and three pieces of toast." Jerry smiled at his son. "Definitely feeling better."

"Kitty? Can I get you anything?" David didn't have anything against Kitty; he just didn't know how to take her, especially this early in the morning.

"No, sweetie, thank you." Kitty smiled and nodded toward Jerry. "I was just trying to convince your husband that his acclaim is in jeopardy. Surely you don't think he should keep certain pieces out of the show because they're portraits of the family, do you? There are at least five that are some of his best work, and you can't recognize faces in them."

"What I think," David said through a tight smile, "is that those are his decisions. If he can live with them, then that's all fine with me."

"Philistines," Kitty opined with a flourish of her manicured nails. "I'm surrounded by Philistines."

"What's a Philis—Philistine?" William turned to David, who only smiled.

"Your father," Kitty snorted with an exaggerated roll of her bright green eyes.

"The Philistines were an ancient people who lived in the Middle East and were considered very good-looking and very intelligent." Jerry lifted his mug to his lips and smirked at Kitty. "Isn't that right, Aunt Kitty?"

42

"Yes, William," Kitty said as she stood up from the table and reached for her bag on the counter behind her. "Your father is a Philistine." David watched as she turned toward Jerry and could barely overhear her remind Jerry not to call her *Aunt Kitty*. "William? You have a nice day at school, and I'm glad you're feeling better. David?" Kitty nodded at Jerry. "I hope you come to your senses soon." And with an annoyed look at Jerry—who was far too amused by all of this—she headed for the door. He could hear her protests anew as Jerry followed her out to her car.

"She's weird." William took another bite of his toast.

David stifled a laugh. "I think the word is *eccentric*."

"What's that mean?"

"It means she's different. And different is sometimes a good thing." David brushed his hand over the short blond hair. "How did you sleep?"

"Good."

"No throwing up?"

"Nope."

"Okay, but if you start feeling sick today—"

"I know, call Dad, and if he doesn't answer, call you on your cell phone."

"Good boy," David said through a smile. He leaned over and placed a kiss on the top of William's head, taking a mere moment to delight in that smell that seemed to be all William. "I love you," he whispered against the short tufts of blond hair.

"I love you, too, David."

"And if you see Cory today, no pestering him about coming over for dinner on Friday." David saw the red cheeks turn and the brilliant blue eyes look at him, but before William could say anything, David added, "Cory's a few years older than you, sweetie, and he probably has his own plans, his own friends."

"But he said he'd think about it."

"I know," David said as he reached out to fix the collar of William's pajama shirt. "And I know how much you like him, but I don't want you to be disappointed if he can't come on Friday."

"Okay."

David placed another kiss, his heart breaking a little at the resignation in William's voice, and made another mental note to talk to Lenore about how he and Jerry could encourage William to make friends. She'd already suggested sports at school, and that was a rousing success, but not in terms of William making friends. The only lasting bond he'd established through soccer was a sixteen-year-old boy who didn't even go to the same school. "Besides, if he can't make it, then you and your dad and I can all go do something crazy like drive to Edmonton and stay in a hotel and eat lots of pizza *on the bed.*"

"Really?" William looked over at David. "When Mr. Boyd brought me here, we stayed in a big hotel in Calgary, but we ate at the table in the room. Or we went out."

"Hey, cowboy," Jerry's unseen reappearance startled David from his efforts to prepare William for potential disappointment. "You've got about forty-five minutes before you have to start getting ready. Wanna see if you can finally beat me at PlayStation?"

David chuckled and then looked at Jerry with a resigned grin when he saw William get out of his chair, plate in hand, and head to the sink before the words were out of Jerry's mouth.

"You go set it up and I'll be right there, partner."

"'Kay."

David stood up and moved to the sink to rinse off William's plate, but Jerry grabbed him before he could get there and wrapped him in his arms. "I'm sorry about that. I didn't know she was so set on making you and William famous."

"Why is she so hell-bent on having those pieces included?"

"I don't know," Jerry sighed. "I think she's hoping the family portraits will make me seem accessible, or maybe she's just trying to stir up some sort of frenzy."

"Is that a bad thing?"

"I'm too old for frenzy."

"And what would you call how you've been in the bedroom lately?" David whispered as he looked toward the living room.

"I love painting, but it's never done for me what you do."

David stood on his tiptoes and accepted the kiss that Jerry was offering. "But William's your son now. You don't have to worry about being too public, so maybe a little frenzy might be good for your exposure."

"Our son," Jerry corrected and grinned when he saw the smile those two words brought to David's handsome face. "And I don't care about becoming famous or having people buy my work." Jerry kissed the top of David's head. "I want people to buy my work because it says something to them, because they love the colors... hell, I'd be happy if they buy my work because it matches the sofa. I didn't start painting to become famous, baby. I paint because it makes me happy." Jerry slapped playfully at David's ass as he headed to the living room. "But not as happy as the two of you."

"Hey," David called as he put William's dishes in the dishwasher, "I'm with you whatever you decide."

"Good to know, baby."

Chapter 6

JERRY stood back from the easel and tried to figure out what was wrong with the painting. He'd already spent most of the day staring at it, then adding or subtracting, but he still wasn't happy with it, and he was getting frustrated. Before he did anything foolish, he decided to head inside and maybe do something else. It wasn't often that his muse abandoned him, but when it did, it was very slow to return. For some reason, he found himself thinking more and more about the mystery that was Cory Flett. It had been two days since David had mentioned that Cory's mother had passed away years ago, and it was only yesterday that David had returned home from school and told him about the conversation he'd had with Lenore. As far as Lenore knew, Cory's dad had never remarried and was still a single parent, at least that's what Cory's file indicated. It wasn't that Cory had lied about something that probably wouldn't have made any difference to William or Jerry or David, it was that William was so attached to someone with a secret. And whatever the secret, and whatever the reason for lying, Jerry didn't like the idea of William getting hurt in all of this; he'd been through enough already. And Jerry was pretty sure that David would feel the same way.

At the thought of David and William and where they were as compared to this time last year, Jerry couldn't help but smile. He wasn't completely comfortable being a parent yet, but he was definitely more comfortable than he was a year ago. He knew that he still had quite a bit of work to do when it came to dealing with William's solitary nature or how to handle some of the people that seemed intent on making William suffer for what Jerry and David had found in each other, but he also knew that he and David made a formidable team; they would be able to handle anything that came their way.

Married and with a child. He'd certainly never imagined that this was where his life would lead him. He shook his head as he descended the thick, wooden ladder that connected his studio to the barn, equally amused and awed by the realization that—each in his way—William and David had saved him from himself. He wasn't what anyone would call a people-pleaser, but when he saw the look on William's face the first time they met last year, saw the look in those sad, resigned blue eyes, Jerry would have done anything to make it all go away.

As he approached the stall of Mountain Lion—William's horse— Jerry tried to imagine how his life would have turned out. He didn't honestly know, but he was quite certain that he would have continued to fumble his way through every day completely convinced that he'd been rich in the only way that mattered. "I am a very lucky man," he whispered to Mountain Lion, chuckling and patting the horse's nose when it whinnied.

Very lucky indeed, he repeated to the open sky as he made his way back into the house. Neither William nor David liked his cooking—and if he was honest, he preferred David's as well—but he felt like doing something for his family. They'd be away in Edmonton for most of the weekend, so Jerry decided to barbecue. Even William and David agreed that Jerry's barbecued ribs were the best they'd ever tasted. It might not be ideal barbecue weather, but the snow was gone and the temperature had peaked today at just under seventeen degrees Celsius. Besides, he rationalized as he fired up the grill, we can go inside if it gets too cold and have a carpet picnic. *We'll do that anyway*, he thought and smiled, catching a glimpse of the framed poster that David had brought with him when he'd moved in with Jerry and William almost a year ago. He couldn't remember who the author was, but he'd read that poster several times, and he would definitely agree with the author's observation to hold hands when going out into the world. And after letting William and David into his life, Jerry now had two hands to hold when he was out in the world.

He felt the vibration against his hip and quickly dug out his cell phone. Glancing at the screen, he could see it was William calling. "Hey, partner, how's practice?"

"Cory's not here!"

"Okay, uh...."

"He's always here, Dad!"

"Listen, William, maybe Cory is busy with other things. We've had this talk before—"

"He told me he would be here." William sounded on the verge of tears. "He always keeps his word, Dad. We have to find out what's wrong."

"Okay, William, you need to calm down." Jerry waited for another interruption; none came. "It's only the first practice he's missed."

"Second." William was probably pouting now, Jerry guessed. "He missed last night too."

"I'm sorry, buddy, but Cory's probably got some things to do."

"He promised."

And here we go, Jerry thought. He took a deep breath and sat at the kitchen table. "I know he did, William, and I'm sorry that he had to break his promise, but he might have a good reason for it. Remember when you told Grandpa Niels that you'd go to the circus with him and you got sick? That was a good reason for not being able to go, right?"

"Yeah, I guess," William conceded. Jerry's heart broke a little; he could just picture William sitting all pinched and closed-off—like he usually did when he felt the world was unfair—and his bright blue eyes would be almost black with resentment.

"I think I've got an idea that might help you feel a little better."

"What?"

Oh, yes, Jerry thought, *my boy is in full pout alright.* "Let's just say you're going to get to do your most favorite thing in the whole world."

"Ride Mountain Lion?"

"Okay, second favorite."

"Stay up past bedtime and watch movies with you and David?"

"Okay, third favorite."

"Eat with my fingers?"

"Bingo!"

"Are we having ribs?" William's voice betrayed the excitement that Jerry'd hoped this news would bring out.

"Sure thing, partner," Jerry laughed into the receiver. "And now that I know that David and I are your second favorite, maybe we can do that too."

"Really?"

"Sure, why not?" Jerry shrugged, knowing full well that David would tease him about being wrapped around William's little finger but not really caring too much. He would do his fair share of teasing in return when he got David alone later in the evening. "Try and have some fun at practice, okay, buddy? We can figure out what to do about Cory later."

"Thanks, Dad."

"Go score a couple of goals so you'll have some news for Cory when you see him again."

"'Kay."

Jerry said his goodbyes and disconnected the call, not as upset as he thought he would be by the inevitable disappearance of William's newfound friend. But how do you explain this kind of thing to an eleven-year-old? He stared at his cell phone, now on the kitchen table. *I wonder what David would think of fixing a play date with Lenore's twins?* He decided to let the inevitable conversation wait until David was home. They were going to have to put some serious thought into this situation; William needed some more friends his own age.

As if on cue, the cell phone vibrated, dancing its way across the thick wooden surface of the kitchen table. "Hi, baby, I was just thinking about you."

"Really? Are you naked?"

"Not at the moment, but now that I know you're interested, I can be there in a couple of seconds." Jerry felt himself grinning from ear to ear. There was nothing he loved more than teasing David.

"A couple of seconds?" David laughed into the receiver and Jerry knew what was coming. "You're slowing down, cowboy."

"Thought you liked it slow."

"Quick and dirty works sometimes too."

"That what you're in the mood for right now?"

"No," David announced bluntly. "I'm heading over to catch the last half-hour of William's soccer game. Wondered if you'd like to meet us and then head out to dinner? My treat."

"Sounds good, and I told you never to call me that." Jerry laughed again, the tension that William's phone call had put in his shoulders gently subsiding.

"What? What did I call you?"

"*My treat,*" Jerry repeated, then shook his head. "Never mind. Maybe we can do dinner out tomorrow night? William just called and I guess Cory's been a no-show at the field the last two days."

"Fuck," David muttered. "We have to do something about this friendless phase of William's. Now, I know that you don't want to—"

"Have I ever told you how brilliant and perceptive you are?"

"No, but you always agree when I say it. Does that count?"

Jerry shook his head slowly, the smile still planted firmly on his face. "I was just thinking about the same thing. That's why I fired up the barbecue, and I sorta promised William he could eat with his fingers."

"Have I ever told you that you're the best father in the world?"

"Many times," Jerry said through his smile. "And maybe one of these days I'll even believe it."

"So back to our son," David announced with a chuckle. "I was thinking of a sleep over with Lenore's twins. Bring them to our place, give her a night off."

"Works for me."

"Okay then, I'll set it up."

"When are you getting home?"

"Same time as usual. Why?"

"Just wanted to know, so I can time the ribs just right."

"Make sure you get the cloth napkins out, the big ones that are in the middle drawer of the buffet," David said with a sigh of resignation. "You know that if you don't, it'll take me a week to get those sauce stains shaped like William's fingers out of his clothes."

"Yessir," Jerry barked playfully. "Anything else, sir?"

"Just one thing, are you naked yet?"

DAVID said his goodbye, disconnected the call, tossed his cell phone onto the passenger seat of his car, and felt like doing a little dance. Jerry was cooking tonight, so David had nothing to do besides eat and thank Jerry in the way Jerry liked best.

He parked the car in the parking lot, as close as he could get to the soccer field, grabbed his cell phone and put it in his pocket, and then stowed his briefcase in the trunk. No need to tempt anyone with the promise of potential valuables. *Sure,* David told himself, *I can see the car from the field, but who wants the hassle of having to run all the way over there to try and stop the thief and then file a police report.*

51

Besides, he rationalized, *if anything gets broken on the car, it would be days in the shop.*

He walked along the edge of the field and finally came to rest a few feet from the coach. "Hey, Don," he greeted, as the tall thirty-something man turned to offer a nod and a smile. "Sorry to interrupt you, but do you know what's going on with Cory?"

"What? You mean not showing up?"

"Yeah," David said as he nodded and looked over to see William with the ball making a run down center field. "Has he left you any messages about why he's missing practices?"

"Haven't gotten one, yet," Don responded as his eyes travelled back to his players on the field. "Besides, we've only got another couple of weeks anyway. And there'll be no practices next week, just a game on Friday night." Don looked at David. "He in trouble?"

"Trouble?" David wasn't sure he understood the question. *Cory's not the kind of kid to get into trouble.* "No, of course not. Why do you ask? Does he have that reputation?" William worked the ball really well, leaving most of the other kids in the dust. He approached the goal and faked out the goalie and landed the ball in the far right corner. "Way to go, William!" David waved quickly as William turned and showed that million-dollar smile.

"Mark!" The coach was yelling at someone David assumed to be the goalie. "You're not coming out far enough." Don turned back to David. "Not that I've seen, but the wife works at the high school—as you know—and when I told her that Cory wanted to do his twenty-five hours of mandatory leadership here with me doing soccer, she expressed *concern* because from what she can gather, Cory's a bit of a pot-head and has an issue with *anger management*."

"Really?" David couldn't believe that he and Don were talking about the same kid. "And you haven't seen him do anything inappropriate with kids, like talk about dope or try to sell it?"

"No," Don said as his head moved up and down the field along with the players. David was no expert, but even he could see that no one was playing defense against the tall brunet who had the ball and was making his way, very quickly, to the same goalie whom William had just scored on and whom Don had just reminded of his need to come out further from the net. "In fact," Don continued after a few moments, "Cory's been a big help."

"I know William thinks he's the greatest." David shoved his hands in his trouser pockets. "That's why I'm asking actually. William wants to make sure that nothing bad has happened to him."

"Sorry," the coach sighed as he shrugged his shoulders. "I wish I knew more, but if I hear anything, I'll be sure to let you know."

"Thanks, Don." David began to back away from the sideline, but then stopped. "Sorry, Don, one more thing? I'm kinda worried that William isn't making friends. Do you see much of him during school?"

"Just for gym," Don answered.

"Does he seem to be socializing well with the other students?"

"Far as I can tell, sure." Don unfolded his arms from around his chest. "He's never been in a fight inside the school, and I'm pretty sure not outside the school either. I mean, he's a really shy kid, but he doesn't seem to be lacking any kind of social skill."

"Okay, thanks again, Don." Again, David turned to walk the five feet where he would sit on the bench until the end of practice.

"And I mean this as a compliment," Don said, his eyes still fixed on the soccer ball and how the players were passing and intercepting, "but I think one of William's issues might be that he's much more mature than the other students, academically and emotionally."

"So, I guess time will tell, huh?"

"How are his marks?" It seemed—to David at least—like such an odd question for the soccer coach to ask, but David just shrugged.

"Eighty-five and above."

"Hmm," Don mumbled as he chewed his lower lip. "So then I guess he's not bored?"

"What do you mean? Bored with school?"

"Yeah, I mean you and I both know that gifted kids tend to get bored pretty quickly with the work that they master far sooner than the rest of the class."

"We've never had him tested, but I've always thought he was probably gifted."

Don nodded in agreement, his arms folded once again over his chest. "I think he maybe needs an environment that is a little more stimulating, make friends faster with some kids who were at his level, if you know what I mean?"

"But he's so small already," David cautioned, "I don't know if moving him into the next grade would help the situation."

"Listen, David, I've been doing this job as long as you," Don said as he offered a lopsided smile. "And we both know that there are other ways of relieving his boredom without sending him on to the next grade."

"Yeah, I know, Don, thanks." David finally made it to the bench and sat down. He knew that Don was talking about advanced or accelerated learning, and he knew that those kinds of courses would probably do wonders. But he also knew that it wouldn't necessarily solve the problem of William not having enough friends of his own.

As he sat and looked at William, legs pumping to catch up to the other player with the ball, David wondered about home-schooling again. He could cut his schedule down to half-time after spring break and work with William in the morning, or afternoon, and then have William back in school for the courses he wouldn't be able to do at home, courses like Metals Shop, Band and Physical Education. But David wasn't convinced that this idea would not just serve to highlight the differences between William and his classmates. If William is having difficulty making friends because he's brighter, putting him in a course that recognized this fact could only serve to alienate him even more.

He was startled out of his thoughts when he heard the coach's whistle. He stood up from the bench and waited for William to remove his cleats and stuff them in his sports bag.

"Hey, William, way to hustle out there. That goal was pretty impressive!"

"Thanks," William said, his blue eyes shining and proud.

"So, your dad tells me we're eating ribs tonight."

"I know, I love it when Dad barbecues." William walked beside David to the car and then hopped in after he'd stowed his bag in the back seat. "Dad said I could stay up late and watch movies with you two."

"He did, huh?"

"Please, can I?"

"Well, if your dad said you could, then there's only one thing I can say." David checked William's seatbelt and William's blue eyes glared at him. David suddenly remembered how much William disliked being fussed over. "Sorry, I forgot. I promise I won't check your seatbelt again."

"What's the only thing you can do?"

"Drive us to the video store, so you can pick out a movie."

Chapter 7

JERRY'S eyes opened, and he stretched, trying to loosen the kink in his spine, his hand brushing gently against the nape of David's neck, the warmth giving him ideas. He rolled onto his side and snuggled up to his lover's naked back, one hand moving slowly, but purposefully, around David's waist so he could pull the warm body closer. While the other hand pushed under the pillow that cradled David's head, Jerry began to touch his lips lightly to the soft skin behind David's ear.

With David held fast against his body, Jerry continued kissing all available skin, the thoughts of where this was going causing his blood to heat and his cock to wake up. He felt David wake up and move his left hand so that it was caressing Jerry's bare hip while his right hand stroked lightly over the hair of Jerry's forearm. "Morning, baby," Jerry whispered against David's ear, feeling even more aroused at the shivers he could bring out in the smaller man. "You looked so warm and inviting. Sorry if I woke you."

"Anytime, cowboy." David turned in Jerry's embrace so that he was on his back. Jerry moved his leg so that he was partially on top. "Sorry, but your hairy chest was tickling my back."

"Can shave it, if you want," Jerry teased as he placed his elbows on either side of David's face and positioned his body so he hovered only a couple of inches above his lover's naked body.

"Don't you dare!" David reached out protectively and ran his hands over Jerry's muscular chest, his fingers teasing and combing the salt-and-pepper hair that thinned out over the belly only to grow thicker again as it formed his treasure trail. "You're perfect just the way you are."

Jerry bent his elbows and brought his mouth to David's, their two bodies shifting and aligning, almost as if by instinct, so that they fit together perfectly. Jerry felt David's hands glide along the long, thick muscles of his back. "Love the way you touch me, David." He nipped at David's bottom lip and then moved his mouth to whisper in one of those sensitive ears, "Never get enough of you." He couldn't believe that it had been almost a year, and he was still able to make David crazy with desire, still make his body writhe and respond like the first time they'd made love to each other.

"Love it when you say things like that." David bent his knees and brought them up toward his chest so that he could wrap them around Jerry's waist. Jerry pressed his pelvis down in between David's thighs and closed his eyes and pressed a little harder when he heard David gasp. "Oh, Jesus, Jerry, so big, so strong."

"What do you want, baby?"

"You," David whispered, his eyes closed and his hands kneading their way over Jerry's back and arms. "Always you, just you." Jerry looked down at the flush of David's cheeks, the rise and fall of his chest as he breathed rapidly and deeply, both of them becoming filled with the need to please each other. He pushed himself up so that he could place first his arms underneath David's knees, then his hands. With his hands on the backs of his lover's thighs, he wiggled his way down to beneath David's thighs, the familiar musk making Jerry as hard as it always did. He pushed his throbbing dick against the mattress, hoping for a little relief as his tongue began to lick and lap at David's entrance. This was Jerry's favorite part: the sight and the sound of David writhing, begging for Jerry to fuck him so that they could both come together. But a very close second was how David managed to contract his muscles, sending those waves of pressure up and down Jerry's dick. Jerry worked his tongue over and around, in and out, his hands maintaining a light but firm pressure on the backs of David's thighs.

"Oh, God, Jerry," David panted as he reached out with his hands and caressed Jerry's head. "Baby, so good, so good."

Jerry closed his eyes as he pushed his cock into the mattress again, feeling the pre-cum as he searched for some relief from the pressure that was building inside him. He felt David relax even more and gave his hole a few more moments of attention before kissing and licking his way up his lover's body until his mouth was at David's ear yet again. "Ready?" Jerry whispered, his prick aching at the whimper that escaped from the younger man. With his hands braced against the backs of David's thighs, Jerry lifted his torso up and made sure his dick was right at David's entrance, and then he hooked his arms under each of David's knees, the movement allowing Jerry to push slowly into his lover's heat. Jerry heard the sharp intake of breath the moment David must have realized what his lover was doing. Jerry had discovered this particular move quite by accident one night, and tried not to use it too often; it was a combination of sensations that usually made David come within minutes. And when David was so turned on that he could come just from Jerry moving in and out of him, Jerry always came within moments of David's muscles clamping down on his engorged uncut dick.

As he pushed himself in, up to the base of his cock, Jerry let his torso come to rest on top of David's, and with his mouth resting at one of his sensitive ears, began to pull out and push in again, slowly. "So tight, baby, so sexy," Jerry whispered against David's ear. Jerry had realized during their first night together that it was a combination of pillow talk, kissing and licking these sensitive ears that made the smaller man lose all control.

As if on cue, Jerry felt David's hands begin moving their way over his back; his right hand would come up and caress the back of Jerry's head and then the left would trail further south, grasping and clutching at the firm ass, encouraging Jerry to move faster and deeper. Jerry heard David's breathing stop momentarily—as it always did— when he thrust deeply enough to peg his prostate. Jerry nibbled at David's earlobe for a moment while he pulled out and then pushed back inside the tight heat. "Breathe for me, baby," Jerry whispered before he let his tongue outline the contours of one sensitive ear. David had no words to answer, but the firm grip that his hands had on Jerry's neck and ass were all the reassurance that Jerry needed.

Raising himself off of David's torso, just slightly, Jerry could get a better angle to continue to peg David's gland as he increased the speed and depth of his thrusts. Their eyes met and Jerry noticed that David's eyes were beginning to lose focus, opening and closing almost involuntarily. "Nothing between us, David. Can feel all of you. So hot, 's like an oven in there, mountain lion," Jerry whispered in David's ear. "So tight, so beautiful, so sexy, baby," Jerry said and began kissing David's ear in earnest.

"Come for me, mountain lion." Jerry brought his knees forward slightly and began to piston his dick in and out in short, controlled movements.

"Oh, baby," David grunted as his hands clenched and released over Jerry's body. "There, right there, oh, Jerry."

"So fucking hot, mountain lion," Jerry whispered into the same ear again and again. "Come for me. I'm not going to come until you do. Come! Come!"

Jerry felt the familiar tightening around his dick as David's eyes began to roll back into his head. David's grip on his ass tightened even more, and Jerry recognized his cue. Pressing his torso down again against the flushed, writhing body beneath him, he let his tongue and hot breath work their way in and around the sensitive ear. "So beautiful when you come, David. I wish you could see yourself."

David's eyes closed at last, and Jerry saw the look he'd been waiting for. He thrust one final time, pushing inside as far as he could, and then felt the liquid heat splash against his belly, his own eyes closing as he felt the vice-like grip roll, like waves, over his rigid cock. He felt himself lose control as David's arms came around his neck and back, holding him there while his muscles began to shake, and his seed spilled inside of his lover.

"Sweet Jesus," Jerry sighed against his lover's ear as the muscle tremors subsided. As David's hands caressed his neck and head, Jerry breathed rapidly, nuzzling his way along the smaller man's neck and shoulders, placing gentle kisses on whatever skin he could reach. "I love you, David," Jerry whispered against David's mouth before kissing him passionately, their tongues finding each other again.

"Jerry, love you too," David sighed as his hands held and caressed his lover's face. "Can't imagine what my life would have been like without you and William."

"My family. Our family." Jerry brought his knees up closer to David's ass and pushed himself up slowly so that he was upright, his own ass resting on his heels while his eyes feasted on the sight of his lover splayed out on the bed beneath him. Jerry brought David's ankles to his shoulders and then softening his grip, guiding his lover's legs back down to the mattress.

He pulled himself gently out of David, and then pushed himself to the edge of the bed, heading for the bathroom. As good and mind-blowing as the sex was between them, Jerry's favorite part was this: he held the washcloth under the hot water until the heat became almost too much. With the washcloth in his hand, he walked back to the bed and stretched himself out beside David, slowly and gently wiping the washcloth over his lover's sated body. There was nothing Jerry enjoyed more than these fleeting, intimate moments just after David had given himself to him.

"I should go and wake William," David sighed as Jerry finished wiping his belly.

"Not just yet," Jerry said as he tossed the washcloth at the hamper and pulled the duvet back up over their bodies, snuggling against David's warm flesh. "Won't get to do this again for a few days, so I want to take my time."

"Love it when you touch me, cowboy," David hummed as Jerry started caressing his skin. "We could always duck into the bathroom at the art gallery tomorrow night."

Jerry chuckled softly against David's shoulder. "Remember what happened that afternoon in the barn just before Christmas?"

The two men dissolved into fits of muted laughter as David turned on his side to be face to face with Jerry. He kissed Jerry tenderly on the lips. "I do remember. And I also remember that I'd never seen you quite so aroused." David's hand trailed down his lover's belly and wrapped itself around Jerry's semi-erect cock. "When I opened your jeans and you were so hard and leaking... what's this?"

"*That* is what you do to me." Jerry's eyes fluttered closed as he pushed his swelling cock into David's hand. He felt a kiss on his mouth and opened his eyes just in time to see the mischievous look in his lover's eyes, the look he had come to know so well. David pushed him slowly to his back and then straddled his hips, running his hands through the salt-and-pepper hair of Jerry's chest and abdomen.

"Looks like a week's worth of exercising has done some good there, cowboy." David planted a kiss on Jerry's mouth and then shifted his legs so that he was now in between Jerry's. Moving slowly, but with purpose, David had his left hand around the base of Jerry's cock while he used his right hand to fondle Jerry's heavy balls. Jerry lay back on the pillows, his arms crossed underneath his head as he watched how David seemed to study his dick. "It's been a while, hasn't it?"

"What's been a while?"

"Since you let me do this."

"Let you?"

"You know what I mean," David said as he squeezed Jerry's balls gently. "You're always so afraid that William might interrupt us that I don't get the chance to taste you, please you... like this." David pushed gently so the foreskin exposed the mushroom head and then put his lips around the glans, licking first the slit and then the ridge that led around to the frenulum.

"Sweet Jesus," Jerry hissed as he watched his dick come back to full erection.

"Or this," David whispered, his lips placing a quick kiss on the frenulum while his right hand continued to massage Jerry's balls. "Or this." David released his left hand so that the foreskin returned to partially cover the swelling head, pushing the foreskin the rest of the way up so that he could take it between his lips to massage it.

"Oh, baby, yes," Jerry muttered as his hands found their way to David's sleep-tousled hair. "Forgot how good you are at that. Please, baby, more."

"You know," David said before dipping his tongue under the foreskin and moving it slowly around the mushroom head. "I never understood why some cultures worshiped the phallus until I met you."

"Jesus, David," Jerry said as his hands traced around the contours of his lover's head. "Please, more."

"So beautiful, so much power, so much strength." David moved his mouth to take each of Jerry's balls into his mouth while the fingers of his left hand alternated between stroking the long, thick shaft and gently pinching and kneading the foreskin. "You have no idea what it feels like to have you inside me, Jerry."

Involuntarily, Jerry's legs came apart even further, his knees bending and his entire body feeling as if it were on fire. "Tell me," Jerry panted as he felt David's mouth return to take him all the way in. "Oh, fuck, David," Jerry panted as he felt his lover's thumb pressing against his entrance. Jerry wasn't into bottoming as a rule, but there was something about having his prostate massaged while David swallowed him balls deep.

"You're so long and so thick that it feels like you're splitting me in half." David pressed his thumb in slowly at first, then withdrew, replacing it with his middle finger. "And when you thrust just so and you tap against my prostate," he whispered before licking playfully at the slit as he began to rub and tap Jerry's prostate, "it feels like my whole body loses control, and all I know is that there'll never be anyone else for me, anyone else who'll ever be able to make me feel what you do."

"Uhh, fuck, David, yes, oh fuck, mountain lion," Jerry panted as he felt his balls begin to pull up. "I love you, David, love you, love you so much."

David relaxed the back of his throat to take all of Jerry's cock into his mouth, feeling the mushroom head hit the back of his throat as he tapped and then rubbed Jerry's prostate. And when he started humming, he felt the familiar pull of his lover's balls, heard the familiar hoarseness in Jerry's voice followed by the guttural cry.

Jerry lay there for a few moments, his arms out to his sides, his legs still bent but relaxed, his body only releasing the occasional twitch. He opened his eyes to see what he knew was one of his lover's favorite acts. David was still between his legs, laving and cleaning away all traces of Jerry's powerful orgasm. He reached out and took hold of David's shoulders. "Come here."

"You can't fool me, cowboy," David said as he snuggled on top of Jerry's chest, his hands resting on either side of Jerry's broad shoulders.

"Huh?"

"Are you feeling a little more relaxed?" Jerry gave him a quizzical look. "You wake me up to make love to me like that this early in the morning when you couldn't have had more than a few hours sleep." David wiggled slightly so that he could kiss Jerry, full on the mouth. "I know you're nervous about the show this weekend."

"Not nervous really," Jerry said as he leaned up to steal another kiss. "Since you and William became my family, I've been doing a lot of thinking."

"About?"

"About being William's father," Jerry said as David rolled off of his chest and snuggled up to his side. He felt the familiar combing of his lover's long, slender fingers through his chest hair. "About being a good husband, a good father."

"Well, if you're asking me, I'd say you're more than just good."

Jerry chuckled and wrapped his arm around David's shoulders, bringing their bodies even closer together. "You have to say that because you're in love with me." He kissed the tip of David's nose. "When my father died, I remember everyone telling me what a great man he was, how important he was, and," Jerry said as he looked into David's eyes, "all I could think was that I'd never seen any proof of any of that."

"But you're a great father to William." David stated emphatically. "You're attentive and loving and kind and patient and—"

"Then how come I can't fix this thing with Cory?" Jerry brought his hand to his scalp and rubbed it as if he could reveal the answer hidden inside.

"What thing?"

"I don't mean Cory himself, but this friend thing."

"You mean why William doesn't seem to have many?"

"Many?" Jerry grunted and shook his head. "Other than Lenore's twins, I don't think he has any."

"But that's up to William." David rubbed his hand over the hairy chest, obviously trying to soothe and comfort, but Jerry didn't feel either.

"No, it's up to me." Jerry placed his hand on top of David's and brought it to his lips, kissing it intently. "But thank you for trying to make me feel better."

"Jerry," David sighed as he smiled at his lover's worried expression. "All you can do is encourage him to do something. Making him do it isn't going to help him or you."

"I know, baby," Jerry agreed as he pulled up the duvet and pulled David even closer. "Okay, enough feeling sorry for myself." As he pulled the duvet all the way over their heads, he smiled and raised one eyebrow. "We've got a whole fifteen minutes before we have to wake William. What do you think we should do?"

Chapter 8

WILLIAM tried not to fidget as he stood in front of his father; he was still feeling a little hyperactive from the last soccer game of the season. He'd scored two goals, and he was excited about that, but he just wished that Cory could have been there to see them. Now, he was being dressed for his dad's art show. He'd tried to do his own Windsor knot, but he'd finally had to ask Jerry for help. Within a few seconds, his dad spun him around so he could look at himself in front of the long mirror in the corner of the bedroom that his two dads shared.

"Everyone ready?" William watched in the mirror as David came into the bedroom.

"Wow!" Jerry turned and stared at David. William couldn't help but notice how nice David looked in his dark navy suit, complete with white shirt and purple tie. "No one's going to be looking at the artwork with you there." William giggled as he saw how red David's face got. William would never understand why David got so embarrassed when Jerry said things like that to him.

"Look at William!" David offered a whistle as he came over and sat on the bed, his hands reaching out to the lapels of William's dark blazer. "I don't know who's more handsome, you or your father."

"We can both be the handsomest, can't we?" William leaned into David's body as he watched his father sit down on the bed.

"Yes, you can," David said almost immediately. "You're such a good boy... young man, I mean."

"Our boy," Jerry exclaimed as he pulled William into an embrace. "Smart and kind and handsome." Jerry let go of his son after placing a quick kiss on the top of his head. "Okay, William, we're taking David's car to Edmonton, so how would you like to go and get his keys and meet us out by the car?"

"'Kay!" William bounded out of the room and was outside with the keys in hand for what seemed like only a few minutes before he saw Jerry and David come out and lock the front door with Jerry's keys.

"Can I sit in the front?" William knew the answer would probably be no, but he figured it was worth a try.

"I don't see why not," David said as he brushed his hand over William's buzz cut. "I've never been driven around in my own car before. This should be fun."

"Thanks, David!" William wrapped his arms around David's waist and squeezed. Not only would he get to sit up front in the car, but he was going to be staying in a hotel attached to a huge mall with a water slide and all sorts of other fun places to visit. He'd helped David load up the trunk of the car earlier today with all the luggage the three of them would need for the whole weekend.

"Just don't drive your dad crazy with all sorts of distractions." David smiled and held up his hand. "And make sure you let him know when we're coming to rest stops or gas stations."

"Okay," Jerry announced as soon as the three of them were in the car and the doors were closed and locked. "House is locked up?"

"Check," David said from the back seat.

"Everyone's got luggage with underwear, shirts, swimming trunks, toothbrush, toothpaste, deodorant, razor?"

"Check."

"Check," William giggled from the front seat. "Except no razor."

"That's okay," Jerry said as he started the car, "you can borrow mine."

"'Kay," William giggled again as he nodded.

"Everyone ready to have a good time?"

"Check."

"Check."

"Everyone tired of these questions?"

"Check."

"Check," William giggled again as he turned in his seat to look at David, who just smiled at him and rolled his eyes. There was nothing that William loved more than when David would tease Jerry about how organized everyone else had to be.

"Hey, William?" As he turned around to look at David, William noticed pieces of paper being passed to him. "I almost forgot. I downloaded some info and pictures about West Edmonton Mall. Why don't you take a look through them and figure out what you want to do tomorrow."

"Cool," William enthused, as he accepted the papers and sat back so that he could study them.

"Have we measured him lately?" Jerry asked.

William looked up and saw his dad looking at David in the rearview mirror. "David measured me last week," he announced proudly. "I'm now exactly four feet tall."

"Forty-eight inches," Jerry whispered, almost to himself.

"I already checked, and there'll be a few rides William isn't tall enough for, but we can go on most of them." David turned and looked at William. "We'll go on those other ones when you're tall enough, right, William?"

"Right!" William put the papers on his lap for a moment and looked up at his father. "Did you know that Cory used to be short like me, and then he grew really tall?" William wondered momentarily at the look that his dad gave David, but continued anyway. "He said that one day I'll wake up, and I'll wonder why the ground is so far away."

"Sounds like a wise young man," Jerry said as he stole another glance at David.

"See any interesting rides?" David asked as he put his hand on Jerry's shoulder. William was flipping between a few of the pages and thought he heard his dad say *Thanks*.

"There's so much to do!" William gave up searching for the page that had the space themed rides and let the pages fall back into his lap.

"Well I like the swinging ship ride and the spinning roller coaster thing... Galaxy Orbiter I think it's called." David held out his hand and William handed the pages back. David flipped through a couple of the pages and then returned them. "This one, right there. Looks like fun, yeah?" William nodded. "And then we can spend some time going to the bookstore or the Apple Store and see what other kinds of stuff we can find there."

"Cool," William said as he settled again in the front seat beside his dad.

DAVID sat back in the plush leather seat and offered up his prayers, for the umpteenth time that day. *Please let him get to be taller than his parents.* He was under no delusions about being a parent; he'd always felt that teaching had prepared him for this inevitable path. The only problem now was that the inevitable didn't involve any of the situations he felt comfortable dealing with as a teacher. William wasn't a behavior problem, he wasn't failing any subjects, and he certainly wasn't involved in illegal activities. William's problem, he realized, would require all of them sitting back and waiting. And David was honest enough with himself to admit that waiting wasn't something he was good at.

At least he'd been able to deflect the conversation again at the mention of Cory's name. Jerry hadn't been happy to hear that Cory might have some connection to drugs and other illegal activities, but David had assured him that Don, the soccer coach, had had nothing but great things to say about Cory. Jerry's protectiveness of William only deepened the feelings that David had for him, and he'd never admit this

68

out loud, but he was sometimes concerned that Jerry wasn't as open to the idea of letting William experience everything he could. David worried sometimes that Jerry was too protective of their son. And if David were to be honest with himself, he still didn't feel as if it was his place to say anything; he still had difficulties speaking up when it came to what was in William's best interest.

It wasn't that David was interested in arguing the merits of William's friendship with Cory, but rather, he had an intuitive feeling about Cory as a person. David had spent enough years in the school system to recognize the signs of a derailed teenager; Cory had none of them. He was polite when speaking to adults—*well, to me anyway,* David thought, *and Jerry didn't seem to have a problem with him either.* Cory was thoughtful; that was evident enough by his riding his bike all the way out beyond city limits to return William's cleats. And Cory seemed to genuinely like William, or at least, it was a safe assumption based on how he'd tried to make William feel better by telling him how he'd grow to be tall.

No, David thought finally, *if I had to put money on any of the possibilities, I'd bet that Cory is a great kid who hasn't yet figured out how to let William down more gently.* The more he'd considered things over the past few days, the more he'd realized that Cory probably had a new girlfriend—or a new group of mates—and couldn't bring himself to look William in the eye and disappoint him. As he heard William talking excitedly about the art gallery and heard Jerry's patient answers to all of his son's questions, David was more convinced than ever that Cory would resurface eventually, and then all would go on as it should.

David turned when he heard Jerry call his name. "Sorry, I was daydreaming."

"I was saying that Kitty was telling me about a couple of gallery owners from Europe being there tonight."

David looked up at the beautiful blue eyes staring at him in the rearview mirror, and he offered a smile. "It'll be a huge success, even in Europe. Right, William?"

"Right."

David leaned forward and brushed his hand over the short blond locks. "Your dad will be rich and famous."

"He's already rich." William said as he reached over and patted his father's shoulder.

"Yes, I am, but because I have you two, not because I have lots of money." Jerry smiled and tried to tickle William's side.

"Well that just leaves famous then." David patted Jerry's shoulder.

"What do you think, William?" Jerry turned to look quickly at his son. "Do you think I should become famous?"

"No," William said as he shook his head. "When I was at boarding school in Switzerland, I was always glad that I didn't have photographers hounding me like some of the other boys." William turned to look at his father. "That's why we make such a good family, us three like privacy too much."

"Amen," Jerry said through a smile as he looked into the reflection of David's eyes in the rearview mirror.

Smiling at the looks on Jerry's and William's faces, David sat back against the soft leather and stole a quick look at his watch. Within another hour or so, they would be dropping off the luggage at the hotel in Edmonton. And after another hour or so at the gallery, he and William would be back at the hotel room watching movies and eating junk food. David had been looking forward to this trip for almost an entire month. A chance to get away from the looks of disapproval he pretended not to notice at the grocery store, or the dry cleaners, or even at school.

He'd almost lost the chance at this life with Jerry and William because he'd always been more comfortable with avoiding confrontation, and it was still a relatively new experience for him to stand up and defend his right to live whatever life he wanted. But there were moments every now and then when he just didn't want to deal with any of it, when he just wanted to forget about everything other than having Jerry and William all to himself. It was times like this weekend that David would plan all sorts of little surprises for both of his men and take a tremendous amount of pleasure in how happy they all seemed just being together.

The first surprise was that they wouldn't be staying at a hotel but at one of the houses owned by David's father. Niels had actually suggested it when David had invited him to the gallery show, encouraging him to spend a few days with Jerry and William at the mansion that had a staff of five full-time employees. The mansion actually belonged to the corporation, not Niels personally, and was normally reserved for visiting business associates and their families. David remembered seeing the mansion only a few times when he was younger, his father having needed him as a translator for certain visitors.

The estate was on Wellington Crescent NW and was mere minutes away from the Paula Redmond Gallery on Jasper Avenue via 102nd Avenue. David couldn't wait to show William the indoor pool and the huge bedroom, complete with its own bathroom and big-screen television that William would have all to himself. Nor could David wait to show Jerry the master suite with a huge walk-in shower that sported seven different types of shower heads and a bench that ran the length of the stall. He felt the heat brush over his face as he thought about the silicone-based lube he'd bought especially for using in that shower.

They would come back after the gallery show tonight and then have two full days to spend lounging, relaxing, and forgetting all the stress and frustration they'd all been through over the last several months: Jerry's nerves about the show and what he perceived to be his own failings as a father, William's worries about Cory, and David's concerns over everything that his two men were going through. This weekend would be exactly what all three of them needed.

Chapter 9

WILLIAM sat quietly in the passenger side of the car as his dad and David changed places. They were dropping off Jerry at the art gallery, would go to the hotel to drop off the luggage, and then come back to the gallery for an hour or so. As William waited in the car—David and Jerry standing just outside the driver's side door—he was beginning to feel the excitement of being in a different city, was beginning to feel nervous for his dad. He closed his eyes and offered a little prayer so that everything would go well for his dad. Jerry'd never admitted to being nervous, but William could tell all the same; why else would Jerry have asked—over and over—about whether the lights had been turned out back home and whether everyone had their cell phones?

Something three or four blocks down the road drew William's attention, but as David pulled open the driver's side door, William heard the last few words of the conversation, and then he and David were heading back the way they came to a section of Edmonton that had large mansions with tall gates and long, winding driveways.

"I thought we were going to stay in a hotel?" William tried not to sound too disappointed.

"We are, sort of," David said as he smiled.

"There's no hotel around here." William sat up straight and looked out all of the windows, disappointment a little more evident in his voice.

"This," David said as he pulled the car into the driveway of a large, three-storied brick mansion, "will be better than a hotel." David stopped the car and then turned to regard William. "There's a pool, your own room, a sauna and," he whispered as he leaned closer, "best of all, you won't have to clean up after yourself."

"A pool?" William asked, his disbelief evident.

David nodded.

"Just for the three of us?"

David nodded again.

"Cool."

David chuckled. "Let's take the luggage inside, and you can pick out your room."

William jumped down from the car and reached inside, grabbed his backpack, and hefted it over his right shoulder. He met David at the trunk and reached inside for his small, black suitcase and then held out his free hand. "I can take one of yours for you, if you want."

"That's very kind of you, William, but your dad and I only have these two small suitcases." David stood aside and let William pass. "I've only ever been here a couple of times myself, when I was much younger." David stooped to take the small suitcase from William's hand, placed it beside his and Jerry's and then pointed to the door knocker.

"Neat," William said as he raised his arms so that David could lift him to the same height as the heavy ring through the lion's mouth. "It's heavy," he whispered over his shoulder as David put him back down. Within a few moments, both of the tall doors opened, and William saw a man standing there dressed in a white shirt and black suit.

"Mr. Loewenberger?" The man extended his hand towards David. William looked at David and then back at the man.

"Yes. This is William. And you are Mr. Sloan?"

William watched the man shake David's hand and then reach to shake his.

"I am, yes." The man stood aside, and William felt himself pushed forward a little by the hand that David had on his shoulder.

"Very nice to meet you, William. Please come in. I'll take your luggage up to your room as soon as I've shown you around the estate."

"Oh, please," David said as he stopped at the foot of the stairs. "Please don't let me make you late. It's Friday evening and I'm sure you have plans at," William saw David check his watch, "almost seven in the evening. Please, we can take care of ourselves from here."

"Very well," Mr. Sloan said as he handed over an envelope. "All of the meals have been prepared and are in the fridge. And the pool and Jacuzzi have been cleaned."

"Thank you, Mr. Sloan." David reached into his breast pocket and William saw several other envelopes, which David passed to Mr. Sloan. "Please accept my thanks. If I could ask one final favor? Could I ask you to ensure that the other staff receive their envelopes as well?"

Mr. Sloan bowed slightly and then exited the large entrance hall. "Is he a butler?"

"I believe he prefers the term concierge." David stooped to retrieve his and Jerry's suitcases and then made his way to the stairs. William grabbed his own luggage and hurried to catch up. "Your Opa Niels's company owns this house," David offered as William tried to look around at his surroundings without tripping on the stairs. "This is where his very important guests stay when they come to Edmonton."

"What if they want to stay in Calgary?"

"There's a big house there as well." David made his way to the end of the hallway and placed the suitcases by the large, wooden double doors. "Now," he said, rubbing his hands together, "which room do you want?"

"Can I have the one closest to yours and Dad's?"

"Of course you can, William."

David pushed open the tall door and stood aside to reveal the bright blues and whites of the nautical themed room. "Hope you don't get seasick, you scurvy dog." David growled out the last few words.

"Cool!" William placed his suitcase and backpack neatly on the nearest chair and stood in the middle of the room. "Can we do this with my room at home?"

"I don't see why not," David said through a smile. "We'll ask your dad after the show tonight."

"Hey, look at that!" William ran across the room to the wide gate-leg table that held a large aquarium. "Look at all the different fish."

"When I was your age, I had an aquarium like that with three different kinds of gold fish."

William turned to look at David. "How long do gold fish live?"

"I don't know, maybe ten years or so, give or take." David came to stand beside William. "Should we ask your dad if we can get an aquarium too?" Before William could say anything, David held up his hand. "It'll mean you'll have to be responsible for them, feed them, clean the aquarium…."

"Is it hard? Taking care of them, I mean."

"No," David said as he sat in the armchair closest to the aquarium. "And we'll help you with the heavy stuff, like cleaning the aquarium."

"Hey," William said, his eyes going wide as the thought came to him. "If I show Dad that I can take care of fish, maybe he'll let me get a dog."

"Maybe," David said with a chuckle. He pulled William to him and planted a quick kiss on the soft blond hair, his hand staying and stroking lightly over the buzz cut. "What kind of dog do you think you'd like?"

"When Mr. Boyd told me that I'd be moving to Alberta to live with Dad, I spent a lot of time searching the internet for stuff about Alberta." William let his body lean against David's; he always felt so sleepy whenever David stroked his hair like that. "I came across this site that didn't have anything to do with Alberta, but showed dog sled races up north."

75

"So you'd like a husky?"

"A Siberian husky, yeah," William said through a yawn. "There were pictures of pure white huskies with really light blue eyes."

"That'll mean I'll be outnumbered," David said with a chuckle. "You and your dad and the dog will all have blue eyes; I'll be the only one with brown."

"We can get one with brown eyes." William started to say.

"I'm just kidding, William, we can get one just like you described when your dad says you're ready." David stopped stroking William's short hair and glanced at his watch. "Okay, we've got fifteen minutes to take a look around the house, and then we have to get to the art gallery." David stood up and William looked up at him. "Something tells me you want to start with the pool."

DAVID watched as William ran for the door and toward the stairs. "Careful, William, the floors are slippery!" David hurried his pace so that he could keep an eye on the little guy who seemed so tired a few moments ago. He was glad that this weekend seemed to have delayed William's preoccupation with Cory and his unexpected absence from soccer practices, but David still found himself worrying about William's progress. Most of the time, David wasn't really sure he wasn't projecting his own feelings onto William's actions.

He'd resisted the urge to wrap the little man in a big bear hug when William had asked to have the room next to theirs. Even though he'd heard no more about Cory for the past several days, David was becoming very aware that perhaps he would need to start encouraging more independence from William, who was no longer the same scared little boy he'd met a year ago. David wasn't sure if he was entirely glad for this transformation, albeit a slight one. On the one hand, he wanted so much for William to grow up and become independent, but on the other, he wished—every now and then—that William could stay this shy, quiet little boy for a few more years. He told himself to be glad that he'd found this family, at last, and he tried to keep things in perspective, but he just couldn't help the feeling of uncertainty that had settled over him since they returned from visiting Frau Zimmerman in Switzerland.

"Hey," David said as he walked down the stark white-tiled hallway to the pool room. "Look at this." William had already beaten him to the room, but David found himself thinking out loud. It had been a while since he'd been at this house, but he certainly didn't remember this wing—in fact, he was quite certain that he'd never even seen the pool before.

"Look, David," William yelled from the other side of the huge room. "They have floaties and noodles and mattresses and rafts and kick boards and—"

"You'll have to come and get one of us if you want to go swimming, right? I don't want any bad decisions to spoil our weekend."

"Okay," William said as he nodded and kept picking through the large chest of pool accessories.

"William?" David suppressed a grin as William stopped searching and turned to look at him, a huge smile still firmly planted on his face. "Or I'll have to lock the door, yeah?"

"I promise," William said as he nodded and made a big X over his heart. "No swimming unless one of you is with me."

"Agreed." David reached into his pocket and pulled out the envelope that Mr. Sloan had given to him. "Do you need to go to the bathroom? We have to get going to your dad's show soon."

William placed all of the toys back in—or nearly in—the chest and came around to the same side of the pool as David. "No," he said after a few moments, "I think I'm good to go."

"Good," David said and pointed to William's shirt. "You're coming undone." David smiled as he watched William tuck in his shirt. "Okay, so one hour—give or take—and then we can come back here and go for a quick swim before you're off to bed."

"'Kay." William stood still as David kneeled before him to fix his tie. "Sorry, I tried to stay neat."

David gave another quick kiss to the top of William's head. "I think you're really neat," he whispered as he pointed to the door to the tiled hallway.

"Not that kind of neat," William groaned as he led the way to the front door.

ONCE they'd arrived safely at the art gallery, David was filled with the same mix of emotions as he noticed William clinging to him, uncertain of these new surroundings and the loud voices. There were probably a few more people than they'd ever had at the family barbecues, but none of the guests seemed to be overdoing it with the wine—a fact for which David was very grateful. David and Jerry had discovered last year that William had not had a lot of experience with adults who were drinking. David felt his stomach lurch at the memory of the panicked phone call he'd received from the frightened and confused little boy who didn't understand why his Uncle Jerry was acting so strangely.

For almost thirty minutes, David had kept an eye on William, finally letting him go exploring. Jerry had done some brief introductions, calling both William and David my family whenever he'd introduced them. And David was so relieved to see so many familiar faces that he was able to relax a little at the thought of letting William out of his sight for more than a minute or two.

And so David stood back, beside a landscape that Jerry had done just shortly after their return from Switzerland, and let himself—white wine in hand—dwell on how he and William had been introduced to the various guests in the gallery. He hadn't expected being introduced as Jerry's family to have such a powerful effect on him. Nor had he expected himself to be so unprepared for seeing Jerry in this environment. There was no doubt that Jerry could handle himself among the members of the wealthy elite. Nor was there any doubt that

Jerry was enjoying this immensely. And as conflicted as he'd been over urging himself to let William gain some independence, David found himself staring into the beautiful canvas in front of him, the Swiss countryside reminding him of a time when he'd had Jerry and William all to himself.

David's mind jumped around, unable to settle itself on any one particular subject. He thought about his father. He'd invited his father—both of his parents actually—but David knew that neither of his parents would attend. David assumed that his mother was still adjusting to her husband having re-established contact with their gay son. And his father? David figured he was far too immersed in his most recent business venture. And as disappointed as David was, he was also rather relieved that he'd have Jerry and William to himself.

"I give private showings."

David was startled at the hand that was snaking its way around his waist. He turned, so lost in his own thoughts that he didn't recognize Jerry's voice—or touch. "Jesus, you startled me." He smiled and leaned into his lover's body, accepting the quick peck that Jerry placed on his lips. "How are you holding up?"

"Me? I'm fine." Jerry left his arm around David's waist and shoved the other one into his trouser pocket. "How are you and William doing?"

"I'm fine, and William seems to be enjoying himself."

"Where is our son anyway?"

"Right over there." David nodded and held up his wine glass in the direction of the table with assorted cheeses, crackers, and imported pâtés.

"I wonder how many of those he's managed to scarf down," Jerry said as he laughed and pointed at the crumbs around William's mouth, David noticing them without any difficulty.

"I'm just glad he's not glued to my leg anymore. But I do wonder sometimes where he puts it all."

Jerry just shook his head, his smile big and broad as he watched William weave his way toward the spot where he and David stood.

"I've promised him a swim in the pool before bedtime, so we'll probably be going before he has a chance to eat too much more."

"Yeah, I was going to ask you about that." Jerry ran his hand over William's head and pulled him in close to his side as he turned back to David. "A little bird told me that our hotel is actually a mansion."

"A little bird, huh?" David raised an eyebrow as he looked down at William's cautious smile.

"Sorry, it just slipped out." William reached into one of his pants pockets and pulled out a cracker. He held it out in the palm of his hand, David assumed as some sort of peace offering.

"It's okay, William." David placed his wine glass on the tray of a passing waiter and reached down to loosen William's tie. "I have to tell you that you have been very, very impressive tonight."

"Thank you." William reached into his pocket for another cracker, looking up when David laughed. "What?"

"Nothing." David undid the tie completely and put it in his suit pocket. "I am dying to go for a swim. How about you?"

William turned to his father and asked, "Are you coming too, Dad?"

"No, sport, I have to stay here for another couple of hours, but I should be home before you fall asleep."

"Oh, I don't know about that." David pulled William to his side, his hand tracing lazy circles across William's slight shoulders. "He seems pretty tired to me. Probably be asleep as soon as his head hits the pillow."

"Then we'll both get lots of rest and play in the pool before breakfast. How's that sound?"

"Good," William said as he nodded. "I'm gonna go say goodnight to Kitty."

They watched, together, as William walked over to where Kitty stood with a couple of elderly patrons. "And what about you?" Jerry sidled up beside David and placed his hand at his lower back. "Will you be asleep by the time I get home?"

"That depends, I guess."

"Oh," Jerry asked, his grin growing a little wider, "on what precisely?"

"On how entertaining your private show promises to be."

Jerry kissed him softly on the lips and was gone.

David saw William making his way back to where he stood. "All set?"

"Yes."

As the two of them exited the gallery, the cool spring air was a welcome relief from the warmth and humidity created by so many bodies inside of the gallery. David walked slowly enough so that he wouldn't lose sight of William, keeping his hand hovering near William's shoulder. The parking garage was only another hundred feet or so, but when David looked up to check the color of the light at the next intersection, William was running off down the sidewalk, yelling Cory's name. David's voice caught in his throat for a moment before he yelled for William to stop. He broke into a run as soon as he realized that William was not going to stop for him.

David finally caught up to William at the traffic light, his mind thanking all higher powers that it hadn't yet changed to green. "William, what are you doing, for pete's sake? You could have gotten hurt or caused an accident." David reached down and took a hold of William's right hand. David hoped that his voice wasn't sounding too angry.

"It's Cory, David. I saw him. He's right there, right over there, by the bank."

David looked down the street and then turned back to him, guiding him across the intersection when the light turned green. "Please

81

promise me you won't take off like that again, William. You scared the crap out of me."

"I'm sorry, David, but it's Cory. I have to catch up to him."

David looked down at the excited face; he hadn't seen William this excited for the last few days, not since Cory seemed to disappear from his life. How would he ever explain to William that—even if this young man was Cory—he was probably here to party with his friends. "Okay," David said at last.

William pulled on David's hand. "Come on, before he gets away."

"What if it's not Cory?"

"It is. I know it is."

William called Cory's name one more time and David looked farther down the sidewalk, trying to figure out which pedestrian could possibly be Cory. And when William began pulling David toward the rather dirty, scruffy young man standing near the corner of the bank and strumming a guitar, David finally recognized Cory. David couldn't be sure, but he would have bet money that Cory wasn't exactly happy to see them. And what's more, David wondered if the bruises on his face might be the reason.

As they approached Cory, David couldn't help the sinking feeling in the pit of his stomach that Coach Lapis's wife had been correct in her assumptions of Cory's wild and reckless behavior. And instead of a weekend for William to have fun and forget about Cory, it would be a weekend spent watching William learn that some people are not to be trusted.

Chapter 10

"HEY, Billiam," Cory said with a strained smile. He took the guitar strap from around his neck and held the instrument out in front of him as if it were a shield.

David watched as William moved closer to the tall teenager and then stop, his smile vanishing. "Cory, what happened to your face?"

"Just roughhousing with some of my friends." Cory shrugged as if to reinforce the idea that his injuries were no big deal. "What are you doing in Edmonton?"

"My dad's art show," William announced, the smile coming slowly back to his confused face. "Do you want to come and see?"

The panicked look in Cory's eyes made David's stomach do flip-flops. And with the clarity that came from spending so much time around lost and confused children, David understood. "William," David said as he placed his hands on the slight shoulders, halting William's return to the art gallery. "I think maybe Cory would like to come over for a swim."

"Oh, no—"

"He won't take no for an answer, Cory." David offered a sincere smile, one that said he knew why Cory was in Edmonton, why a sixteen-year-old was busking on the street corner. And more importantly, David hoped his smile let Cory know that there would be no questions until the young man was ready to share whatever information he wanted.

Cory nodded only once, and David couldn't help the feeling that the dirty and bruised young man was fighting back the urge to run—or cry. He took the backpack from Cory and slung it over his shoulder while William helped his friend pack up the guitar. And within a few minutes, the three of them were headed into the parking garage.

"HOW come you never told me you played guitar?" William had decided to sit in the back seat with Cory.

"Sorry," Cory said after a few moments, "I guess it just never came up."

"Will you teach me?"

"Sure, I guess—"

"William?" David waited until he saw William's wide blue eyes staring back at him in the rearview mirror. "There's plenty of time for all that. How about we just let Cory enjoy the pool for a bit first, okay?" He smiled at William in the mirror and returned his gaze to the traffic light just in time to see it turn green.

"'Kay. Can you stay over? There's lots of rooms. And then we can go swimming again tomorrow. And David and Dad and I are all going to the mall with all the—"

"William, why don't you ask Cory what he likes to eat?"

"I like mac and cheese, especially the way David makes it. Do you like mac and cheese?"

"Who doesn't?"

David couldn't be absolutely sure, but Cory seemed to become a little less nervous since his unexpected reunion with William. "Mac and cheese it is then." David pulled the car into the long, winding driveway of the mansion. "So," he began as soon as the car was in park and the engine turned off, "William, you can help Cory with his things and with picking out a bedroom for tonight, and I'll be in the kitchen getting all the food ready. Okay?" David held up the house key for William.

"'Kay." William grabbed the key, pushed open his door, and reached back in for Cory's backpack. "Come on, Cory, you can have the room next to mine. You should see how big the beds are!"

David exited the vehicle, closed his door, and steered his way to the front door. As he came around the other side of the vehicle, Cory stopped in front of him and turned around. For a moment, it seemed as if Cory was about to say something, but then he just stood, his eyes staring into David's.

"I'm here if you need to talk to someone," David said quietly. "But I think, right now, you'd better go with William before he blows a gasket." Cory nodded and turned to follow William through the front door.

DAVID was busy in the kitchen preparing mac and cheese, french fries, and chicken salad sandwiches. Occasionally, he heard William's excited voice as he gave Cory a tour of the house. They stopped in the kitchen and Cory asked if he could help with anything. David declined, but then turned to William. "Hey, William, how about you go and get Cory some towels and stuff for his room?"

"'Kay." William, still in his dark suit, ran toward the door, but then stopped. "Cory, do you have swimming trunks with you?"

"No, but I have a pair of shorts I can use."

Satisfied with Cory's answer, William dashed off to make sure Cory's bathroom was fully stocked.

"Thank you." Cory's voice was a whisper and—David noticed—he didn't seem to know what to do with his hands. "I don't know what to say to him."

"You've run away, haven't you?" David didn't wait for confirmation. "Is there anyone I should call so they won't worry?"

"No," Cory said as he pushed his hands further into his pockets. "There's no one."

"I'm sorry, Cory; I know your mother passed away years ago, but what about your father?"

"He's not around anymore." David was sure Cory could see his confusion.

"You've been living by yourself?"

"No, my... I mean, my dad is usually there, but he was...." Cory's voice trailed off, and David felt like letting the subject go. It seemed quite obvious to David that Cory was embarrassed or ashamed, or both.

"I meant what I said, Cory. I'm here if you need to talk to someone."

"Thank you, but I don't want William to find out why I left."

"I won't say anything to him." David walked around to the side of the counter where Cory stood. "But when it comes to you, I think you could tell him you have three heads and he wouldn't care. He's become quite attached to you." David felt a little bit relieved when he saw the smile tug at the corners of Cory's mouth. "Has anyone checked your bruises? I mean...." David drew a circle around his own face.

"They're okay." Cory looked down at the floor again when he added, "This isn't the first time."

David resisted the urge to ask the question that immediately came to mind and was thankful when he heard William's thundering footsteps coming down the hall. He moved back behind the counter to check on the food just as William rushed into the kitchen. "Okay, towels, face cloth, soap, toothpaste, and there was even a robe in there."

"Okay, well, I think Cory's looking forward to a swim, so I'll come and get you when the food is ready." David watched the two boys exit the kitchen and head left to the pool, and then found himself staring at the frayed bottoms of Cory's dirty jeans. "Cory? If you want to bring me your clothes, I'll make sure they get washed."

William was explaining, excitedly, about all of the pool toys he'd found earlier as he pulled Cory out of the kitchen and down the hall toward the pool, leaving David alone with all of the many questions that he'd not been able to bring himself to ask. Where was Cory's father? Why had Cory run away to Edmonton and not Calgary? What had really caused the bruises on Cory's face? Was it related to drugs? Was Cory being abused? Was letting Cory around William the worst judgment call David had ever made?

JERRY turned after shutting his car door and headed up the stairs to the mansion, waving to Kitty as she guided her bright red BMW to the opposite end of the semi-circular driveway. He knew that he was a little later than what he'd told David earlier in the evening, but he was still pretty sure that he'd be in time to say goodnight to William and spend some quality time with David in the pool or their bed—or both.

He tested the door and found it open. Pushing the heavy door aside, he entered the darkened foyer, surprised by the squeals of laughter coming from the other side of the house. It wasn't that he'd expected to find no life in the house at just after 10:00 p.m., but he hadn't anticipated hearing this kind of noise until their trip to the mall tomorrow.

The smell of the food guided him to the kitchen. Shrugging out of his suit jacket, he turned the corner to find David, William, and Cory sitting at the expansive kitchen table, all three of them sharing a laugh. "I'm home," Jerry said, his lips curling into a smile almost involuntarily.

"Dad!" William was out of his chair within seconds and had his arms wrapped around his dad's waist; Jerry couldn't help but notice that William and Cory were both wearing damp swimming trunks. "Look who I found."

"Hey, chief," Jerry said as he smoothed his hand over his son's head, wondering where the bruises on Cory's face had come from. "Cory," Jerry nodded at the young man, "I'm glad to see you're safe. William was quite worried about you."

He noticed the nod that Cory offered. "I'm sorry if I caused anyone any worry, sir."

"Sir?" Jerry laughed and watched William return to his seat beside Cory. "Jerry's fine." Jerry finally moved to sit beside David, leaning over quickly to plant a kiss on his lips. "Looks like we've both had a busy night."

"Are you hungry?" David asked. Jerry considered the question while he shut his eyes and felt David's hand massaging the back of his neck. "William and Cory have already eaten their weight in mac and cheese, but there's still some left, or I could make—"

"I'm good, thanks, baby." Jerry leaned in for another quick kiss and then turned to William. "How about you two go for another quick dip before bedtime so I can talk to David?"

Jerry was surprised at the look that Cory gave to David, but kept his mouth shut. When William and Cory were gone from the room, Jerry leaned in and gave David a proper kiss. He held on to the soft skin at the nape of David's neck for a few moments and then pulled back to look into those nervous brown eyes. "Looks like Cory might be worried about what I was going to say to you."

"I think he's very confused. He's run away from home."

"Yeah, I kinda figured it would turn out to be something like that," Jerry sighed and let his chin fall into his palm.

"Are you angry?"

"Angry? Why?"

"Well, some people might think it shows a lack of judgment letting a stranger into the house, especially around a young boy."

"He's not a stranger to William," Jerry said as he scrubbed his hand over his face. "Besides, I trust your intuition when it comes to kids before anyone else's." Jerry leaned forward when he saw the smile spread across David's face. "How long is he staying?"

"I don't know," David said after he stole another kiss from Jerry. "I guess we'll have to check with Sara or someone else at Child and

Family when we get back. Cory says he has no other family." David shrugged and let his hand move its way slowly up Jerry's forearm until he felt the soft, thick hairs of Jerry's beard. "I think there might be a very sad story attached to that young man."

"And you want to make it all better, don't you?"

"I'm not that obvious, am I?"

"I'm just teasing you, baby." Jerry pulled David to him until David was sitting in his lap.

"I know." David went willingly and settled himself on the firm muscles of Jerry's thighs. "So, was it all a huge success?"

"Kitty seems to think so. Sold most of the pieces that I had there and had a few people ask about special commissions. She looked very smug when she brought over an elderly couple—big time rich—who were interested in seeing samples of portraits. Apparently, they want one done of their new grandchildren."

"I was very proud of you tonight, Jerry." David leaned forward and ran his hands over Jerry's scalp. "And how cute was William when you introduced him to that couple from France?"

"And what about that tall, blond kid who had you cornered for a good half-hour?" Jerry chuckled as David pulled a face, obviously trying to convey that he had no idea to whom Jerry was referring. "I seem to remember him touching your arm and shoulder several times."

"Please," David said as he punched playfully at Jerry's bicep. "I'm old enough to have been his kindergarten teacher."

"I know, that's what I'm saying." Jerry wrapped both of his big arms around David; he knew there would probably be another slap for that observation. He took a deep breath and relaxed his grasp a little as he felt David's body settle against his.

"Were you happy with the show, Jerry?"

"It's nice making money, that's for sure, but I just don't care about the socializing part of it." Jerry felt himself cringe inwardly at the memory of the many hands he'd had to shake, the forced smiles. He knew that most people had an impression of him as antisocial and curmudgeonly, and he knew he didn't really do anything to correct this impression. And Jerry had always been fine with that, had always been content to stay on his ranch, alone and free from the drama that other people tended to bring. But even Jerry had to admit that when he felt David and William so close at the art gallery, when he'd been able to look up and see them, all of the socializing and smiling and hand shaking hadn't really bothered him as much as he'd dreaded. "Listen, David, I want to thank you for bringing William tonight. I never realized what a difference it would make to have the two of you there."

"You're very welcome, baby." David was able to move his arms a little more and took advantage of Jerry's loosening grip to lose himself in the sensation of moving his hands slowly over the silk shirt that Jerry was wearing. David leaned in for a slow kiss, his lips curling in a mischievous grin when he felt Jerry's growing erection beneath his own. "After we get the boys to bed, I'll have a surprise for you."

"Ooh," Jerry said as he moved his hands under David's thin cotton T-shirt. "Like that?" Jerry pulled David closer when he felt the smaller man shiver. "Wonder if I'll still be making you shiver like this when we're old and in rocking chairs."

"As long as we're in the same rocking chair, I'd say it's a pretty safe bet."

Jerry smiled at that thought and let his head fall back while David's tongue and lips traced a trail from his ear to his collar bone. Jerry closed his eyes as he pulled David even closer and felt the long fingers lose themselves in his hair. "Can't believe it's been almost a year," Jerry whispered against a sensitive ear.

"I know," David muttered against the heated skin of Jerry's neck. "Okay," he said after he pulled himself away from Jerry's body a little. "I'll go and get the boys ready for bed, and you can go and get naked and meet me in the shower."

"I don't get to try out the pool?" Jerry couldn't hold his playful— yet indignant—expression for too long before he was grabbing at the waistband of David's jeans. "Our only plans for tomorrow were to go to the mall and then do a barbecue here for dinner." Jerry pushed himself up to his feet without relinquishing his grasp on David's jeans. "Why don't we let the boys live a little. We'll let them wear themselves out, and then you can take me upstairs and wear me out. Then we'll all sleep in until noon and be really rested for the mall." With his legs on either side of David's, Jerry walked both of them out of the kitchen and down the hall, stopping at the large double doors to the pool area. Jerry asked Cory to keep an eye on William while he and David changed upstairs.

Despite his best efforts, Jerry could not convince David to do a little fooling around on the pristine, duvet-covered king-sized bed. Even his usual pout didn't work and only led to David repeating himself over and over that he'd planned a nice surprise for Jerry later. And so, appeased—but not sated—Jerry followed his lover back down to the pool.

They found William in the shallow end of the pool tossing a waterlogged nerf ball back and forth with Cory, who was perched on the side of the pool with his feet dangling in the warm, clear water. Both William and Cory were completely drenched, laughing each time the ball was caught and more water sprayed over their heads and torso. David threw his towel on one of the cedar lounge chairs and headed for the boys, but Jerry grabbed his arm and guided him in the opposite direction. "We're going in here first," Jerry said as he led David to the Jacuzzi.

After entering the water first, Jerry pulled David in so that the younger man was sitting beside him, Jerry's arm draped lazily over the soft skin of his lover's shoulders. "Should we be doing this in front of Cory? I mean, since we don't know how he'll react and all."

Jerry wasn't sure what David meant at first, and then caught up. "It's wrong to show affection?"

"That's not what I mean, and you know it."

"Doesn't matter what you mean, David. Thought we weren't going to let people control how we behave anymore."

91

"I'm not talking about that." David moved a few inches away from Jerry so he could look directly at him. "I'm talking about not doing something that might make our guest feel uncomfortable."

"You want me to find out?"

"Don't you dare," David warned as he stood to exit the Jacuzzi. "You'll embarrass him." He walked to the edge of the pool with Jerry not too far behind. As he prepared himself for an elegant dive into the pool, Jerry wrapped his arms around the slim waist and fell backwards, pulling David along with him into the calm waters of the deep end.

David surfaced first, his legs and arms working to widen the gap between him and his lover. He made it to the shallow end a few seconds before Jerry did, trying to use William as a shield. With only his eyes above the surface of the water, Jerry made his way slowly to his son. Grabbing William around the waist, Jerry lifted himself out of the water and flipped William onto his shoulder in one seamless movement. With William and Cory both laughing at his antics, Jerry moved his long legs through the shallow waters and managed to take hold of David's swimming trunks before he could escape the pool. With his family safely in his arms now, he let himself sink back into the water.

"For the record," Cory began when his own laughter died down, "it doesn't make me uncomfortable."

Jerry looked at David, quite certain that he would be embarrassed at being overheard. "Told you so," Jerry said through a self-satisfied smirk.

"Wow, good ears," David muttered as he felt Jerry's big hand push his head below the water.

Chapter 11

JERRY'S eyes fluttered open. There wasn't anything that woke him up, but once his eyes opened, he became aware of the sound of David's breathing, the aroma of the soap and shampoo that still lingered on his lover's body from the night before. As happened every morning, Jerry ended up on his back, one arm outstretched and draped somewhere over David's body. He rolled onto his side and snuggled up against David, who always ended up sleeping curled up on his side, both hands in loose fists in front of his face on the pillow. He felt his erection grow as David wiggled his body backwards and closed the distance between them. "Did I wake you?" Jerry asked.

"No," David whispered, "I've been awake for a little while, wondering if I should wake you so that I can ravage you again."

"You have, have you?" Jerry said as he wrapped one arm around David's waist and pulled him tightly against his body. "Well, for future reference, the answer to that dilemma will always be yes."

"Good to know." David chuckled as he turned to lie on his back.

Jerry raised his head and rested it on one hand while he looked past his lover to the digital clock. "It's only six thirty in the morning. Do you want to get some more sleep? We've got a day full of a happy eleven-year-old at a mall with other screaming and excited kids and rides and junk food and—"

"Don't worry about me," David said as he turned on his side, wrapping one arm around Jerry's back and pulling himself a little closer. "I'll be fine."

"Okay," Jerry said as he nodded and brought a kiss down to David's forehead. "In that case, I think we need some more practice with my surprise toy."

"You liked that, did you?" David pushed against Jerry's shoulder and moved his body so that he was positioned in between Jerry's legs. As he brought their lips together, he pushed each of his legs forward, delighting in the sound of anticipation in his lover's moans. "It was incredibly erotic for me too." David reached down between Jerry's thighs, a muted whimper escaping his own lips when he felt how rigid Jerry had become. "Knowing that I'm the reason you're making those noises, knowing I'm the reason you're leaking so much pre-cum right now." David kissed Jerry passionately, their tongues moving slowly against each other, as he brought his thumb to graze across the slit of Jerry's prick. He spread the clear liquid around the mushroom head of Jerry's cock, being sure to keep the thick foreskin pulled up, just the way Jerry liked.

Jerry imagined seeing himself right then, knees bent, his sensitive hole exposed. He opened his eyes when their kiss ended and saw David moving slowly down his body, planting languid kisses on his neck, shoulders, and all along his belly. Finally, Jerry felt the long, slender fingers pushing against the heat of his hole. His eyes closed involuntarily and he heard the sharp intake of breath into his own lungs. "Fuck, David," Jerry sighed as he pulled his own knees toward his chest. "Feels so good." After a few moments licking and kissing the sensitive flesh, David replaced his tongue with his fingers and then— and Jerry had no idea where it had come from—the dildo that had been his surprise last night in the shower.

Almost instantly, Jerry felt himself harden even more, his balls aching almost at the memory of how the slender dildo had felt as David—on his knees and with his mouth around Jerry's erection—had pushed it slowly inside of him. He'd been lying on the ample bench inside the shower when David had explained softly and slowly what he would do with him. It's not that Jerry had ever objected to having someone entering him, but rather that he'd never found anyone whom he thought enough of to allow himself to be as vulnerable and trusting as this intimacy required.

He and David had discussed it often enough, what David felt when Jerry was inside him, and Jerry had always wondered—out loud even—whether he would enjoy it or not. They'd tried a couple of times just after David had moved into the ranch, but Jerry had found that he'd been far too uptight and had not been able to relax enough. But lately, he'd found himself looking forward to having David fingering him or rimming him. Jerry found he enjoyed it especially when David was able to nip and bite at his foreskin while pushing inside him with his fingers or a thumb. And then last night? Jerry opened his eyes to see David concentrating intently on hitting all of his erogenous zones. When he felt his prostate tapped for the fifth time in what seemed like mere minutes and hours all at the same time, Jerry knew he couldn't hold on any longer. "Won't last, David, so good."

As the slender dildo was pushed and pulled tantalizingly slowly, Jerry felt the vibrations of David's response, and felt the heated, rigid tip of that tongue dip one more time into his slit. Then, as if he could sense Jerry's climax building deep inside of his belly, David touched his teeth against the sensitive head as he pushed the dildo in and used it to massage Jerry's prostate over and over again. The combined sensations of David tonguing his slit, massaging his prostate, and nipping at the sensitive head of his cock sent Jerry over the edge, and he cried out as an orgasm—more powerful than last night's—came from somewhere outside of himself. The sensations of feeling David's throat work to swallow his release did nothing to soothe Jerry's overheated and sensitive body.

He felt David petting his overly warm skin, placing kisses as Jerry continued to come down back to earth. "Come here, baby," Jerry whispered as he reached for his husband.

"Good morning," David said as he snuggled beside Jerry. "I'm going to go down and get breakfast ready for the boys. You sleep some more."

"Or...." Jerry pushed against David's shoulder and then let most of his body weight work to pin David in place, preventing him from getting out of the warm bed. "We can both stay in bed and make out?"

"I don't know. I was really looking forward to breakfast. Maybe you can convince me to stay here."

Jerry's mouth lifted at one side, a small sneer to let David know he'd accepted the challenge. Jerry lowered his body slowly, positioning it so that David would not be able to escape and knowing exactly what he could do to keep him from leaving the room. Letting his arms support him, his torso suspended a few centimeters above the silky skin, Jerry let his lips find their way to the sensitive ears, kissing first one and then the other, finally whispering in the more sensitive of the two, "Until I met you, I never realized how great morning sex can be." Jerry kissed the ear again and nibbled at the ear lobe for a few seconds. "You're even more sensitive in the morning." He positioned his legs so that their hips and cocks were aligned perfectly, and then returned his lips to David's ear. "I love you, mountain lion," he whispered, and then kissed around the shell of his lover's ear, closing his own eyes as he felt the shudder pass through David's body. "You make me happy." Jerry felt David's body push up to meet his, felt his hands pull against the thick muscles of his back. He kissed the sensitive ear once more and whispered, "Love to see your face when you come. Come for me, baby."

Jerry lowered his body slightly so that David was able to get a little more friction going between their bodies, Jerry's own cock hard again,and leaking beside David's. He could tell by the rhythm of his panting that David was close. Taking this as his cue, Jerry moved his body, his movements opposed to David's, his lips continuing to kiss at the sensitive ear. He heard his name, a mere puff of air against his neck and then felt the heat spill out between them. He held himself there, knowing how sensitive his husband was after every orgasm. "So pretty, baby," Jerry whispered as his body felt David's body relax back against the mattress. "Never get tired of that, David, never." Jerry moved off to the side of his lover and petted and stroked the sensitive skin, pushing himself down a little so that he could rest his head on David's chest.

"Think we might have to get a shower like that for home," Jerry said and felt his head bounce as David laughed.

"Something tells me that if we do, poor William would never see us again."

"Don't think he'd notice," Jerry said as he raised his head and smiled. "I don't think he's ever going to let Cory out of his sight again."

"I'm just glad he's actually putting himself out there trying to make a friend." David's hand came up, almost on its own, and stroked Jerry's hair. "But I'm not sure I like the fact that Cory ran away."

"Does seem to raise more questions than it answers, that's for sure."

"I told him that if he felt like talking, I'd be more than willing, but I have this feeling that he's a closed book, and a very tightly closed book at that."

"So what are we going to do?" Jerry raised himself on an elbow. "Take him home and call Sara?"

"He says he doesn't have any other family, so I don't see what else we can do." David smiled at Jerry and tried to sit up, but was stopped by a large, beautiful hand on his chest.

"No, don't go yet," Jerry said calmly. "The boys won't be up for hours, and I feel like spooning." He rolled David onto his side and snuggled up behind him, wondering what surprises lay in store for his family. If Cory did run away, there must have been a good reason for doing so. And if the reason was something bad enough to cause the teenager to find his way 300 kilometers from home, then what did that mean for Jerry and David and William? Were they in any danger? Could Cory's presence here jeopardize the new family that Jerry had found and worked so hard to keep? As he closed his eyes, content to feel David safe in his arms, Jerry contemplated the most important question of all: Would Jerry be able to fix whatever Cory broke?

As HE leaned against the metal railing, David watched Cory and William take another turn on the swinging ship and was impressed at how attentive and protective Cory was with William. Jerry had disappeared to the bathroom only minutes before, and David could hear the whistling before he felt the hand at the small of his back. "How are the boys doing? They haven't thrown up yet?"

David laughed and shook his head. "I don't get how William can eat everything he's eaten—including that huge breakfast—and go on these rides again and again."

"Stomach of iron, I guess," Jerry said as he pushed closer against David's body. "So, I was thinking that maybe one of us should have a little sit-down with Cory and talk to him about what his plans were before we found him in Edmonton. I mean, I remember you telling me he was busking outside of a bank, so I'm guessing that he hadn't really spent too much time planning his getaway."

"I know we should, but what if he runs away again? Maybe we should just call Sara and see what she says."

"Could do that too." Jerry let his hand stroke lazily up and down David's back. "But whatever he wants to do, we can't really stop him. He's not ours, not any relation to either of us. And for all we know," Jerry said as he shrugged, feeling a little more than helpless, "he could have some family that he's not admitting to."

"I just hope this doesn't end up hurting William," David said as he watched Cory and William, both smiling, come toward them.

"Can't protect him from that." Jerry said as he nudged David's shoulder with his.

"David?" William was standing in front of him and looking up, a big, happy smile on his face. "Will you come on the Orbiter with me? Cory says he wants to take a break."

"I'd love to."

"It's no wonder Cory wants a break there partner; you've kept him going for almost an hour straight." Jerry put his hand on David's shoulder. "Cory and I will meet you over in the food court in about twenty minutes."

"Why so long?" David asked as William pulled him toward the next ride.

"I need to head up to DeSerres for a few art supplies." David watched Jerry turn to Cory and ask, "Hope you don't mind?" And with Cory offering a quick shake of his head, David watched the pair of them head off to the art supply store.

"Come on," William grunted as he continued to pull on David's hand.

"How can you keep going on these rides, William? Don't you feel even a little sick?"

"No!" William stopped at the gate and held out the correct number of tickets for both himself and David. "I love feeling like I'm flying. And on this one you spin around while you're going fast on the roller coaster at the same time."

"I love roller coasters." David sat beside William in the chair and the young employee closed the bar on them and then turned his attention to securing the other two passengers who'd gotten on just after David and William. "I used to drive my parents crazy every time we went somewhere with a roller coaster, begging and pleading until my dad usually gave up and took me on the roller coaster."

"I know," William announced, "Opa Niels told me how much you used to love going riding on the horses and how you'd beg to go off the highest diving board at the pool." He looked up at David's bewildered expression. "When we go out on the horses or when he babysits, I always ask him questions about you." William suddenly looked panicked. "Is that okay?"

"Of course it is," David smiled down at the flushed face and ran his hand over William's short, blond hair. "But you know that you can ask me anything you want, right?"

"'Kay." William smiled and then brought his hands up to grip the security bar in front of him as the car started to move. "Here we go! Hang on, David!"

David barely took his eyes off of William during the entire ride. There was something about this little boy's enthusiasm for grabbing every minute of happiness that life had to offer that continued to keep David dumbfounded and amazed. He still had a hard time believing that this little bundle of energy was the same little boy who'd stood in front of him almost a year ago with his eyes downcast, seemingly defeated and lost. In truth, David found himself worrying less and less about William's size; the possibility of William being short—like his biological parents—did not seem to be causing William any concern, so David and Jerry had stopped worrying about it—well, almost stopped. What had them concerned now was William's lack of any social network.

In many ways, David felt as if he'd been a part of Jerry's and William's family forever, but there were moments—such as sitting beside William on this ride—when he realized that he didn't feel as if he understood this young boy at all. It had been a time for adjustments for all three of them, and during this time, they had grown very close to one another. Each of them had come to care for—and love—each other very much, and there had never been any question that Jerry and David would be there for each other and for William. But David was also enough of a realist to know that, sooner or later, William would not tell them everything, would cease to make them the center of his world, and would eventually choose to leave them out of certain important moments of his life.

During the first parent-teacher interview that David had attended—at Jerry's insistence—back in October, David and Jerry had both been surprised to discover that William had begun to fall behind in his homework. Being one of William's former teachers and then one of his two dads, David had made the conscious decision to retreat into the background when it came to William and his new school. It was during that interview when David realized that William was changing; he was venturing outside of comfortable limits to see what else was out there.

And at first, David had been happy to see William taking risks, trying his wings. But sitting there in front of William's new teacher, David was filled with a feeling of dread; it filled him so quickly that he actually felt nauseous and had to curb the urge to run for the door. It took him several days to discern that what he felt had not been dread at all, but rather an inexplicable sense of solace when he admitted that William would always need him. It had been David who'd always been far too independent to admit that he could need anyone else.

It was this independence that had cost David so many years of happiness, had kept him from giving his heart to someone else. And then William had arrived, and David had found it almost impossible not to let William in; David had found someone more lost and lonely than himself. William had had a way—and probably would always have a way—of endearing himself to everyone who met him. There was something about William's sincerity that few people had been able to resist. So, why did someone so energetic and outgoing have so few friends? And then there was Cory. Did William see something in Cory that David and Jerry couldn't? Had William been able to sense that Cory was in need of protection? Or was it all as simple as William having a crush on Cory? Jerry and David had never really discussed the potential for William to be gay or straight or even bisexual; it was a nonissue for both of them. William would become what he would become.

It wasn't William's attachment to Cory—another boy—that worried David and Jerry, but rather the attachment to someone who seemed to be such a mystery. Both David and Jerry knew that every boy goes through phases of hero worship or adulation of someone other than a parent, but each of them also knew that there was the inevitable moment of disappointment. There would be that moment when William would come to realize that Cory wasn't infallible, that Cory was capable of making mistakes just like everyone else.

David knew full well that he couldn't protect William forever, but still there was a part of him that wanted to keep this lovable, earnest, and endearing little boy for as long as possible.

Chapter 12

WILLIAM put his hands around his dad's neck and waited for the feeling of exhilaration. He felt the first bounce and let out a little giggle. He felt the second bounce and felt his dad's grip tighten a little around his small foot. When he heard his dad say three, William sucked in a breath and straightened his arms over his head. He felt himself fly through the air and dive into the clear, warm water of the deep end.

He blew out through his nose, like he'd been taught at the boarding school so many years ago, and kicked his way to the surface. As his head broke the surface, he let out a whoop of delight, and then he swam back toward the shallow end where David had now joined Cory and Jerry. "David, did you see me?"

"I sure did," David said as his face broke out into a broad smile. "That was amazing. Maybe you'll become a world-famous diver, huh?"

"No," William panted as he felt his feet touch the tiles of the shallow end. "Maybe a world-famous horse jumper?" He'd talked about his future with Opa Niels a couple of times, and once with his dad, but William didn't know if he'd ever be able to decide on becoming just one thing; he wanted to do everything. "Or maybe a world-famous painter like Dad," he said as he put his foot into his dad's hands and his hand around the strong neck.

"Good choice, son," Jerry smiled at him and began his series of three bounces.

"This will have to be the last one." He heard David say as he counted along with his father. "Supper's almost ready."

William went flying through the air again, found himself under the water again, and swam back to the shallow end, just like he'd been doing for what seemed like such a short time. They'd returned from the mall a few hours ago, and they'd spent most of that time here in the pool. "Cory," William called as he approached the side of the pool where Cory sat. "You try, you try, Cory!" William pulled on Cory's T-shirt. "Come on. My dad's really strong. He can lift you, I know he can!"

"That's okay, Billiam; you can take my turn."

"No, come on, Cory, you have to try!" William pulled harder on Cory's T-shirt.

"No, thank you, Billiam."

"Dad, you can lift him, right?"

"William, that's enough. Cory doesn't want to take a turn, and we have to dry off for dinner anyway."

"But Dad—"

"William," Jerry said as he raised his eyebrows and his voice, "that's enough, now. You're making Cory uncomfortable."

William looked over at his dad and then at Cory. He felt his face going red from embarrassment and the sting behind his eyes. "I'm sorry, I didn't mean to." He didn't want to be in front of Cory right now, didn't want Cory to see the tears that would probably come anytime now. It had been a long time since William had done anything to make his dad angry, the last time being back in October when he'd been caught leaving his homework undone. He'd tried to explain that he understood everything and did really well on the tests, but Jerry had still been very angry that William had lied to him.

He'd run off to his room after he'd been made to sit there, his eyes stinging as they were now, disappointment too much to bear. He could handle just about anything—had handled a lot in his young life—except the look of disappointment on his dad's face or David's.

As he'd done that day in October, William found himself running to his room, the tears streaming down his face at the thought that Cory would be angry with him as well. He'd had enough time to change out of his swimming trunks and put on his favorite sweat pants and T-shirt before he heard the knock at his door. He knew it would be David; it was always David. It had been David who'd come to check on him that October evening. It was always David who came to check on him when he had a bad dream.

"I'm sorry," William said as he felt his face going red again.

"I know you are and so does your dad and so does Cory." David sat beside William on the bed, his hand going immediately to caress his back. "No one is angry with you, William."

"Dad said I made Cory feel uncomfortable." William looked up, trying to figure out what David was thinking. Were they really angry and David was just telling a white lie to make him feel better?

"Maybe you did, but that doesn't mean anyone's angry with you." David moved his hand to William's head, his fingers, his touch familiar and comforting.

"I didn't want to cry in front of Cory." William admitted finally.

"Do you think he'd think less of you if he saw you cry?"

William didn't have an answer to that question. His first instinct was to say yes, but then he remembered David telling him in October that crying wasn't a bad thing, and everyone needed to let out some emotion from time to time; sometimes, there was just so much built up inside that it had to come out somehow. Finally, he looked down at his feet and shrugged, not really sure if Cory felt the same way David did.

"I think you know the answer to that question, William." He looked up to see David's smile. "He's spent almost an entire day going on rides with you and playing with you in the pool. I think you know he wouldn't think less of you. But what you may not have figured out is that Cory probably doesn't know how to swim."

"Why didn't he say something then?" William had never even considered the possibility that Cory didn't know how to swim; he just assumed that all kids learned how to swim. "I could have helped him to learn how to swim." William saw David smile again and felt David's arms wrap around his shoulders.

"I know you would have, William, because you're a very special young man." David's fingers snaked around to his sides, William quite certain that David would try to tickle him to get him to laugh. This was how David tried to get him out of bad moods. "You're the best son anyone could ever have and Cory is very lucky to have you as a friend, but right now…," William squirmed when he felt David's first efforts to tickle him, "we have to get you downstairs, so you can eat something and show Cory and your dad that everything is okay." William managed to get away from the tickling, but was quite sure it was because David let him. "Okay?"

"'Kay," William said, as David stood up from the bed. After hugging him quickly, William ran to the stairs and headed to the kitchen.

JERRY and Cory had just finished setting the table and were about to start dishing out one of Jerry's favorite meals when William entered the kitchen, followed a few moments later by David. Jerry saw the smile on David's face before focusing his attention on how William stepped up to where Cory sat and looked him in the eyes.

"Cory, I'm sorry if I made you uncomfortable. I promise I won't do it again."

Jerry's heart skipped a beat at how earnest and sincere William was, and watched with rapt attention as Cory held up a fist. "It's okay, Billiam, no harm done." William's smile was bright enough—from relief Jerry supposed—to light the whole mansion, and he lifted his own fist to bump it with Cory's. "I guess I should have told you that I don't know how to swim."

"That's okay," William said as he took a few steps back and looked at his dad. "Dad and I can teach you. I'm a really good swimmer. It'll be my turn to help you like you helped me with soccer."

Jerry nodded at William and took his seat at one end of the small rectangular table. "My swimming instructor in Switzerland always said I must be part fish." William laughed as he made his way to sit beside his dad. With a somber expression, William looked at his dad. "I'm sorry I made you angry, Dad."

"Not angry, son, just concerned." Jerry wrapped his arms around William and stole a glance at David who had taken a seat at the other end of the small table. Jerry looked back down at his son and put his big hands on either side of William's flushed face. "I love you," he whispered.

"Love you too."

And with that, Jerry was happy to see that everything was back to normal. It was something he'd feared had to happen sometime today; William had a way of getting himself so excited that he seemed incapable of controlling himself. It was as if all of the filters in his brain shut off. It was something he'd been consciously working on with William, and—if Jerry were to be honest with himself—tonight's little episode was probably as much his fault as William's; he'd known it was a possibility, but not paid close enough attention to the signs.

"Cory?" David's voice snapped Jerry out of his own thoughts. "Before we eat, we like to join hands and then we each say our own silent prayer of thanks. But as our guest, we don't expect you to join in, unless you would like to."

Jerry took William's hand in his left and was quite surprised to see Cory's hand come out and take his right. Jerry looked over and saw David smiling. As had become the custom, William's *amen* signaled the end of the silent prayer of thanks and the rather less organized ritual of figuring out whether the food was being passed clockwise or counterclockwise, or whether it would just be passed around—as was usually the case—to the person with empty hands.

Jerry made a conscious effort to ensure that Cory—as the guest— was offered most of the dishes first, but William managed to get to the bread basket before anyone else and was already buttering two slices before seeming to remember that they had a guest. It wasn't a frequent occurrence for the McKenzie-Loewenberger clan to have dinner guests, but it was frequent enough that William would know to offer the bread to Cory before taking any himself. Tonight, however, Jerry didn't have the heart, nor the desire, to point out yet another faux pas to William.

"This is really good," Cory said, or tried to say through a mouthful of food, and Jerry looked over to see Cory's cheeks fairly bursting with food, wondering again—as he had during lunch—whether Cory ever got a decent meal at home. "This is almost as good as my mom's. Where'd you learn to cook like this?"

Jerry caught David's brief glance at him and couldn't help but remember that night when he'd learned about David's grandmother, how she'd never known of his sexual preference and therefore, had never known to disown him like her daughter and son-in-law. Jerry smiled at the memory; it had been the night when he'd begun to see the future he could have with David and William. That had been the night when Jerry understood that he had been slowly falling in love, not only with David, but with the idea of having the family he'd always wanted. He'd never admitted that desire to himself, but something about the honesty and the compassion that David had shown in sharing that part of his life sent Jerry's mind groping to explain the inexplicable urge to protect both David and William.

"My grandmother was a very good cook." David offered the large Dutch oven to Cory for the second time. "I loved being around her."

"I'm sorry," Cory whispered, taking the pot from David's hands.

"Thank you, but it was a long time ago."

"This is my very favorite meal." Jerry offered as he passed the bread to Cory. "Actually, I don't think there's anything that David makes that I don't like."

"Liver," William grunted before stabbing another big piece of roast with his fork. "I hate liver."

"But you've got to admit, cowboy, that the way David makes it… it's almost good."

"Never!" William stuck out his tongue and shook his head, as if to emphasize that nothing would ever make him like liver, in any form.

"Liver's good for you," Cory offered after his own laughter subsided. "My mom used to make it with onions that she'd fry up with butter and a little bit of brown sugar. It was good."

Jerry looked over at his son, hoping that he hadn't caught the *used to*, hoping that he wouldn't begin to ask questions that Cory might not be ready for. David had explained to him about Cory not wanting William to know too much about his situation, not wanting William to know that he'd run away because of problems at home. And as he looked around the table at his son and his husband, Jerry wasn't sure he even wanted to know what those problems were. He didn't want to think about what it would mean for Cory if there was no relative to take him in, like Jerry had been there for William. He didn't want to think about having to live the rest of his life knowing that things didn't always work out for everyone. Of course he knew they didn't, but he'd never had one sitting at his table, sharing his food.

"So then what's your favorite meal, William?" Cory put down his fork while he waited for an answer. Jerry felt like laughing, knowing full well that his son wouldn't have to think very long.

"Lasagna!" William looked up at David, his eyes wide and his mouth full of bread. "Hey, tomorrow's Sunday."

"We have lasagna on Sunday," David explained as he looked over at Cory's empty plate. He pushed the pot of beef stew toward Cory, and Jerry noticed how Corey looked around the table as if asking permission to have more.

"Help yourself," Jerry said as he sat back in his chair. "I'm not allowed to eat too much anymore. Apparently, I'm getting fat." Jerry looked over at William, whose smile disappeared as he looked up at his father. "I'm just teasing you, cowboy." Jerry looked over at David, the admonishment clear on his face.

"There's nothing wrong with beef stew," David said as he stood and took first his plate and then Jerry's. "It's the desserts you have to watch out for."

Jerry swatted David's ass as he walked past. "I know, I know." He turned to Cory and shrugged his shoulders. "Just my luck I had to marry a gourmet cook."

"How long have you two been married?"

Jerry noticed the genuine curiosity on Cory's face. "David and I met a year ago. We were married last October."

"Cool," Cory said as he sat back in his chair and rubbed his belly. "I'm stuffed."

"I hope you saved room for some blueberry pie and ice cream." David returned to the table and placed the steaming pie in the center before taking the remaining two plates. Jerry stood himself and helped clear away the remaining pots and pans before returning with the two-liter tub of ice cream.

"Maybe a little piece," Cory offered with a lopsided grin.

"You should try his Sachertorte," William said as he stood so he could begin scooping ice cream onto the small dessert plates. "It's almost as good as Frau Zimmerman's."

Jerry noticed the look of confusion pass over Cory's features. "The cook at the boarding school William attended in Switzerland."

"She answered my e-mail the other day," William announced to no one in particular. "She sent me pictures of her new grandson. She said his name is Heinrich." William finished filling the fourth bowl with two scoops of ice cream and looked over at Cory. "That's Henry in English."

"Thanks," Cory said as he accepted the bowl that William held out to him. "And you speak French as well? That must be so great to be able to speak another language."

"I can teach you, if you'd like," William offered as Jerry filled his plate with a big piece of pie.

Jerry noticed David fight the urge to smile at how caring and mindful William had become of Cory and finished depositing pieces of pie on his and David's plates. "Great," Jerry sighed playfully, "that'll just leave me as the only one who won't understand what anyone is saying."

"I was never very good at languages," Cory said as he tried to pick up a piece of pie without the little dollop of ice cream on top falling off. "Never very good at math either."

"What are you good at?" William asked and then added quickly, "Besides sports, I mean."

"Drawing, mainly," Cory said once he'd swallowed. "And I always got good marks in English."

"And gym class." William added as he looked up at Cory.

"Sure, and gym class."

Jerry ate his pie slowly, wondering why Cory had suddenly begun to refer to his life in the past tense, as if he'd already decided that he would never be going back to the life he'd run away from. And he wanted to ask Cory about it in the worse way, but knew the trust needed for those kinds of questions had not yet been established. "Hey," Jerry said finally. "I have an idea. Why don't you and Cory go and look on top of the television in the family room." Jerry nodded in the direction of the huge family room to the right of the kitchen. "There's a huge screen in there, and I bought some movies when we were at the mall today." Jerry looked to William. "And I do believe one of them is the sequel to *The Fantastic Four*."

Chapter 13

JERRY stretched his long body in the plush leather theatre-style reclining chair and looked over at William. Fast asleep. It was no surprise; William had had another very busy day full of excitement. And the fact that each of them had his own individual reclining seat with console complete with cup holders probably helped to lull both William and Cory to sleep long before the movie ended.

He stood at the same time as David and headed for William. "I'll get the boys to bed and meet you in the Jacuzzi in about ten minutes." Jerry stood close to David so he could whisper, "I'll bring the suits in case the boys wake up and come down, but I was hoping to get you naked." Jerry kissed David's ear and then bent to scoop up his son as David touched Cory gently on the shoulder.

"Sorry," Cory said as he shook his head to wake himself up. "I'm awake."

"Time for bed, Cory," David said as he pointed to Jerry, who had William in his arms.

"'Kay," Cory murmured as he stood and followed Jerry and William upstairs. Before leaving the kitchen, Cory turned back to David. Jerry stopped to see if there was anything wrong. "I wanted to thank you for being so nice to me. I haven't had a lot of that lately."

"I'll let you two talk a bit," Jerry explained as he started for the stairs. "I'm just gonna get this guy to bed."

As he walked up the stairs, Jerry could hear Cory's hushed voice. Perhaps, Jerry hoped, Cory was finally opening up about what he'd been through. And he hoped more than anything that Cory would be able to find some peace of mind, not only for himself, but also because William still seemed so intent on keeping him in their lives.

AFTER spending almost ten minutes trying to put an unconscious William into pajamas, he had to stifle the laughter as he imagined the strange picture the two of them must have presented. Every time that Jerry managed to get a limb free of clothing, William would roll onto his side and reach for Jerry and hamper his efforts in freeing the next limb.

It took him a little longer than he'd anticipated to finally get William into bed, and he'd expected to find David alone—and near or in the Jacuzzi—but Jerry found him and Cory sitting at the table. Jerry could tell, immediately, that Cory had shed some tears or had been fighting hard to keep them inside. He couldn't help but feel sorry for the young man. Cory's home life had been so horrible that he'd felt the need to run away and leave everything he'd known behind. And as he took a seat at the table, Jerry realized that Cory's home life must have been so bad that running away and starting again—with no one and nothing offering any kind of support—seemed like the best of all possible options.

"Sorry," Jerry said when Cory finally noticed him, "should I come back later?"

"It's okay," David began to explain while Cory looked away and took a few quick swipes at his eyes. "Cory was just heading off to bed, but he did give me permission to let you know what we were talking about." David turned back to look at Cory, his hand coming out to rest gently on Cory's shoulder in a reassuring way. "I promise, William won't find out. And I meant what I said about you being welcome here any time."

Cory nodded slightly, his eyes darting quickly between the two adults, and then he was heading for the stairs. Both David and Jerry watched Cory ascend the stairs, ready with compassionate smiles if he looked at them, but he didn't; Cory kept his eyes on the stairs until he reached the top and disappeared into his room.

"Oh. My. God." David said as he closed his eyes and leaned into Jerry.

"That bad?"

"I need something to drink." David headed to the fridge, and Jerry began to wonder what Cory could have possibly said to make David drink. It couldn't be too bad, could it? After all, David had extended an open invitation. He wouldn't have done that if he'd discovered something too awful. Jerry was sure of that, at least. "Where are the suits?" David asked as he came back to stand in front of Jerry with an unopened bottle of white wine and two glasses. "Did you forget them?"

Jerry reached into his back pocket and pulled out two pairs of boxer shorts. "Forgot that our suits were already down here and probably still damp." Jerry put his arm over David's shoulder and the two of them walked to the Jacuzzi. "Don't start without me. I'm going to run over to the bathroom and get a couple of towels." Jerry turned back to look at David, who was already stripping out of his clothes. "Is it something that could hurt William? Or you?" Jerry didn't feel reassured that David had to think a few moments before shaking his head.

Even though his trip to retrieve the towels took mere minutes, Jerry found his mind racing to consider all the possible complications that Cory's confession could mean for him and his family, especially William. He returned to find David already sitting in the warm, bubbling water of the Jacuzzi, his head tilted back and both wine glasses filled almost to the brims with the white wine. It didn't seem that David had taken even a small sip of his wine yet.

"You're not going to fall asleep on me, are you?" Jerry was free of his T-shirt and was stepping out of his pants and boxers at the same time when he noticed David's eyes come open.

"Absolutely not," David said as he stood and stepped over to where Jerry was entering the Jacuzzi. "And most certainly not when you're naked."

Jerry smiled, sat down in front of one of the jets, and then pulled David onto his lap. "Good answer," he sighed as he leaned forward a little so that their lips could skim over cheeks and chins and necks and ears. Jerry's hands roamed over the smooth, slick skin of his lover's back for what felt like only minutes and finally settled on David's ass. "What do you want, baby?"

"This," David moaned and pulled his head up from Jerry's shoulder to look at him with those bedroom eyes. He continued to move his hands slowly over Jerry's chest and shoulders. "I want this. This is good." Jerry closed his eyes as David's long, wet, slender fingers came up to caress his cheeks, his forehead and then finally settle themselves on Jerry's close-cropped hair. "I have to tell you something, and I don't want you to be worried."

"Okay," Jerry said cautiously.

"Cory's father has been beating him for almost six years now." Jerry opened his mouth, furrowed his brow, ready to offer a comment. But David placed a finger across his lips to silence him. "His father is a big man, like you." David's caresses grew even more gentle, and Jerry couldn't help but wonder what he had to be worried about; all of this information had very little to do with him. "Cory is a little intimidated by you... your size."

"Okay," Jerry repeated.

"It's why he's kind of standoffish with you and not me."

"Cory thinks I'd hit him?"

Jerry heard his own voice, heard the disbelief and disappointment. It was no surprise to him then when David's voice became hushed, as if he were speaking to William after a particularly bad day. "He knows on some level you never would, but he's been... trained, I guess, to be very guarded around men your size and what they've represented in his life up until now."

114

"Okay," Jerry said for a third time, not really sure how he was supposed to react, what he was supposed to say to all that.

"He wanted me to tell you that." David dipped his hands into the warm water and brought them back to Jerry's shoulders, soothing and pacifying. "He wanted me to thank you for all you've done for him this weekend."

"Guess I should have realized that," Jerry admitted after a few moments. "When we were in the art supply store, I told him he could pick out anything he wanted. After a few minutes of him looking on his own throughout the store, I went to find him. I came up behind him and touched him on the shoulder as I called his name. And… he flinched. I mean, he brought up his right arm. I thought it was just that I'd scared him, but now I understand."

"There's more."

Jerry wasn't sure he wanted to hear the rest of it, but he pulled David's body closer to him as he listened.

"His mother passed away about six years ago, and his father came back to be closer to his own mother, so that she could help take care of them." David's hands moved to the back of Jerry's neck. "And Cory said that everything was great, but then his grandma passed away, and his father started to spiral out of control. Alcohol, drugs, yelling, screaming… or crying. Eventually, he lost his job, and that's when he turned to growing and making and selling drugs."

"Jesus," Jerry murmured, shaking his head in disbelief.

"Cory ran away to Edmonton this past Wednesday."

"I guess that explains why he wasn't there to help William's soccer team."

"He told me that his father was drunk, drunker than usual. When Cory got home from that last soccer practice a little late, his father showed his disapproval with his fists. So, Cory called the police to report his own father and then ran away before they arrived; he was afraid they'd arrest him too."

"I'll have to call Sara first thing tomorrow."

115

"He says he won't go back. Says that he'll run away if we try to make him go back."

"You believe him?"

"There's no doubt in my mind that he'll take off if he sees us as betraying him."

"So," Jerry said as he brought his own hand to rub at the thick hairs of his beard, "I shouldn't call Sara?"

"I don't think we have a choice." David shrugged and smoothed some more water over Jerry's chest and shoulders. "I can check with Lenore about protocol, but I think I already know that she'll tell me it has to be reported to the police."

"Is there any other family?"

"He mentioned something about an aunt, his father's eldest sister. She apparently lives in the south end of Calgary."

"Should we call her? I mean, did he say anything about calling her or going to live with her?"

David shrugged. "He's still pretty reluctant to share too much information. I would watch his face when he was telling me all this, and I could almost see his brain working really hard to sort out what he should tell me and what he shouldn't. I think he's more spooked than anything else, like the horses during thunderstorms."

"Was he crying?"

David nodded and then got off of Jerry's lap so that he could drape his long legs over his instead. "He was crying because he said that his dad used to sell to some of the students at his school, said that everyone knows what his dad does for a living." David shrugged, a sign of frustration Jerry assumed. "He's been harassed, ridiculed, bullied, and even suspended once because he smelled like pot. Apparently, the principal didn't believe him when he tried to explain about his home life."

"Didn't you tell me once that if a school employee—like a principal—even suspects abuse, he or she has to report it?"

"Maybe it was easier for him to believe that Cory was just making it all up."

"Asshole," Jerry muttered.

"That may not be fair," David said as he continued to stroke his hand over Jerry's shoulders and neck. "We don't know what kind of information he had, so he may have made the decision he felt best at the time."

"That doesn't mean he's not an asshole." Jerry took hold of David's hands and pulled him so that he was once again sitting on his lap. "Now," Jerry said as David settled against him, "what would you say to forgetting about everyone else until tomorrow." He covered David's lips with his own and let his hands find their way back to the sensitive flesh of his husband's back.

IT TOOK David a few minutes to realize that he wasn't hearing—or feeling—Jerry; he must already be out of bed, David realized as he turned over on his side again to look at the amber digital numbers of the clock. It wasn't even seven in the morning, and he was alone in bed. It wasn't that he was alone in bed that seemed to bother David, but rather that he had managed to sleep through the departure. He wasn't what anyone would call a light sleeper, but any movement from Jerry had usually woken him, even out of the deepest of sleeps. As he stretched, David remembered that they hadn't made it to bed until just after midnight.

The boys had gone to bed just after ten, and then David and Jerry had found themselves in the Jacuzzi until their skin began to wrinkle, at which point they'd made their way to the bedroom but had been far too busy continuing their romantic evening to realize they'd stayed up far too late. He didn't know what shape Jerry was in, but David was already planning his afternoon nap.

He allowed himself to doze for another few minutes before he heard William giggling in the hallway just outside the bedroom doors.

As if by force of habit, David found himself smiling at the sound of William being William and swung his legs over the side of the bed. It took him a few moments to splash some water on his face, drag a brush through his unruly hair, and then he was on his way to the kitchen.

Before heading into the kitchen, David decided to see what Jerry and the boys were up to in the pool house; there seemed to be an awful lot of laughing and carrying-on happening for so early in the morning. "What does everyone want... for breakfast?" David had thought he would get everyone's order, but Jerry's absence from even the pool area made him a little nervous. *Where is he? Where did he have to be so early? And why didn't he tell me about it? Why didn't he wake me?*

"Chocolate waffles, please," William was already in the water, toys bobbing in the wake of his energy. "With blueberries and syrup." David felt his pancreas protest in sympathy of William's.

"Sounds good to me," Cory said as he smiled over at David.

David hadn't realized until that moment that Cory was shirtless and in the water beside William. Nor had he noticed the death grip that Cory seemed to have on the inflatable killer whale that was bigger than William. "William, where's your father?"

"I think he's in the study. At least he was there a couple of minutes ago."

"Okay, thanks." David moved closer to the edge of the pool and picked up the long buoy line and tossed one end to William. "Remember, you don't take Cory in the deep end until Jerry and I are here to make sure nothing goes wrong. Okay?"

"'Kay." William swam back to where Cory stood.

As he left to find Jerry, David stifled a laugh when he heard William explaining how they would start with getting Cory to put his head under the water for a count of three.

He stood next to the office door but didn't immediately hear Jerry's voice, only the tapping sound. That sound, David would always—forevermore—associate with his husband. Not being a terribly patient person, Jerry was far too often found bouncing his left leg and tapping a pencil—or pen or ruler or paintbrush—on the closest horizontal surface.

David knocked and then pushed the heavy mahogany door; it opened quite easily and revealed Jerry sitting on top of the ornate desk tapping a letter opener against the well-worn leather insert. Jerry smiled at him, and David took a seat on one of the two love seats covered with dark green raw silk upholstery, waiting for Jerry to finish his phone call. It wasn't difficult for David, after a few minutes, to figure out that Jerry was speaking with Sara. Nor was it difficult for David to figure out the topic of conversation.

After another one or two-word exchanges, Jerry thanked Sara and promised to have her and her partner—whose name Jerry could never seem to remember—out to the ranch soon for what was quickly becoming a biweekly dinner. Outside of his time spent with Jerry and William, those dinners with Sara and Lynn were some of David's favorite evenings. Before he'd met Jerry, it seemed his social life was defined by expensive restaurants, gallery openings and other late-night activities that seemed to typify the men he'd thought he'd been attracted to. And then there had been the evening he'd spent with Jerry and William.

Watching Jerry's expression as he hung up the phone, David couldn't help but feel that his life was about to change again, much as it had after he'd met Jerry and William for the first time.

"Sara said she'll have to do some checking, but she doesn't see any reason we can't take care of Cory until…." Jerry blew out a lungful of air and let himself slump down beside David. "If Cory's dad is facing criminal charges, he could lose his parental rights, and Cory would become a ward of the court, then child services would become involved, and they'd try a kinship placement. If there was no kin, they'd have to put him in the foster care—"

"Or with us," David stated matter-of-factly.

"Oh thank God," Jerry said with a sigh of relief, gathering David into his arms. "I've been trying to decide what you would think of all this, and I was pretty sure you'd be okay with the idea of having another kid in the house, but then...." Jerry didn't bother finishing his thought, opting instead to kiss David thoroughly.

"When will Sara know anything?" David pulled back from Jerry, the smile coming as the thought occurred to him. "Can you imagine what William will do if Cory ends up staying with us?"

"Speaking of our little boy—"

"Oh, shit," David sputtered as he pushed himself off the love seat. "I put the buoy line up, but we should get in there."

"Whuh?"

David laughed as he reached down for Jerry's hand. "Our little boy is teaching Cory how to swim."

"Right behind you."

Chapter 14

DAVID watched as William led Cory from the car to the house; the little tour guide was so intent on explaining about Cory's new room and movie night and his new computer and everything else William could think of that he forgot about his own luggage. David hoisted it over his empty shoulder, not noticing that Jerry had come to stand beside him.

"Well, Dad," Jerry whispered in his ear, "at least he's probably forgotten about getting a dog."

"You're terrible," David said with a smile. "I just hope this doesn't all go horribly wrong."

"Wrong?" Jerry pulled William's backpack off David's shoulder and put his arm around the smaller man. "What could possibly go wrong?" As he led his husband back to their house, Jerry said with a smirk, "Nothing ever goes wrong here."

"Knock on wood," David sighed as he tapped Jerry's temple. "What time is Sara supposed to call?"

"She said she'd call when she had something to tell us."

"In the meantime, I'll try to ignore that gnawing in the pit of my stomach."

Jerry and David were almost bowled over by William. He was pulling Cory along behind, yelling that he was going to show Cory the barn and Jerry's studio. David turned to see Jerry open his mouth to deliver his usual warning, and then laughed when William reassured his dad that nothing would be touched.

"Do you think Cory will mind if I go and get his laundry?" David asked.

"I'll let him know when I head out there."

David stopped on the stairs and turned to look at his husband.

"What?" Jerry asked as he found his progress halted by that look that David always gave him whenever David thought he was hovering. "I want to check on the horses and my studio."

"Liar," David laughed before continuing to their bedroom.

"I'm not lying." Jerry insisted as he threw the bags on the bed and began to unpack. "We've been gone for two days and I want to make sure nothing is wrong."

"And during those two days, Lenore and Harvey were out to check on the place. Remember?" David balled up the dirty laundry from his, Jerry's, and William's luggage and threw it in a pile near the hamper. "So either you think they didn't check on everything or you think they did and didn't do it right."

"You know, Mr. Teacher-man, you don't know everything." Jerry organized the remaining clothing in piles on the bed and then turned to look at David. "There is also a third option."

"A third option?" David repeated as he gathered unused socks and underwear and put them back in the drawer. "Well don't keep me waiting."

"Or... Lenore and Harvey were here and did a fantastic job and I'm going out to the barn because I don't want to have to help with laundry."

David closed the drawer to the mahogany bureau and turned, moving back to the bed to retrieve William's clothes. "Well, of course," he said with a solemn expression. "Yes, that does seem much more the likely option." He passed Jerry, who was readying the suits for hanging in the closet, and leaned up to kiss him gently. "I'm surprised your eyes aren't brown." He watched Jerry's brow furrow and quickly added as he walked toward the bedroom door, "Because you are so full of shit. I'm not sure you even know where the laundry room is."

"David!" Jerry declared in mock horror. "Language!"

"Oh, by the way," David said just before he reached the door, "the laundry could always still be here when you get back."

"Mountain lion, you are the love of my life, the sweetest father to William, an incredible source of inspiration for my art, and the most incredible lover I've ever known." Jerry walked toward him, his eyes full of mischief. "I love you more than you will ever know." Jerry kissed him gently on the lips. "But you and I both know that you couldn't let that laundry sit for more than five minutes before it drove you to distraction."

"Oh really?"

"Uh huh," Jerry said, and took the pile of clothes out of David's arms. "Five minutes, I'll bet you."

"And if I win?"

"Then I'll do laundry for a month."

"You know, Jerrod McKenzie," David said as he stroked his lover's arms, his hands working to encircle the pile of clothes. "I'd take that bet, but either way I'd lose." Taking back the laundry, David turned to the door, calling over his shoulder, "I don't think William and Cory would appreciate pink clothes three sizes too small." David watched Jerry head out. Alone in his thoughts, he didn't hear Cory approach.

"Ah, David?" He was snapped out of feeling rarified by Cory's voice. "I was wondering if there was anything you needed done, you know, so I don't feel so guilty about taking so much from your family?"

David offered a sincere smile, the word *family* still not losing its charm. He looked around for a moment, his smile disappearing. "Where's William?"

"Oh, he's still in the barn. I told him I was going to come in and see if I could help with anything." Cory seemed nervous for some reason, but David let it go.

"You could go up and get your laundry." David nodded to his left. "If you don't mind my doing it, I'll be in here for the next little while sorting and getting the first load going."

"Sure thing," Cory said with a smile and then disappeared up the stairs.

David plopped the pile of laundry on the long, narrow table that served for folding and sorting and had barely begun before he heard Cory's voice again. "If you ever need help, I know how to do washing and ironing, even dress shirts and pants."

"It's pretty state-of-the-art here," David said as he turned to indicate the bright red washer and dryer. "I even have one of those clothes presses." He opened a lower cupboard and pulled out the clothes press and placed it on the table. "Jerry bought it for me as a Christmas present. He has a very strange sense of humor."

"That must make ironing a lot easier, yeah?"

"I haven't used it that often. We're kind of a jeans and T-shirt family."

"Yeah," Cory chuckled, "me too."

"Well," David corrected himself, "except for weekends like this one where we're getting dressed up to do something fancy."

"William showed me some of Jerry's art." Cory was rubbing his hands over his jeans and David couldn't help notice how ragged and worn they were. "It's really something."

"Thank you." Neither of them heard Jerry come back into the house. David noticed Cory jump as Jerry appeared behind, one large hand landing on Cory's shoulder. "Sorry, didn't mean to scare you." Jerry took a step back, and Cory backed up toward the door, his demeanor changing almost immediately.

"I'm just going to, uh, go see if William is okay." David's heart broke a little when he saw Cory almost run for the front door and the look that the hasty exit left on Jerry's face.

"Sorry, I know," Jerry admitted suddenly, "I shouldn't have touched him. I know."

"Give it time, baby, he'll see what a teddy bear you are." David finished sorting the pile he had on the table and began loading the machine. "I think that boy needs some new clothes."

"You want me to take him out tomorrow after school?" Jerry asked as he came up from behind and wrapped his arms around David.

"How about we all go?" David turned around and brought his hands to his husband's face. "Dinner, shopping, maybe a movie?"

"On a school night?"

"Why not?" David kissed him gently. "Spring break isn't that far off. Maybe we could even take them out of school on Friday and do something spontaneous and fun."

"Spontaneous and fun, huh?" Jerry brought his hands so that they rested behind David's thighs. "I like spontaneous and fun." Within one swift movement, he hoisted David so that the smaller man was sitting on the washing machine, its noises muffled by the extra weight. "We could be spontaneous right now."

"Do something we've never done before?" David shoved his hands under the waistband of Jerry's jeans, his hands exploring the contours of his tight butt and put his lips to Jerry's neck.

"Yeah, I could lock the door."

"Yeah, and then," David whispered against Jerry's ear, "you could help me finish the laundry so I can start dinner." David felt the hands on his back still, then slide slowly to his sides. "Jerry? Don't! No tickling!" David pulled away to see the look on his husband's face. "I'm serious!" David found himself stuck on top of the washing machine; he couldn't get away, his own legs being trapped in between Jerry's muscled thighs.

"That wasn't very nice, you know." Jerry backed up a few paces to let David dismount, his hands never leaving David's torso.

"I'll make it up to you. Promise." David tried to back away, tried to get to the door, but Jerry was too quick and scooped him up into his arms. "Jerry, put me down."

"How were you planning to make it up to me?" Jerry carried him out the door and into the kitchen, putting him down slowly as he listened to what David whispered in his ear. "Okay," Jerry said finally when there was no more whispering, "you're forgiven." He smacked David on the ass. "Do you know how hard it's going to be to wash the car in this state?" Jerry put his hands in his jeans pockets and rearranged himself.

"I'll be out to help in a minute." David rolled his eyes at the look that Jerry gave him. "With washing the car, you sex fiend!" He busied himself with gathering the necessary ingredients for their usual lasagna dinner, having it all down to a science by now. By the time he'd boiled the noodles and sauteed the beef and prepared the sauce, he heard the buzz of the first cycle of laundry.

He got the first dryer cycle going, had shredded enough cheese for the lasagna, and even had enough time to get the load of colors going in the washing machine before he heard William giggling outside. When he exited, he found his three boys soaking wet and the vehicles not much cleaner than they'd been before the washing had begun.

"Dinner is in the oven," he said as he took a seat on the veranda. "Why don't those cars look any cleaner?"

"He started it!" Jerry stood ramrod straight, pointing at his son, and David thought that he would lose it completely.

"Did not, you big fibber!" William's indignation was clear, but he threw a sponge and nailed Jerry in the side of the head anyway.

"You're the fibber!" Jerry picked up the sponge and threw it back at his son, William's giggles filling the cool night air.

"How did you get all wet?" David stood and took a few steps closer to Cory.

"Collateral damage, I guess." Cory picked at his wet T-shirt.

"He was trying to save me," William shouted as he dodged the spray from the hose that Jerry was holding.

"You two tried to gang up on me," Jerry yelled with a tone that almost had David believing he was the victim in all this.

"Well," David said as he made his way over to Jerry, "I'm here now, so the big bad savages won't hurt you anymore." He'd almost gotten to Jerry's side when he felt the first drops of biting cold water.

"See?" William shouted as he took cover behind Cory. "I told you so!"

"Jerrod Austin McKenzie!" David kept walking toward his husband, trying to keep his face serious, with that look that told Jerry he'd gone too far. "Are you trying to make more laundry for me?" David could see the uncertainty in Jerry's eyes. "Do I have to do everything around here? The cars still need to be washed."

"We were just playing. I'll do it."

"Right," David said through a frown. "Give me the hose." The laughter erupted from David almost as soon as he had the hose in his hand. "Reload the torpedo tubes. Fire sponges at will!" David backed up so that Jerry couldn't get at the hose, ignoring the jibes from Jerry about playing dirty. David howled with laughter as both Cory and William proved too quick—and far too accurate—with the sponges for Jerry to escape them.

And as the giggles and laughter filled the air that glowed purple and orange with the setting sun, David forgot that it hadn't always been like this.

DAVID and Jerry heard the giggles as they climbed the stairs. Jerry had told them to go to bed almost a half-hour ago, but David knew he'd probably make a few more trips upstairs before he actually succeeded in separating them. Jerry walked softly, trying not to alert them to his presence, and stood outside William's bedroom door for a few seconds

127

before pushing on it gently. David backed up a little, content to watch Jerry be the dad.

William and Cory sat side by side at the computer. They were both huddled there in front of the screen, doing their best to keep their voices down as William was translating an e-mail from Frau Zimmerman. Jerry watched as one photo after another of little children flashed across the screen, listening to William tell Cory about Frau Zimmerman and her grandchildren. He couldn't see the photos very well, but Jerry assumed that the children must have been doing something goofy to have William and Cory as amused as they were.

He waited as long as he could and then knocked on the door, pretending that he'd just arrived. He couldn't even open his mouth before William was holding onto Cory's arm and looking up at him forlornly, as if they were victims of some cruel injustice that would see them separated forever.

"Please, Dad, just another five minutes. Please?"

"You asked that a half-hour ago." Jerry stood, arms crossed over his chest, and smiled at their bright, shining faces. David had to suppress a smile as he watched William wrap Jerry around his little finger.

"I know, but now I mean it."

"So, you didn't mean it before?"

"Yes." William frowned as if he wasn't quite sure what the question meant. "Well, no, but I mean it now. Please?"

"It's okay, Jerry," Cory said as he stood up, his hand patting William's. "We'll listen this time." Cory turned to William. "We can finish them tomorrow, Billiam. We don't want to make your dad mad."

"He's not mad," William corrected and turned further in his seat. "He's the best dad, ever."

"Nice try, cowboy," Jerry chuckled. "Okay," he said finally after a deep sigh, "the next time I come back up, it's lights out. Right?"

"Thanks, Dad!" William hopped off his chair and ran to wrap his arms around his father's waist.

"Right," Jerry huffed, "just make sure you remember that the next time I come in here."

"We will," William said reassuringly.

Jerry shook his head as he exited the bedroom to find David standing a few feet behind him. "What?"

"I didn't say anything," David protested as he walked toward the stairs. "But I would have to agree. You're the best dad, ever."

"I think I scared him again," Jerry whispered as they made their way to the kitchen.

"Who? Cory?"

"You should have seen the look on his face when I was in there." Jerry eased himself into one of the kitchen chairs. "Am I that scary?"

"Of course not," David said with a consoling laugh. "But until we know what he's been through, we won't know why he's so...."

"Shit scared?"

"No," David said as he slapped at Jerry's forearm. "Why he's so hesitant around you."

"I don't get it." Jerry scrubbed at his face with his hands as David moved back to the counter to finish fixing each of them a mug of tea. "He's not that way around you."

"Ah, yes, you see because I'm adorable." David turned and beamed, pushing his fingers into his cheeks to make dimples.

"And sexy as hell," Jerry muttered.

"Well, there is that too." David walked back to the table, and Jerry pushed his chair out so that David could sit on his lap. David wrapped his arms around his husband and buried his face in the soft cotton of Jerry's T-shirt, inhaling deeply the scent that made him feel both electrified and safe at the same time. "I tell you this, Mr. Jerrod

Austin McKenzie, you are the most incredible man I have ever met. I love you, William loves you, and Cory will love you too."

"Yeah, but you have to say that. You're contractually obliged as my husband." Jerry pouted but only because he knew it would get him a cuddle and a kiss.

"Poor baby," David said after kissing Jerry's pout away. "Should I get you a pacifier?"

"If I'm not mistaken," Jerry said, his voice husky, as his hand moved to between David's legs, "I do remember someone promising me a night of... what were the words?" Jerry's other hand came up to rest behind David's neck, their lips touching lightly. *"Whatever I wanted."* Jerry pushed his lips to David's, his tongue coming out to find its partner. He deepened the kiss as he squeezed gently with his other hand, delighted when David's hands came around his neck and began caressing his head. He'd never thought of his scalp as an erogenous zone, but David had a way of touching him—everywhere and anywhere—that made him lose all focus.

He felt the writhing stop, heard David's moans stop, and then his lap was empty. Confusion battled with the lust he'd felt mere moments before. He looked at David and saw him straightening his clothes just before he heard the footsteps coming toward the kitchen.

"I'm sorry for interrupting," Cory said as his eyes flitted around the room, not sure where to look. Jerry crossed his legs and pretended that he wasn't flushed and excited. "I just wanted to mention that, uh, well, since my father was... since I, you know, ran away, I, uh, haven't been to school, so...." Cory fidgeted with the hem of his T-shirt and looked at Jerry then at David. "I've been in some trouble there before, so I, uh...."

"Cory?" David said as he came back to the table with two mugs of tea, placing one in front of Jerry. "Would you like to stay home until we can meet with the principal?"

"I'm not sure that will do any good." Cory's fidgeting grew more intense, and Jerry pushed out a chair for him and motioned for him to sit. "Thanks, uh, Mr. Husack doesn't really like me and Ms. Rogers, the, uh, vice-principal, and he already thinks that I—"

"Cory, were you involved—in any way—in what your father was doing?" Jerry offered his mug to Cory, taking it back when Cory shook his head.

"No, but they don't believe me." Cory looked up, and Jerry began—probably for the first time—to understand the complexities of what had been Cory's life. "Some of the other kids thought that since my dad was a dealer that I must be just like him, and no matter what I did… I mean, I tried to ignore them, but then they'd be saying stuff about—"

"If you didn't have anything to do with it, then you just go to school, ignore them, and let me handle the rest." Jerry put his hand slowly on Cory's shoulder. "Okay?"

"O… okay, okay," Cory stammered and then looked up at Jerry and offered a small smile. "Thanks, Jerry."

"I'll tell you what, Cory," David said after a few seconds. "Why doesn't Jerry go with you tomorrow? You two can meet with the principal and get things going on the right path again?"

Cory nodded, thanked them each by name, and headed for the stairs but stopped short. "Maybe I should just go by myself." Cory had returned to the kitchen, and the look on his face had Jerry wondering just how he should handle all of this.

"I don't mind coming with you," Jerry said, his eyes shifting quickly between Cory and David.

"I know, and I appreciate it and all, but…."

"You want to see if you can handle things yourself first." Jerry understood; he'd been the same way when he was Cory's age, so desperate to prove that he could handle anything, that he was a man already at sixteen.

"Kinda, yeah," Cory said as he began backing up towards the stairs. "Can I call if I need your help?"

"I'll be waiting by the phone." Jerry wished Cory a good night's sleep, and Cory disappeared up the stairs. Jerry turned to find David smiling, the big grin eliciting a smile from Jerry himself. "What?"

"Told you," David said as he brought his mug to his lips. "Best dad in the world."

Jerry wasn't sure he believed it yet, but as he reached for his husband's hand, he thought—probably for the first time in a year—that he wasn't the worst.

Chapter 15

JERRY was contemplating a nice large helping of leftover lasagna and maybe even a beer for lunch when he felt the vibration on his hip. He stabbed the bale of hay with the pitchfork, took off his gloves, and grabbed for his cell phone. "McKenzie."

"Yes, Mr. McKenzie, this is Mr. Husack." Jerry thought he'd heard the name before, but decided to wait for the man to finish. "I am the principal at Shaftesbury Collegiate."

"Mr. Husack, what can I do for you?"

"I have Cory Flett sitting here in my office, and he tells me that you are his guardian now."

"In a manner of speaking."

"Well, I'm afraid there's been some trouble here at the school this morning. Are you available to come and pick him up?"

"Pick him up?" Jerry checked his watch. "It's not even eleven. What's he done?"

"Please, Mr. McKenzie. It will be easier to explain to you in person."

"Be there in about fifteen minutes, then." Jerry didn't bother waiting for the pleasantries to end. He snapped his phone shut and wondered if he should call David. After all, this was his territory; he probably even knew this Mr. Husack. He flipped his phone open, ready to call, but then decided against it. He stuffed his gloves into his back pocket, grabbed the keys off the hook just inside the barn door, and headed for his truck.

He'd only ever been to the high school once, to give a talk to one of the art classes, and was pretty sure he remembered how to get there. And after a couple of wrong turns and some cursing when he found the city had changed even more than he'd thought since he moved away almost twenty years ago, he found the visitor parking, pushed his hat back on his head, and took a few long strides to the front doors.

He found the office, took off his hat, pulled open the door, and waited for the secretary to acknowledge him. She didn't really seem to notice him, so he cleared his throat. He was just beginning to wonder if the job description of a school secretary had changed since his days when a door to his right opened, and a small, haggard man strode out and offered his hand.

"Mr. McKenzie?"

"Jerry, please."

"Right. Jerry, then." They shook hands, and then the man stepped aside and motioned toward the office he'd just left. Jerry could see Cory sitting inside the office that looked about the same size as one of the bathrooms at home. Cory didn't look too happy to be there, and Jerry could hear David's voice in his head. *Listen to everyone before you start calling them dipshits.* Jerry found a smile for Cory, who only looked up briefly, and took the seat beside him.

"I'm afraid to tell you that Cory is being suspended for fighting."

"I defended myself!"

Jerry looked over at the look of utter disgust on Cory's face and put a hand on his knee for a few seconds, hoping he'd be able to avert any kind of yelling match. "That's fine if he was fighting. He should be punished."

"This is Cory's third suspension this year, and I will be recommending to the school board that an expulsion should be seriously considered."

Jerry's hand went again to Cory's knee when he saw Cory's body bristle and flinch. "Suppose you bring me up to speed on the other suspensions. They for fighting too?"

134

"Yes, I'm afraid they were." Mr. Husack sat back in his chair, and Jerry couldn't help but wonder where the smug expression had come from.

Jerry turned to Cory. "Can you tell me your side without yelling?"

"Why bother? He's already made up his mind."

Jerry studied Cory's expression of disgust as well as his bouncing knee. "Why bother? Because I'm asking. You don't wanna say anything? That's fine, then I guess I'll have to take his word for everything." Jerry leaned back in his chair and waited, not really caring that he hadn't called the man by his name. He didn't know what it was, but there was something he didn't like about this Mr. Husack.

"Wasn't even in the school for ten minutes this morning, and some of the other kids were bad-mouthing my dad, calling him names, calling me names." Cory sat up a little straighter in his chair and looked over at Mr. Husack before continuing. "I ignore them like you and David told me last night, and Brad Martens comes up behind me and pushes me into Ms. Barker. Next thing I know, I'm here, and he's calling you."

"That what he told you?" Jerry looked over at Mr. Husack, who was leaning against his desk again.

"Almost verbatim."

"And what's this Brad fellow have to say about what happened?"

"We don't discuss other students in these kinds of situations, Mr. McKenzie. We are concerned only with Cory right now."

"As am I, Mr. Husack." Jerry leaned forward in his chair, straightening his back so that he looked down on the principal. "But I'm not about to take everyone else's word when there's an obvious discrepancy here."

"I can assure you, Mr. McKenzie, that with Cory's history—"

"And I can assure you, Mr. Husack, that I can go find a bunch of people who will tell me that Cory's one of the nicest guys in Calgary." Jerry leaned over, grabbed Cory's backpack, and stood to his full height. "Now if you're telling me that you've already looked into this, talked to this teacher and the other students that were in the hallway, and Cory's version is a lie, then I guess I don't have any choice but to trust you."

"There was no need for me to investigate any of—"

"That's all I needed to know." Jerry turned toward Cory, put a hand on his shoulder, and moved him to the door. "I'll do some investigating of my own on other options for Cory's schooling and be in touch." Jerry nodded and put his hat back on his head. "Appreciate your taking your job so seriously, Principal Husack."

"Oh, that's right." Jerry heard the smug tone and turned back to the principal. "Your wife is a teacher."

"You have a good day, Mr. Husack." A thought occurred to Jerry, from deep down inside his brain. It was something he thought he remembered from all of the frenzy of dealing with the Bennet Brigade last year. "One more thing, Mr. Husack? Am I correct in assuming that Mr. Loewenberger doesn't need to be present to hear that remark in order to file a complaint of unprofessional conduct against you?" Jerry pushed his hat back on his head again. "It would appear I've said something to upset you, Mr. Husack, and if I did, your problem is with me. Best to leave my *wife* out of this. Something tells me you couldn't best him on his worst day."

Jerry didn't wait for any kind of reaction at all before pulling his hat back down and exiting the tiny office to find Cory already outside the main office in the hallway.

"I'm sorry, Jerry, but he is such a prick." Cory picked up his pace to keep up with Jerry's long strides. "I heard what he said about David."

Jerry stopped dead in his tracks, half of his brain telling him to go back into Mr. Husack's office and beat the smile off the smarmy little shit's face and the other half telling him to be a better man than that. "Listen, Cory," Jerry finally said when he got the two of them walking again. "Don't matter what he is, 'cause I ain't angry with *you*, okay?"

"Really?"

Jerry couldn't help the muted snort of laugher. "Really," he said as he pressed the key fob and opened his door, throwing Cory's backpack in between them. Once he was settled, he turned to Cory. "I just hope David doesn't rip my head off."

JERRY had spent a frustrating afternoon between finishing his chores in the barn and going back to the house to check that Cory was doing his schoolwork, all the while trying to get the thought out of his head that David was going to tan his hide when he heard about the meeting. He'd debated with himself for the better part of three hours before he finally decided not to phone David and tell him everything. He would wait until David had been home for a while, giving Jerry a chance to snuggle and kiss him senseless before dropping the bombshell.

David and William arrived home just after he'd finished fixing the two loose posts on the corral fence. He delayed the inevitable by jumping in the shower after a quick greeting to William and offering a quick kiss to David. He left the three of them in the kitchen, debating which restaurant they would eat at tonight. Neither he nor David had mentioned anything to Cory about clothes shopping, and as he stood under the hot water and smelled the soap and shampoo he'd come to associate with David, he hoped that the whole evening wouldn't be ruined because he still couldn't couch his remarks to the idiots of this world.

DAVID waited for Jerry to exit the shower. He'd left the decision about the restaurant to the boys and waited, towel in hand, for his waterlogged husband to reappear from behind the frosted shower door. When the water stopped, he saw Jerry's hand come out, his eyes closed as usual, and reach for the towel. David handed it to him and waited for Jerry to dry his eyes.

137

"Hey," Jerry said nervously, jumping when he noticed David standing there in the steam.

"Hey yourself," David said as he took the towel from Jerry and started drying Jerry's muscular chest. "Anything you want to tell me?"

"How…?"

"Cory told me the highlights." David looked up into the bewildered expression. "And… you've been in that shower for almost twenty minutes." He moved the towel lower and kneeled down as he dried Jerry's legs. "I would have known something was up just from that alone."

"Okay," Jerry said as he turned to let David dry his back and ass. "Let me have it. I know I fucked up."

"Oh, you're going to get it, that's for sure." David schooled the smile that threatened and stood up as Jerry turned around. He draped the towel around Jerry's neck and pulled gently. It wasn't resistance that he felt when he brought his lips to Jerry's but rather uncertainty. He let go of the towel and placed his hands on the beard, his fingers combing and teasing. He finally felt Jerry relax and accept his tongue, felt his own growing erection aligning itself with Jerry's. After a few moments, he pulled away. "Have you learned your lesson?"

"I don't… what did Cory tell you?"

"He told me that you stood up for him. He told me that he was pushed and the principal didn't believe him." He pulled the towel from around Jerry's neck and fastened it around his waist. "And he told me that you weren't willing to punish him without knowing all the facts."

"So…." Jerry fixed the knot in the towel and looked down at David, who was combing through Jerry's wet hair with his fingers. "You're not angry with how I handled it?"

"Now what kind of wife would I be if I didn't support my husband?"

"He told you that too?"

"Do you honestly believe I've never heard that kind of garbage before?" David pressed himself to Jerry's chest. "But thank you for wanting to protect me. Besides, Ed Husack is a miserable shell of what he used to be. He was the third person to sign Bennet's petition last year and has applied to be the superintendent five different times and was never even granted an interview. He's a bitter, disillusioned alcoholic."

"You have no idea how much I wanted to wipe that smarmy expression off his face."

"You wouldn't be alone, baby." David kissed his husband and then backed up slowly to the door. "Now, get dressed. It's time for us to forget about Ed Husack and spend an evening out as a family."

DAVID was relieved that that was exactly what they managed to do: spend the evening out as a family. They had dinner at one of William's favorite restaurants, one of the many in Calgary that offered an all-you-can-eat buffet, and David actually felt guilty about the check at the end of the night. Between William's fascination with croutons and bacon bits and Cory's inability to get enough pizza, David wondered if the restaurant could possibly make any profit after their visit.

William managed to pick up on some of the scattered conversations between his fathers and figured out that Cory had been suspended due to fighting at school, chiming in just after dessert that it wasn't right to fight. Jerry and David tried not to look at each other as they heard their own words coming back to them through the sage wisdom of their son. "I know," William was saying around a mouthful of ice cream. "I was in a fight last year and got suspended. I couldn't go to the zoo because of that." William took another mouthful of ice cream. "Dad wasn't mad at me either because I was defending my friend. But it's still wrong to fight."

Cory looked at David and smiled. "I know. I won't do it again."

"You're both very wise." Jerry pulled out his wallet as the check was placed on the table. "And if you do it again, you'll be mucking stalls for a year." Jerry smiled at the waitress as she took the credit card and the bill back to the cash register. He stood, stretched his back for a moment, and then followed her.

"Does that mean what I think it means?" Cory looked to David for an explanation, whispering his question quietly, but not quietly enough.

"Cleaning up the horses' stalls," William said just as quietly.

"Don't worry," David said with a smile, trying to assuage the look on Cory's face. "It's not as bad as you think. And besides, he's mostly full of hot air."

"I'm what now?" David knew that Jerry was behind him. He could tell by the look of concern on Cory's face and the look of amusement on William's.

"You're just the smartest and most generous person I've ever met." David looked over at William. "Isn't that what I said?" William giggled and nodded exaggeratedly.

"Asking the boys to lie for you?" Jerry said as he shook his head. "That is just too...." Jerry shrugged his shoulders as if there were no words to convey his feelings.

"You're not the smartest and most generous?" David widened his eyes and looked up at Jerry, all innocence and playfulness.

"I'll deal with your punishment later." Jerry turned back to the boys. "Okay, we've got some shopping to do, and if you're like me, you hate it. So, let's get going 'cause the sooner we start the sooner we can be home watching a movie and eating popcorn."

"Can Cory and I pick out the movie?"

"Affirmative," Jerry said as William scooted out of the booth. "We'll need jeans and boots and hats and underwear and socks and shirts and sweat pants and more jeans and maybe some rubber boots for mucking out stalls and gloves for helping me fix—"

"But I already have all that stuff," William protested.

"Not for you, cowboy." Jerry brushed his hand over William's head. "Cory needs all that stuff if he's going to be staying with us."

Cory stopped dead in his tracks just after exiting the restaurant. David noticed right away and backtracked to where Cory was standing. "I don't have any money," Cory said. David looked ahead to see Jerry had noticed as well but kept walking beside William, his big hand still on the little blond head. He exchanged a smile with Jerry for a moment before turning back to Cory.

"It's okay." David put a hand on Cory's shoulder. "Think of it as payment for helping out with some chores."

"I can't... I don't...."

"There are no strings here, Cory." David pushed against his shoulder, trying to get him moving again. "Jerry and I want to help you."

"Why?" Cory took a step forward and then turned to face David.

"Why not?" David shrugged and offered a sincere smile. "It's what people are supposed to do for each other, isn't it?"

Cory nodded, but still seemed confused by it all. David managed to get him walking again, and they quickly caught up with Jerry and William, who were waiting outside of the nearest jean store.

"I'd get Wranglers," William said as he entered the store beside Cory. "They've always held up for me." David exchanged a look with Jerry; he could tell that Jerry was enjoying this outing as much as he was. It all seemed so normal and not at all where he thought he would be. He'd always wanted this, but never thought he would ever actually get it.

David finally saw Cory smile and relax a little as William began to extol the virtues of the various styles of Wrangler jeans, which seemed to occupy almost an entire section of the store. As Jerry looked through the hats and shirts section of the store, David sidled up beside him. "He was worried about how he would pay for his new clothes."

"Figured that's what you were talking about." Jerry picked out a few cowboy-style shirts and a couple of Stetsons. "He'll settle in soon, when he realizes that we're not like his old man."

"Just breaks my heart, Jerry," David said as he watched William picking out jeans for Cory to take to the dressing room. "What if there is some relative out there? All of this will be for nothing."

"Not for nothing," Jerry corrected, and then exchanged the cream-colored Stetson for a black one. "Even if there is a relative, we'll make sure he visits. We'll make sure he knows we still care about him."

"I guess," David said as he followed Jerry to the changing room. "I just hope William will see it that way."

"He will," Jerry said with a lopsided grin.

"I love you," David whispered, accepting a quick kiss on the forehead from his husband.

"Love you, too, mountain lion."

Chapter 16

JERRY had breakfast on the table by the time he heard the other three men in the house begin to stir, the sounds of showers and toilets giving him a pretty good indication of who was almost ready for a good, hearty breakfast. He'd been sure to make extra, especially for Cory. The poor kid had gone full hog on all the chores he'd been given and was aching something fierce, Jerry was certain, but Cory never complained and did his best to keep up. He was nursing some pretty serious blisters on his hands since he kept forgetting to wear his gloves, but Jerry couldn't have been prouder of the kid if he'd been Cory's real father.

In fact, he had forgotten completely that Cory might have to leave, had forgotten about Sara's investigation into whether he had any other living relatives. Cory had become such a part of their lives already. David had been spending his lunch hours at school visiting websites that offered explanations about how the foster care placements worked. With David's lunchtime Internet surfing, Jerry had learned enough now to know that Child Services would try for a kinship placement before a foster placement, and he understood that. He would certainly question anyone who would want to place a child—regardless of age—with a total stranger before a blood relative. It was what they'd done with William, and he was not about to question that decision. Of course, it wasn't exactly the same situation since Pamela, Jerry's cousin, had stipulated in her will that William should be raised by his only living relative—Jerry—if she and her husband were no longer able to care for him.

Whatever placement Cory would live with would have to take so many things into consideration that it all seemed like far too much to bear in mind for Jerry. There were the familial ties; the cultural history of the child; the opinion of the child; the age of the child; the continuity that family could provide to the child; and the mental, physical, and emotional needs of the child. It was all too much to absorb. There were no percentages, no way of assessing how much impact each category would eventually have in determining the placement of the child. And so, before he drove himself to distraction with scrutinizing every possible combination and permutation, Jerry decided to stop considering anything but the moments Cory would be part of the family.

David had even been to the school—he waited until Wednesday before going to see the principal. He was—if the truth was known— quite intrigued to see how he would be treated. He and Jerry had already made the decision to keep Cory out of the school for that week, so David had decided to speak to the principal about organizing all of the work that Cory would need to complete instead of speaking to each individual teacher. And he was glad that he had decided to do it that way. The e-mail that he received from Mr. Husack listing all of the work Cory would have one week to complete seemed impossible to David; he had completely forgotten that high school blocks were almost ninety minutes long. Missing one period could well represent a significant portion of a unit.

Jerry had been a little disappointed to learn that David had decided to play the whole thing straight and professional, never mentioning Mr. Husack's insult even once, but he'd not been surprised by it. Jerry had meant what he'd said to the principal about David being out of that man's league entirely. No doubt about it, Jerry had found himself one classy, refined man, who just happened to be a wildcat between the sheets. And the way David was with William. Jerry would always be too proud to admit it, but he sometimes felt that David made a much better father; he had a way of talking to William, of comforting him, that made Jerry a little bit envious sometimes. But luckily, most of the time, Jerry figured he was doing pretty good for a middle-aged man who'd never really thought he'd have a husband, let alone a husband and a kid.

"Morning," Cory muttered as he took a seat at the table.

"Morning yourself, there, sunshine," Jerry said with a big smile. Cory wasn't really a morning person, but he was a lot better at pretending than David or William. "David told me that you got some corrections to do for math?"

"Yessir," Cory said with a moan.

"You get those done, and then you can come out and help me fix the last few fence posts." Jerry deposited a heaping plate of bacon, eggs, hash browns, and toast in front of Cory. "Bet that math doesn't sound so bad now, does it?"

"Rather do fence posts," Cory sighed as he picked up his fork and dug into the food. "Sorry," he said around a mouthful of bacon. "Thank you for breakfast."

Jerry let out a chuckle and opened the fridge to pour him a large glass of orange juice, depositing it in front of him before retrieving his own breakfast. "You're welcome, Cory." Jerry put his own plate on the table and sat, taking a few sips of his coffee before digging into his own bacon and eggs. "Math not a good subject for you?"

"No, I get it, but I just don't see how it'll ever be useful, all those angles and the Pythagorean theorem." He looked up at Jerry and offered a weak smile. "The teacher always says it's the process that matters and not what we're learning, but I still don't see the connection."

"You don't, huh?" Jerry put his fork down and picked up his mug, taking another couple of long, slow sips while he did some figuring in his head. "Any idea what you want to do when you finish school."

"I like drawing." Cory put down his own fork and picked up his orange juice, downing half of it in one long swallow.

"What kind of drawing?"

"Graphic novels, anime, that kind of thing."

"Love to see your work some time." Jerry smiled, truly intrigued that he'd finally found something in common with Cory at last. "But in the meantime, let me ask you a question, a math-type question." Jerry's smile grew when he saw Cory look toward him, giving him his full attention. "If you're serious about pursuing your art, then you'll need to have a head for math. For example, which is the better deal, buying two ten-inch pizzas at $8.99 each or one twenty-inch pizza at $18.00?"

"I don't like pizza, so neither."

"Liar," Jerry laughed, surprised at how Cory was opening up and cracking jokes. "I've seen you eat, and you'll never convince me that you'd turn down any food." Jerry sat back in his chair. "Come on, which one is the better deal?"

"The two pizzas, I guess."

"Why?"

"Two are better than one, right?" Cory picked up his fork again, and Jerry got the impression he was pleased with his reasoning. "Besides, it all works out to twenty inches of pizzas for only the difference of two cents."

"And if you don't care about your money, sure, that's one way to look at it." Jerry leaned forward again. "But if you break it down to cost per square inch of pizza, you're getting twice as much pizza if you buy the twenty-inch."

"No way," Cory huffed, his eyes wide with disbelief.

"You know how to find the area of a circle?"

"Yeah," Cory said indignantly. "Pi times radius squared."

"So," Jerry said quickly, pleased with himself. "Work it out. And if I'm wrong, I'll let you go back to bed and I'll do your math homework for you." Jerry could see the wheels begin to turn as Cory's expression became pensive and earnest. "Eat up. Something tells me you're gonna be fixing fence posts after all."

DAVID shook his head as he hollered to William one more time from the bottom of the stairs and grabbed his briefcase from the bench in the front hall. He went into the kitchen to grab a bagel or something to eat in the car before he had to meet Lenore and was surprised—although he didn't know why—to find William dressed and finishing his breakfast while Cory worked on homework.

"You little monkey, when did you get down here?"

"When you were in the shower." William popped the last little bit of toast in his mouth, scooped up his plate, and deposited it in the sink. "You should see the math that Cory has to do. It's really hard."

"Oh yeah," David said as he walked over to stand beside Cory. "What is it? Trigonometry? Congruency?"

"Functions." Cory looked up and rolled his eyes.

"I loved math when I was in school."

"Can you help me with it later?"

David wanted to laugh at the sheer desperation in Cory's voice. "Sure thing." David shifted his briefcase to his other hand and then put his hand on top of William's head and flexed his fingers as if his hand were a spider crawling away. "But first, we've got to get Sir William to school... after he goes up and gets his backpack."

"Which would be the better deal, David. Two ten-inch pizzas at $8.99 each or one twenty-inch pizza at $18.00?"

"Is that one of your questions? Seems like a middle school word problem." David didn't wait for an answer, looking instead to the ceiling as he tried to crunch the numbers in his head. "If you figure cost per square inch—"

"Never mind."

David took a seat opposite Cory. "What's wrong?" David's smile grew exponentially as Cory explained the math problem that Jerry had left for him to figure out. "Well, I hate to burst your bubble, but he's right."

"Is he ever wrong about anything?"

147

"Listen, Cory," David said as he leaned forward, "he may downplay his intelligence, and why, I have no idea, but Jerry is probably one of the smartest people I've ever met; and I mean book-smart *and* street-smart. You could learn a lot from him."

"Jerry said he'd like to see my drawings."

"There," David announced as he stood. "See? He'll help you with art, and I'll help you with math." He reached out and placed a hand on Cory's shoulder. "Are you still upset about the suspension?"

"No," Cory sighed. "Well, sort of. I mean… it's nothing."

"'Kay, I'm ready."

At the sound of William's voice, David looked toward the hallway and then back at Cory. "Do me a favor, Cory?" When Cory looked up at him, David continued, "Why don't you give Jerry a chance. He's a really good listener, and I know he would really like to help you."

"Okay," Cory said and offered a smile. "Bye, Billiam. Have a good day at school."

"You too, Cory. Remember about tonight."

"I won't forget." Cory looked back at David and whispered, "Sorry, he's sworn me to secrecy."

"Fair enough." David shifted his briefcase once more and then let go of Cory's shoulder. "And if Jerry starts to gloat about the pizza question, just remind him that he still has trouble counting to twenty in French." David winked and smiled at Cory, pleased that he didn't seem as glum as he had only a few minutes before.

"William?" David found William out by the corral, talking to his father. "William?" He called again as he moved to the corral. "Time to go. Come and get in the car while I say goodbye to your dad." He scratched the short blond locks as William passed him and stepped up to Jerry. "Pizza?"

"Hey, he wanted to know how he'd ever use math."

"I'll call you at lunch today once I know what Lenore wants to see me about." David leaned up and kissed Jerry on the lips, quickly, just in case William was watching. "Cory seems a little down-in-the-dumps about something. I told him what a good listener you are."

"Did you now?" Jerry pushed his hat back on his head and showed that smile, the one David could never get enough of. "I was thinking that maybe he and I'd spend some time in the studio this afternoon. Seems that Cory likes to draw."

"I know," David said as he reached out and rubbed his free hand over the cotton of Jerry's T-shirt, the sweat Jerry'd worked up already starting to soak through the well-worn fabric. "I'm so glad that you two finally found something in common." David stole one more quick kiss and then backed away a few feet. "I can't wait to hear about your afternoon when I get home tonight."

"I can't wait for you to get home tonight." Jerry licked his lips playfully. "Been a few days, mountain lion."

"I know, baby, and if Lenore didn't want to meet with me, I'd be dragging you into that barn to clean your stall, but...." David pouted and then blew his husband a kiss. "Love you."

"Love you back."

David turned around and headed for the car, flushing a little at the whistle that he heard from behind him. And not for the first time, he couldn't help but marvel at the twists and turns that life constantly threw his way. Ten, five, even two years ago, he never would have looked twice at a man like Jerry. He could be refined as anyone else from the monied elite, but Jerry was also very... down-to-earth just didn't describe him.

Matter of fact, pragmatic, honest. None of those words were able to encapsulate everything that Jerry was. There was no doubt that Jerry was sexy and an incredible lover, but it was the Jerry outside of the sex, beyond the lust, that had David completely enthralled. For the first time in his life, David was sure that when the lust did dwindle and lose its hold on the two of them, there would be something else of substance between them. And it even went beyond William and the family they'd built. For David, it even went beyond the idea of growing old together in this house, surrounded—perhaps—by grandchildren.

He had found in this one man, this one gloriously funny, idiotic, goofy, sincere, and loving man, someone who had shown him what his life could be. David had learned from Jerry how to be himself, how to ask for what he needed and wanted, how never to settle for less than he deserved. Jerry had taught David that loving someone didn't mean expecting the other to make him happy. He'd learned from Jerry that it was okay to take from people sometimes, that it was acceptable for him just to be. Jerry never expected—nor asked—him to hide his flaws.

David pulled the car out of the driveway, and as he listened to William whistling some song that he knew but couldn't place, he felt his heart would burst with the love and acceptance he got from the two of them. He would give anything to Jerry and William, do anything for them. And even if he had the chance, David knew that he wouldn't ever change a thing about his family or his life.

Chapter 17

DAVID found himself replaying the conversation with Jerry over and over again. Jerry had been spending the past few days getting to know Cory, working with him in the studio. Jerry was impressed with Cory's talent; he didn't necessarily understand the fascination with superheroes and villains and weapons and lots of blood, but he was becoming quite attached to Cory. David knew it wasn't easy for Jerry to wear his heart on his sleeve, but he would never tire of watching Jerry allow himself to open up a little each day. Since he'd met Jerry, David found himself discovering things about the gruff cowboy every day, found himself loving him a little more every day. It was always a bit of a surprise to David when Jerry would get up in the middle of the night. David was usually the one to go and check on William, but now it seemed Jerry no longer slept through William crying out after a nightmare. David would wake up the next morning to find Jerry in William's room, sitting on the bed with an arm placed protectively near his son's head. Sometimes, Jerry was awake and just staring off into space, and sometimes Jerry was asleep, his body poised nearby to protect their boy.

As he sifted and mixed and poured, moving between the oven and the cupboards, wondering just how much food three eleven-year-old boys would actually eat over two evenings and three days, David forced his mind to focus on anything but the research he'd been doing on becoming a foster family. It wasn't something that he'd ever thought about; he'd always assumed that if he ever had children, they would be his own biological children. Then he fell in love with William and Jerry. And now, he was realizing his need to protect Cory was transforming into a deep desire to take care of the young man, to have him become part of the family. But whether or not that happened would depend on what Sara had discovered during her research.

After about an hour of multi-tasking in the kitchen, David stood back from the counter and surveyed the smorgasbord of snacks. It wasn't every day that he had three eleven-year-olds in the house for a sleepover, so everything had to be perfect. The urgent early morning meeting of a few days ago with Lenore was so that she could ask David and Jerry to watch her twins for a day or two. Harvey's father had been rushed to the hospital after having suffered what they believed to be a heart attack. Lenore was sketchy on the details and more frantic than David had ever seen her. Of course, there was no question that David would watch the twins for the weekend, so with only a couple of days, David and Cory had managed to throw together a weekend sleepover that would keep Lenore's twin boys and William amused and entertained.

It was also, unfortunately, going to happen at the same time as Sara's visit. And from the tone of her voice and her unwillingness to share any information, David knew it wouldn't be good news. Jerry had been busy playing phone tag with Kitty; it was something to do with special commissions from potential clients. David couldn't really be sure because they had both been so tired at the end of the day lately that they fell asleep in each other's arms as soon as they hit the bed.

"'Kay," Jerry said as he stole through the kitchen and pecked David on the cheek. "I'm off to the barn. I'll do a little work and be back before the kids get here."

"No worries, baby." David turned and insisted on a proper kiss; it was the closest thing they'd had to sex in the past four days, and he wasn't about to do without even that. "Cory'll be here to help, and Sara won't be here until the kids are watching the movie."

"I'll definitely be here by then." Jerry kissed his forehead and was out the door.

"Can I help?" Cory came into the kitchen, and David was pleased to see that he was wearing more and more of his new clothing. When they'd first arrived home after the shopping trip, he hadn't been able to help noticing that most of the clothes just stayed in their bags. But today, Cory was wearing new jeans and a beautiful western-style shirt in blue and turquoise over a brand new white T-shirt.

"Uh, I don't think so. I don't think I missed anything," David said as he turned on the faucet and washed his hands again. "Bored?"

"Kinda," Cory said with a smile.

"I was hoping to talk to you." David dried his hands and motioned to the table. "Jerry was telling me last night about how the two of you have been spending the days together in his studio and working on the ranch. It takes a while for Jerry to express his deeper feelings for people, Cory, but I just wanted to make sure you know how much he thinks of you. He thinks you're one of the bravest young men he knows." He looked in Cory's eyes, noticing the flush spread across his cheeks. "And I do as well. And I just wanted to be sure that this is what you want. Living with us, as your foster family I mean."

"It is," Cory said, nodding his head slightly.

David knew it was still going to take time for Cory to open up and trust himself enough to let his new family in, so he wasn't surprised at the short answer. To the point and as few words as possible. Another trait that Cory shared with Jerry. "Sara will want to speak with you first before she speaks with Jerry and me, so if you change your mind and don't want to stay, I want you to know that we won't be angry and that you're welcome here any time." David exhaled, his heart beating so quickly he was sure that Cory would hear it. "I know William will want to see you, a lot." He laughed when Cory smiled at that thought.

"I really like being around you guys." Cory studied his fingernails as he spoke. "And I promised William that I wouldn't tell you and Jerry what we've been doing each night, but I hope you'll like it."

"If you and William made it, I'm sure we'll love it."

"Well," Cory said after a few moments. "I promised William I'd play guitar and sing some songs with the twins, so...." He lifted himself out of the chair.

"Okay." He watched Cory leave the kitchen and felt the tension in his neck and shoulders ease slightly. He had no idea if Cory was nervous about Sara's visit, but David felt like he was pulled as tight as an elastic. He stood, turned back to the counter full of snacks, and busied himself—for the hundredth time—with fixing and arranging and more tinkering in the hopes of keeping his mind off what he'd come to fear as an inevitability: Sara had found a relative for Cory to live with.

JERRY had been in the house, showered, and was now sitting at the kitchen table, his leg bouncing nervously. Sara had called from her cell phone to say that she would be a little late and that it would be best to meet with all three of them together. Other than that, she'd given no further indication if she had good news or bad. It wasn't only that they were looking forward to adding Cory to their family, but also what Cory had come to represent for each of them as individuals within the family.

William obviously saw Cory as a brother, something that neither of the boys had ever had. As an only child himself, Jerry often understood the laments he heard from other only children; he knew what it was like to feel alone, *be* alone. Jerry knew that he'd come to see Cory as a younger version of himself, as a chance to be a mentor to Cory's talent as an artist and a friend to the lonely and confused young man. Jerry had been only a few years older when he'd lost his own parents, and Jerry had never really had anyone. And David? Jerry couldn't really be sure what David would get out of having yet another person to worry over, but he was very sure that these two boys would never find a better friend and ally than David. He knew this because *Jerry* had never found anyone better.

"Is she here yet?" Cory came into the room, breathless and smiling.

"No," David said with a smile. "Sounds like you have your own little fan club in there."

"Oh, they're great!"

"I haven't heard some of those songs in years," Jerry offered, looking from Cory to David. "'There's a Hole in the Sea'? I remember singing that one in music class. None of us could get through it without laughing or making rude noises when the frog developed a hole."

"My favorite is the 'Risseldy, Rosseldy' song."

"Isn't that the one from *The Birds*?" Jerry looked over at David with a quizzical expression. "That movie gave me nightmares for months afterwards."

"You don't have to wait here with us, Cory. You can go back and enjoy yourself; we'll come and get you when Sara arrives."

"I don't mind," Cory responded as he shrugged his shoulders. "I'm kind of nervous."

"No need to be," David said as he leaned back in his chair. Jerry could tell he was trying to be nonchalant about the whole thing, and maybe Cory was buying it, but Jerry knew better. "No matter what happens, we'll always be here if you need us."

"Cory!" William came running into the kitchen, face flushed. "Come on, the movie's starting."

"Right behind you, Billiam."

"Hey, you," Jerry said as he reached out and took hold of his son by the waist. "You better slow down or you're going to run out of steam, and we'll be peeling you off the floor in the morning." Jerry pretended to take bites out of William's neck. Jerry welcomed the change of mood; he'd begun to feel a little oppressed by sitting in the kitchen. "Okay, cowboy, you take it easy in there," Jerry was explaining as William seemed to take off again just as quickly as he'd arrived, "and remember, it's lights out in another two hours!"

"I'll make sure that they're all in bed by ten," Cory said. And with a quick, parting glance at both of them, he went to join the three energetic eleven-year-olds in the living room.

Jerry watched David get up, touch Jerry on the shoulder, and then wander out of the kitchen without saying anything at all. He wasn't sure if David was feeling the same kind of anticipation and frustration as he was, but Jerry knew him well enough to know that he wasn't happy about having to wait either. He stood and was about to go and find David, sure that he'd gone outside to wait for Sara, when he felt the vibration of his phone against his hip. As he spoke into the receiver, he continued by the living room, popping his head in to check on the activities. He spoke softly when he saw that there were three little boys on top of their sleeping bags, prostrate on their stomachs, eyes glued to the television. He noticed Cory lying on his stomach beside William and thought of calling to him, but decided against it.

"Hello, Sara," Jerry whispered as he exited through the front door and found David sitting on the steps. He sat down beside his husband and put an arm over his shoulders. He listened for a few moments and then closed his phone. "Sara's only about ten minutes away."

"Are we crazy to think that we're the best thing for Cory right now?" David asked as he leaned against Jerry, not giving him an opportunity to answer. "I mean, what if there is a family out there that Cory didn't bother mentioning? What does that mean? And maybe he's better off with them."

"I don't know, baby," Jerry said after kissing David's temple. "I just want—we both just want—what's best for him right now." Jerry shifted position so that their hips were touching. "Did I tell you that he finally opened up about some of what he's been through?" Jerry knew he had, but he felt a strange compulsion to live the experience once more. "It was amazing. I don't mean what he went through, but that he felt safe enough to tell me about the beatings and the getting to school early so he could shower and get the smell of pot off him."

David didn't say anything, and Jerry was grateful. "He would stow some clothes in a plastic bag and put the bag in his backpack and then ride his bike to school." Jerry pulled David a little closer. "After he'd showered, he'd put the smelly clothes in the same plastic bag so he could wash them when he got home and then do the whole thing over again, day after day." Jerry placed another kiss on David's temple. "He told me that he finally called the cops when he couldn't use the kitchen anymore because of the little lab his father had started." Jerry took a deep breath and continued. "Said that his father almost beat him unconscious when he refused to help him start a meth lab. A *meth lab*, for fuck's sake."

"Cory had to face those kids every day, knowing what his father was." David's hand went to Jerry's hand on his shoulder, his long fingers playing with the gold wedding band. "Makes what my family did to me sound almost civilized."

"Speaking of which," Jerry said as he interlaced his fingers with David's. "Does Niels know about what's going on?"

"No, I haven't told him yet."

"William will need all the support he can get if this thing goes south."

"I know." David agreed. "He sent William an e-mail this afternoon. He gets back from his trip tomorrow, and he said he wanted to come over for dinner some time this week, so it'll be great timing." David pulled away from Jerry slightly and looked up into his eyes. "It's been almost four days since William sent Frau Zimmerman those most recent pictures of our trip to Edmonton."

"Our son needs to learn some patience, I think."

"I don't know," David said as he shook his head. "She's never taken this long to answer any of his e-mails. I hope everything is okay."

"She's European," Jerry said with a smile, as if that explained everything. "They're a little more laid back, from what I recall." Jerry turned when he heard the familiar crunch of gravel under car tires. "Show time."

157

"I'll go get some coffee and food ready." David turned to head back to the kitchen.

"Hey?" Jerry stood, his hands out at his sides, palms up. When David turned to face him, Jerry smiled mischievously. "What, no kiss?"

"Sorry," David said as he stood on the top step and wrapped his arms around Jerry's neck. "I kind of like being taller than you." He kissed Jerry softly on the lips and then pulled back a few inches, his hands resting on Jerry's shoulders.

"You want to be taller *and* sexier *and* smarter?" He watched David's expression soften even more, felt the hands on his shoulders offer a quick squeeze.

"You big flirt," David said as he pushed against the solid shoulders and headed back into the house.

Jerry turned as Sara exited her vehicle and met her as she opened the passenger side door to retrieve her briefcase. "Thanks for coming, Sara."

"I'm not here," Sara said as she slammed the passenger side door. "I know it won't make any sense to you now, but officially, I'm not here."

"You feeling okay?" Jerry took Sara's briefcase for her and led her to the veranda.

"Just listen carefully to what I have to say once we get inside and you'll understand." Sara turned to look at Jerry as he opened the door for her, her grin mischievous. Jerry knew that grin very well; she was about to make him feel stupid. "And David will be able to explain it to you when you don't."

"Why did I know that was coming?" Jerry laughed and followed her into the kitchen, appreciative that Sara—as always—would be able to put smiles on their faces.

For the next hour, Jerry and David sat—Cory between them for the first fifteen minutes—and listened to Sara as she explained the inner workings of Child Services in Alberta. Jerry understood almost immediately what Sara meant before entering the house. She wasn't here as a category B supervisor, but rather as a friend, since what she was explaining to them was probably unprofessional if not illegal.

Chapter 18

"IT MUST be those beautiful eyes of yours," Lenore said as she accepted the mug of coffee from Jerry. "You have the gift to turn lesbians. But it's a powerful gift, Jerry. Use it wisely." Lenore wasn't terribly successful in hiding her smirk.

"You know you're the only love in my life." Jerry took his own mug off the counter and took a seat opposite Lenore.

"Okay," David said as he entered the kitchen and sat beside Jerry. "I've got the twins all packed, and I put their sleeping bags in your car already. They'll be down in a few minutes." David looked at the two of them, reaching for Jerry's mug and taking a quick sip of tea. "What?"

"Your husband is hitting on me." Lenore did her best to look offended.

"Again?" David used his best disappointed teacher voice and looked at Jerry. "How many times do I have to explain this to you? You like men, not soccer moms."

"Hey!" Lenore leaned across the table and swatted David's arm. "I'll have you know that there are a lot of men who find me irresistible."

"So that's why you get all those messages from Barnum and Bailey's."

Lenore laughed, that fake laugh that meant that she was about to say something rude. No matter how long Jerry knew this woman, he would never really believe that she'd once been a nun.

"You know," Lenore said as the fake laugh trailed off, "my grandmother, that sweet old woman, had a saying for times like these."

Lenore dragged out the suspense, and Jerry could feel the corners of his mouth lifting in anticipation.

"What was it?" Jerry asked, and he shot a look at David, who seemed quite unimpressed with all this buildup.

"I want to get it just right." Lenore snapped her fingers, her timing impeccable. "Oh that's right. *Bite me!*"

"I'll give you a ten for timing, but a five for content," David said, his attitude one of beleaguered tolerance.

"Ten out of ten, that's not bad."

"Out of twenty," David said just before the kitchen was invaded by three eleven-year-olds, all of whom had consumed far too much sugar and had not had enough sleep over the last two days. Jerry was certain the only way he hadn't dropped dead of exhaustion was that neither he nor David—nor Cory, he was sure—had had much sleep either and were running on pure adrenaline. And despite Lenore's visit to pick up her twins and the promise of sleep and a return to a normal schedule, Jerry was still fairly certain that no one in the McKenzie-Loewenberger household would be back to normal anytime soon. The next few weeks would be very stressful, for him, for David, for Cory, and especially for William.

Jerry and David knew how this would all end, as did Cory, but they'd all agreed that William was too young to understand. William would have a hard time understanding everything that would happen tomorrow, and all three of them would have a hard time watching him go through it, but this was how it needed to be.

Lenore had said something earlier in the evening that had stayed with Jerry—would stay with him for a long time. *Being a parent means helping your children understand the fair and the unfair, even if that means they hate you and think you're the cause of all of it.* Jerry and David and Lenore had sat in the kitchen for a little more than an hour while William and the twins finished their games and helped Cory clean up. All things considered, it had been a very good weekend for

William, one that Jerry hoped would help him get through the next couple of weeks.

"Jerry?"

He looked up to see David standing at the end of the kitchen table. "Sorry, I'm coming." He lifted himself off the chair and walked out to the veranda to say goodbye to the twins and to Lenore. It was as if he was seven years old again, the endless possibilities for fun and play on Saturday morning seeming a million miles away on Sunday night, the night before he had to return to school. As soon as Lenore and the twins drove away down the winding driveway, he and David and Cory would have to sit down with William and explain why Cory was leaving them to live clear on the other side of Calgary. But unlike those Sunday nights of his youth, Jerry knew that this night would be with him for much longer than the few days it took for the next weekend to arrive.

He stood on the veranda, one hand on David's shoulder and the other tracing lazy circles over William's soft, blond hair. They waved goodbye as the car disappeared down the driveway and then headed inside, David and Cory heading straight for the kitchen, both of them seeming so much stronger than he.

"William? How about a smoothie?" David stood at the counter and smiled at Jerry as he walked in and pulled out William's chair.

"'Kay," William said as he hopped up on the chair. "Can I have bananas and strawberries?"

"You got it," David said and turned to the blender to fix the smoothie just the way William liked it. The whirring and the noise of the blender lasted for several seconds as David dropped the banana and strawberry slices into the cold milk. Once the pink concoction was in front of William, Jerry proceeded.

"Listen, partner," Jerry said as he took the seat beside his son. "You remember on Saturday night when Sara came over?"

"Sure," William said, his head bobbing as he swung his legs back and forth, the straw dancing inside of the large tumbler in time to his movements. Jerry had already noted several times how—if William sat just a centimeter or two closer to the edge of the chair—his feet would reach the floor. "She looks pretty with her hair short like that." William got a look on his face, and quickly corrected himself. "She always looks pretty, though."

"Well, she was here to talk about Cory and his family."

"We're his family now," William said, face so earnest and sweet that Jerry took a deep breath to keep his voice from cracking.

"Yes, you are," Cory said as he smiled at William, reaching out to bump fists. "But Jerry means my biological family."

"Cory's dad had to go away for a while, and so Cory is going to stay with his father's sister, Aunt Linda." Jerry moved his hand closer to William's little arm that was holding the tumbler, ready to comfort and do whatever he needed to do.

He watched as the straw fell out of William's mouth, the little blond head turning slowly to look at him. "But he's staying here; he's part of our family now."

"William?" David moved to sit on the other side of the confused little boy, whose legs had stopped bouncing and whose breathing had become faster with each passing moment. "He'll still come and visit, and we can go and see him—" Jerry reached out a hand and put it on his son's shoulder.

"No! No!" William shouted, looking only at Jerry. "You said he could stay here! You said you liked him!"

"I do, partner, I do, but—"

"Didn't you mean it?" William pushed himself away from the table, David having to catch him as the chair threatened to fall backwards. "You lied to me! You said he could stay! And now he's leaving!"

"Sweetie," David said as he reached for William, "your dad didn't lie—"

"Yes he did!" William pushed David's hands away and ran for the front door. "He lied!"

"I'll get him," Cory said as he got up and left the kitchen.

"He hates me," Jerry said as he brought his hands to rest on the top of his head. "He hates me." Jerry's voice was a mere whisper, the disbelief clear, even to him. He'd known—anticipated—that this would not be an easy conversation, but he'd not been able to prepare himself for actually hearing the words, the disappointment, the confusion, and the accusation in William's voice.

"He doesn't hate you, baby," David said as he sat beside him and put an arm around his shoulders. "He's confused right now. He's tired, over-tired from the weekend and confused. We knew that he wouldn't take it well." David kissed his forehead. "I know it doesn't make it any easier, but we just have to give him time."

"I won't make it another couple of weeks with him looking at me like that."

"It won't take that long."

"God," Jerry whispered again. "Did you see how he looked at me?"

"I know, baby, but it'll get better. I promise." David took one of his hands and kissed it tenderly. "You just have to wait for him to come around. And he will. He loves you. You're his *dad*."

"More like *cad* at the moment."

"See?" David sat back in his chair and rubbed the hand he held between his own. "You still have your sense of humor."

Jerry leaned over and kissed his husband, grateful that he hadn't had to go through this alone.

IT WASN'T easy, but David convinced Jerry not to go looking for his son. Cory would be with William and help him to understand that it wouldn't be forever, that nothing had really changed except geography.

But as satisfied as he was with Jerry's ability to refrain from interfering, David had no such self-discipline. He wandered out of the house about thirty minutes after Cory left to check on William, and he found them both sitting on the large, padded swing at the south end of the veranda.

"He cried for a bit and then just conked out," Cory said as he smiled down at the red-faced little boy whose head was in his lap. "Poor little guy, he was just way too tired. All that sugar probably didn't help either." David nodded, amazed at how good Cory was with William. "I hope Jerry's not too upset."

"He's a big boy; he'll get over it." David leaned against the railing. "No one ever said it would be easy being a parent."

"I remember Jerry telling me out in the studio one day about how the three of you came to be a family." Cory's hand stroked absentmindedly, as if by reflex, over William's head. David was sure that he must be getting tired of maintaining the soothing rhythmic swinging that had lulled his little friend to sleep, but did not dare disturb either of them. "It's a beautiful story, how you two found each other and made a home for William."

"I think I fell in love with the little guy the first time he took my hand and led me out to the barn to show me the horses." David felt a chill pass through him as he remembered everything that he'd gone through to make sure that William and Jerry would not be hurt because of the Bennet Brigade. "It wasn't easy and I still count my blessings every day."

"That's kind of like something my mom used to say to me when she'd tuck me in at night." David watched as Cory looked down again when William snuffled and rolled onto his other side, head still on Cory's thigh. "She used to tell me that every day is a gift and that you have to do everything you can to show how grateful you are for it."

"I'm sure she'd be very proud of you, Cory."

"I like to think so, yeah."

"I've often thought that William has a sixth sense about people." David repositioned himself on the railing. "He seems to be able to tell—almost instantly—if someone is worth getting to know. And I think he knew right away that you were someone good... and kind." David looked away when he noticed that Cory was blushing; he looked up at the sky, at the purple and gold and pink hues that he'd come to love so much now that he was living out in the country. He'd never really taken the time to look up at the sky when he'd been living in his condo in the city. But out here, it was as if he was looking up into heaven itself.

"When she was tucking me in, my mom used to ask me if I'd done something good for someone that day." Cory stopped and closed his eyes for a second. "It's one of the few things that kept me going after she died. My dad just seemed to lose his way. He was so angry all the time and started drinking, and then he lost his job and we had to move."

"I'm sorry, Cory."

"Thanks, but I guess we all get some things we have to deal with, huh?"

"If you don't mind my asking, why didn't you run away to live with your Aunt Linda?"

"We'd sort of lost touch with her after we moved, and when Dad started getting... started beating...." Cory stopped again and cleared his throat. "It was too late by then. She's very religious, always has been. I remember Mom would just go nuts when we had her over or if we had to go to her house." Cory offered a lopsided grin and shook his head at the memories. "Mom would always complain about how controlling and manipulative Aunt Linda was. Nothing was ever good enough, Mom wasn't raising me right and all that. I guess I didn't know who I could trust, didn't know if I wanted to take the chance."

"Will you be able to handle it for a couple of weeks?"

"No problem," Cory said with a smile. "Even if she's mellowed and I could live with her, I know where I belong now."

David felt the familiar sting behind his eyes, but found himself smiling in spite of it. It was only a year ago that he'd thought he had so few blessings. But right then, looking at two of the three people who had come to define his life in so many ways in such a short time, he realized that he'd been wrong to assume that he would never be as blessed as Lenore, that he would never have the family that he'd always yearned for. It was his turn now; he was getting the blessings that he was ready to receive. And he had Jerry and William to thank for that. And in another couple of weeks, he would have one more blessing. In another couple of weeks, he and Jerry would add another member to their family. In another couple of weeks, William would have a brother.

As he held the swing so that Cory could scoop up William to take him inside, he looked out at the purples and golds and pinks of the sky and sent a silent thank you—as he'd done almost every night since he'd moved in with Jerry and William—to whomever was listening. He thanked them for not only sending him the many blessings, but for waiting until he was ready to learn how to care for them.

Chapter 19

NO MATTER how hard he tried, William could not bring himself to eat anything. He'd been distracted enough throughout the day, what with two tests and a science experiment at school, but then he'd found himself at home again. And Cory wasn't there. They had said their goodbyes early that morning before Jerry left to take Cory to his aunt's house on the other side of Calgary. William had asked to go with them, but he knew that his dad would say no, and he did. *We'll be back too late, and you'll miss school*, he'd said.

William didn't care about missing school. He didn't really care much about anything. He'd gone to school with David, as he always did, except this time, he didn't much feel like talking. In the car, a thousand times during the day, and even now as he sat at the dinner table, he reminded himself about what Cory had told him last night and this morning, but it just made him sadder.

Every night, when my mom tucked me in, she would ask me if I had done something good for someone that day. My mom always said that you had to be grateful for each day, live it like you were thankful for everything you got. You've got three people who love you very much, Billiam. And even though one of them won't be living with you anymore, it's not anyone's fault. Your dad loves you very much, so does David, and so do I. As William pushed the mashed potatoes around on his plate, he remembered how hard he tried not to cry in front of Cory, but he couldn't help it. *We won't see each other every day, but we can still be grateful for the times we do see each other. You can still be grateful that you have two great dads who will let you come and see me, or let me come and see you. So, you make sure they know how much you love them, okay.*

Cory had bumped fists with him one last time before he turned and got in Jerry's truck, and William couldn't help but wonder who else he would lose. He didn't have his parents anymore. He didn't have Frau Zimmerman. And now he wouldn't have Cory. He knew that what Cory said was right; he should be grateful for Jerry and David. It wasn't that he didn't feel grateful, but he felt alone most of the time. He loved camping and the horses, and he even loved cleaning day when all three of them would make a kind of game out of it all. He loved how much attention he got from his two dads, and he loved them. He still did, even with how Jerry had lied to him.

"How was school, partner?"

"Fine," William said as he continued to push his food around on his plate, not even bothering to look up at Jerry.

"Do you think you did well on your tests?"

"William always does well on his tests," David said. William looked up and managed a smile for him. "I'm sure he'll do really well."

"Listen, William, David, and I were wondering if there was anything special you wanted to do after your final soccer game on Friday?" William didn't answer right away, didn't look up. "Spring break is coming up and it'll be a full year since you moved here."

"It doesn't matter," William said finally.

"We were thinking of going back to Edmonton, or maybe drive to Banff and go to the hot springs. What do you think?"

"It doesn't matter," he repeated.

"We were thinking of letting you decide for the whole family," Jerry said after a few moments of silence.

"I'd like to stay here with my horse," William said, finally looking up at his father. "If it's all the same to you, I mean." He noticed his dad look over at David. William knew they were worried about him; they'd said it often enough in the past ten hours, but he didn't know what he was supposed to say to make them stop. And it made him feel worse.

"We can do whatever you want, William." David stood up from the table and crossed to the fridge, opening it and pulling out the large cake plate. "Maybe we can go camping out by the lake? Take the horses?" William saw the Sachertorte on the plate. "I bet you want a big piece, right?"

"No thank you," William said as he finally pushed his plate away. "I'm not hungry."

"David made that just for you, cowboy."

"Thank you very much," William said as he looked up again and smiled at David. "May I be excused?"

"Of course, William," David said as he put his hand to William's forehead. "Are you sick? Do you feel sick?"

"No," William answered as he got off his chair and headed for the stairs to his room. "Just tired."

He walked into his room at the top of the stairs and closed the door. He went straight to his new computer and clicked on Safari so that he could check his e-mails. He'd sent one to Cory as soon as he'd gotten home from school, but he was sure that there would not be a response so soon. And there wasn't. Neither did he have a response from Frau Zimmerman. He'd sent her pictures of his trip to Edmonton, including some of Cory, but that was almost five days ago. It never took her this long to respond to his e-mails. Having no news and no messages that hadn't been there since after school, he put his computer to sleep and sat on the edge of his bed. He didn't know what to do. He didn't really feel like doing anything other than going to bed.

"William?" David knocked on his door, but he wouldn't come in until William gave him permission.

"You can come in," he said after the second knock.

"Your dad's watching one of those shows you like," David said as he sat down beside William. "It's all about nature and helping animals. You love those kinds of shows. I can make you a sandwich if you'd like. You must be starving by now."

"No, sir," William said as David put an arm around his shoulders.

"I'm so sorry you're sad, William." He closed his eyes as he felt David move his hand gently over his scalp. "Your dad's really sad right now too."

"Why's *he* sad?" William didn't understand why his father would be sad; he's the one who let Cory go away.

"Because you're sad," David said. William opened his eyes and looked up at David. "You know how much we love you, William, and we don't like to see you so sad." David leaned down and kissed his forehead. "I miss Cory, too, and so does your dad, but we'll still get to see him."

"Not the same."

"I know, but it's better than not seeing him at all. And who knows? Maybe Cory will come back for sleepovers or be able to stay for a couple of days when he visits." David pointed to the new computer. "Maybe you can send him an e-mail, or call him, and ask him."

"I sent him an e-mail after school today, but he hasn't answered me yet."

"He will, you just have to be patient." David pulled him a little closer. "Now, how about we go down and watch some of that show with your dad?"

"'Kay," William said. He didn't really want to, but he didn't like the idea of his dad being sad because of him. "What's it about?" he asked as he walked downstairs with David.

"I think it's about volunteers who help rescue sea lions and seals in California," David said as he followed William into the sunken living room. "Look who I found," he said with a big smile. William took a seat beside his father on the large sectional, and David walked around to sit on the other side. "We thought we'd come down and watch with you."

"Well, I'm so happy that you did," Jerry said as he wrapped an arm around each of them. "I was getting kinda lonely down here all by myself, and now I don't need to get a blanket if I get cold." William was surprised to find himself giggling as Jerry tried to pull him onto his lap as if he were a blanket.

JERRY looked over at David and mouthed a thank you to him. He didn't have to ask to know that William coming down here had been all David's doing. He kissed his husband, then his son, and settled in for what he hoped would be at least an hour or two of having his family with him. He wasn't foolish enough to think that William had forgiven him or had weathered the worst of this particular storm. Even if they could tell William the truth, there was still the fact that he was far too young to be trusted with information that had the potential to come back and land them all in a lot of trouble.

They sat and watched, all three of them giggling at the antics of the sea lions and seals. Some of the animals had been abandoned by their mothers, or had found themselves stranded before they were completely weaned from their mother's milk. There was a custom in the shelter of allowing the person who rescued the animal to provide a name, and the first ten minutes of the program was focused on a young elephant seal named Kira. She'd been discovered abandoned and stranded far up the beach, too far to get back to the water on her own. Jerry felt his heart rate quicken as it seemed the story would be about how Kira had been too far gone to be saved, but he soon relaxed when Kira was shown cavorting in the large shallow pools at the shelter.

She was playing with two of the volunteers, elderly women who had more than enough energy and compassion to spend twenty hours a week at the shelter. Jerry felt William snuggling in a little closer as Kira swam and barked and high-fived a few of the volunteers with her flipper. There were a few sniffles, Jerry noticed, although he couldn't really tell from which one of his two men, when Kira was finally released back into the wild and was shown swimming and playing with some of the other seals, making new friends. The next story was about Bob.

Bob was a harbor seal, with a beautiful shiny, spotted coat that reminded Jerry of those Rorschach inkblots. Bob was less than a year old and had been found on one of the beaches, abandoned. It wasn't immediately clear why Bob had been abandoned, but then the camera panned away from his shiny, dark eyes to reveal the large tumors that seemed to be growing out of his bottom lip. Jerry felt both of his men flinch when they saw it, William wondering out loud what would happen to the baby.

The show spent more than ten minutes explaining how the veterinarians would need to X-ray Bob's mouth to see what kind of tumors he had and whether there was any hope. Instinctively, Jerry crossed his fingers, but was disappointed when the veterinarians began to explain that the tumors reached far into Bob's mouth and that there was very little they would be able to do to ensure that Bob could survive on his own in the wild.

He felt the hand that David had placed on his stomach form into a fist as the veterinarians began to talk about euthanizing Bob. At only nine months old, Bob's life would be over.

"You mean they're going to kill him?" William's body, Jerry noted as he paused the program, had become rigid, and his eyes were beginning to fill with tears. "Why can't they just operate so he'll be all better?" Jerry looked over to David for help, hoping his expression was as panicked as he felt.

"Sometimes, William, no matter what doctors try to do," David said as he reached over across Jerry to fix William's collar and let his hand find its way to his shoulder, "it won't help the patient. Sometimes, the most humane thing to do is make sure the patient doesn't suffer anymore."

"But they could feed him with a bottle and let him live in the pool," William said, tears beginning to stain his rosy cheeks.

"That's not the kind of life that Bob was meant to have, sweetie." David pulled his hand back and looked back at the television screen. "Bob was meant to live in the ocean with all of the other animals and chase his food and—"

Without saying anything else, William closed his eyes, pushed himself off of the sectional, and ran to the stairs. Jerry turned to look at David. "I'm sorry. I should have known that there might be something like this."

"It's not your fault, Jerry." David stood up. "I'll go and talk to him."

"No," Jerry said after a few moments. "I'll go."

"I'm sorry, Jerry," David said while his eyes studied something at his feet. "I should never have invited Cory to stay with us."

"Hey," Jerry said as he wrapped his arms around his husband. "One broken heart at a time here, please?" Jerry lifted David's chin and kissed him softly on the lips. "I wish we could protect him from this kind of stuff forever, but…." Jerry held David's head in his hands and looked into his eyes. "And besides, if you hadn't helped Cory, that wouldn't have been like you."

"I'll find something else for us to watch… that is if you can get him down here again."

"No, hit the record button." Jerry moved toward the stairs and then turned. "There's got to be some happy moments in this show." Of course, Jerry knew that there were, since they'd just finished watching quite a few.

He made his way up the stairs, wondering what he would actually say to William. He'd been much older when he'd had to learn about death and the disappointment that life can sometimes provide, but he'd never really had someone to talk to about the loss of his parents. There'd been more than enough money—still was—but there had been no one in whom Jerry could confide. As he knocked on William's door, Jerry couldn't help but marvel at life and this perverse turn of events: he was happy that he would be there for William, to help him through these sad and lonely moments.

"Hey, partner," Jerry said as he knocked again on the door. "May I come in?" Jerry wasn't sure where William was, but the yes seemed very muffled. Did William have his head in a pillow? Was the poor little guy so choked up that he could only manage a whisper?

Jerry opened the door and walked inside. He could tell right away that William was not on the bed, or under it since that space was occupied by drawers. He looked around quickly trying to figure out where William could be, suddenly remembering last year when he'd gotten drunk and William had called David for help. The closet. William was probably in the closet.

Jerry opened the closet door and saw two little hands wrapped around bent knees, the only movement coming from the occasional hiccup or sniffle. He got down on his knees and made his way slowly to sit beside his son. He put an arm around William's shoulders and was surprised at the almost immediate reaction.

Jerry listened as William's breath quickened and waited as his little arms hugged him a little harder. Jerry didn't really know what to say, so he said the only thing that was on his mind. "I'm sorry, buddy." Jerry wasn't really sure whether he was sorry for Bob or for Cory, and then realized that William would take it in whichever way he needed it most.

Jerry sat there, the tears from William's beautiful blue eyes soaking through the thin cotton of his T-shirt, for almost two hours before he heard the rhythmic breathing and the snuffles that meant his little boy was fast asleep. He picked William up in his arms slowly, so as not to wake him, and put him on the bed, putting the duvet over him and then sitting beside him, caressing his troubled head. He didn't know how many more evenings like this they would have, nor did he know what—precisely—it would take to make William feel better, but he was glad that the first one was over. There hadn't been much talking, and he knew that William would be hungry and tired tomorrow, but he'd find a way to get them all through.

With his son beside him and the light from outside dying slowly, Jerry sat there, his head resting against the headboard, and smiled coyly as the plan formed inside of his head. David would probably object, but this would be something for William; there was a way, Jerry realized, to help all three of them right now. Of course, this is what he would tell David to convince him, but Jerry knew that he was doing it for William, to help his son learn about love and loss and being grateful for whatever the day gave you.

175

Chapter 20

IT WAS almost four in the morning, and David found himself awake. It was another three days until spring break, and David wasn't sure how they would all make it. He and Jerry and William had been so tired lately that it seemed all they did was watch television for an hour or so before they fell asleep. David had never been more thankful for the coming of spring break. Just thinking about that sweet, little boy and everything he'd been through over the past couple of weeks made David want to do anything he could for William. At least, he thought, as he pulled his arms back under the covers and turned toward Jerry, he'd managed to get the two of them together last night. There might not have been much talking, but there had been some release of emotion, finally.

He moved carefully, slowly, and snuggled up against the broad, muscular back, inhaling deeply the scent of his husband, a scent that was uniquely Jerry.

"I'm awake," Jerry whispered as he rolled onto his back. "I have been for about half an hour."

"I'm going to have to do something drastic to keep my family rested and healthy," David whispered back as he slid his hand across Jerry's belly to his chest.

"Thank you for getting him to come and watch the rest of that show." Jerry looked down, his brilliant blue eyes seeming so tired and resigned. "I've been so worried about him, but he seems to be doing a little better now."

"My heart is just breaking for the poor little guy," David said as he looked up at Jerry, his hands sweeping over the expanse of the hairy chest. "I think my father coming for a visit will help William."

"I do believe," Jerry said with a tired smirk, "that you told me I had to wait for William to come around, so what's with all of the event planning?"

"Don't you know me well enough yet," David asked, his tone teasing, "to realize that what I meant was that you should wait until I could get him to come around?"

"Ah, yes," Jerry sighed, "you'd think I would know that by now, but you never cease to amaze me, baby."

David ducked his head and kissed any skin he could find. "I love you, Jerry. And I love the family that we've made."

"Me too," Jerry said and then ducked his own head to kiss David's forehead. "Speaking of, have you heard from Cory yet?"

"No, and I hope we don't."

"How so?" Jerry asked, obviously puzzled.

"I was thinking about that all day today... well yesterday, at school and when I was driving home, it hit me. If we don't call him or e-mail or whatever, then it will actually look better in the long run." David lifted his head and scooted up beside Jerry, their heads even and on the same pillow. "When he finally does run away for whatever reason... then having little or no contact with him will make it seem as if we couldn't possibly have influenced his decision."

"I see," Jerry said, drawing out the last vowel. "But I thought it didn't matter what happened. If the criminal code specifically mentions that parents are only responsible for their children until the age of sixteen, and that if the kid runs away, there's not much that the police and courts are willing to do about it...." Jerry's voice trailed off, the question having been implied.

"It does, but this way, it's even more ammunition if Aunt Linda turns out to be as controlling and pathological as Cory remembers and Sara suspects."

"Gotcha," Jerry turned on his side, their lips finding each other as if by force of habit. "Can I interest you in a little fooling around?"

"Funny," David smiled as he pushed Jerry onto his back and pulled himself so that he was straddling the narrow hips, "I was just about to ask you the same thing."

"It's been so long, baby," Jerry sighed as David reached down to stroke him. "I missed this."

"Me, too, cowboy." David kissed his way down Jerry's neck. He continued stroking with one hand while his other hand went to caress Jerry's head. "Tell me what you want, Jerry."

"Mmm," Jerry murmured into David's ear. "Was hoping you'd ride me."

David brought both hands up and planted them beside Jerry's head, then raised himself up to look down at the sleep-softened features. "Now here's one of my favorite positions."

"Love watching you ride me," Jerry sighed and pulled on the backs of David's thighs. "Love watching your face as you take me inside you. Love being able to touch you."

David raised his torso, Jerry's hands finding their way almost instantly to caress and explore and tweak and stroke. "I think the last time we did this, we were still using condoms." David sat back and felt Jerry's erection jump between his cheeks. He squeezed once and heard Jerry's muted grunt. "Know what it does to me feeling you inside me without anything between us?" David reached behind him and found Jerry hard and leaking pre-cum.

"I want you, baby." Jerry pushed himself up into David's hand as he reached to the side for the tube of lube. "Can you get me ready?"

David took the tube and squeezed some of the slick onto his own hand, reaching around to get the two of them ready. When he positioned the head of Jerry's dick at his hole, David watched his lover's face. "Love that look on your face, Jerry. Love that I'm the one that puts it there."

"So good, so tight, David." Jerry caressed his way down the lightly-furred chest and belly until his hands came to rest at David's hips, his forearms feeling the flex and release of the long thigh muscles as David started to raise himself up and then slowly lower himself down onto Jerry's shaft. "Lean forward, baby." Jerry circled his hands around David's waist, sliding them to his back as he leaned forward. "If I remember correctly, all I have to do is put my heels...." David felt Jerry moving his body around for a few seconds and then nothing but the sensation of having his prostate pegged and massaged by the engorged head of Jerry's cock.

David sucked in a quick breath, his head automatically falling forward. He felt Jerry's hands on his back, felt the enormous head of that uncut cock tapping and massaging his gland, and wasn't sure how much more attention he would be able to take from Jerry before his orgasm exploded between the two of them. He was panting now, leaning forward, the flushed skin of his cheek moving languidly against the heated beard on his lover's face. "Jerry, not gonna last... wanna come with you."

"Keep squeezing me, baby," Jerry muttered against David's ear. "So hot inside you, like an oven... feels incredible, baby."

"God, Jerry, I'm gonna come soon," David lifted his head, his lips finding Jerry's as if by instinct.

"Yeah, mountain lion, come for me, come on my chest," Jerry hissed as he increased the speed of his hips pistoning in and out of David's hole, his hands pushing against David's chest so that one hand could wrap itself around David's rock-hard cock and the other could fondle the sensitive balls. He looked up at David, both of them so near the edge. "Come for me, baby, come for me," Jerry sucked in another breath and felt his balls pull up, the sensations of being in and around David all at the same time too much for him. The fire coursed up and down his spine and settled in his belly, and he felt himself let go moments before David's heat clamped down on his dick.

David felt Jerry buck up against his ass, knew that Jerry would be especially sensitive after such an intense orgasm. He honestly couldn't remember the last time that Jerry had called out to him like that. He leaned forward and kissed Jerry's swollen lips. Jerry was panting heavily now, his chest heaving and his arms cast out to the side of his body. He made a trail with his kisses up and down Jerry's neck, delighting in the aftershocks that coursed through his body when Jerry touched him. "Maybe we ought to go without more often," David sighed against Jerry's neck. "I haven't seen you that turned on in a long time."

"I don't know," Jerry said with a chuckle. "You do that to me every time, but this morning?" David felt Jerry's hands wrap around his back, holding him safe and secure. "Was... something... different in there? You feel it too?"

"I'll say... and then some," David said with a mischievous smile. He felt Jerry slip out of him, felt the big beautiful hands stroke slowly up and down his back, and closed his eyes, only for a minute, he told himself.

AS HE exited the school, David checked his watch again. He would be home with plenty of time to make dinner for his father's visit tonight. It had been a rather uneventful Thursday at school, but the events of the past couple of days still weighed heavily on his mind. He was looking forward to an evening with his family. Jerry had mentioned that he might take William out after school to see if he couldn't lift his spirits a little bit. Neither Jerry nor David had known that the television program about the seals and the sea lions would feature such a sad story as Bob's. Despite the three of them watching the rest of the program and seeing and learning about all of the wonderful successful rescues and releases back into the wild, William still had the occasional question about why some animals died while others lived. But, all things considered, David and Jerry had both been rather relieved that it helped William get rid of some of the emotion he'd been holding on to. David wondered out loud last night as he and Jerry lay in bed if some of this emotion from William was a delayed reaction to losing his parents. Neither David nor Jerry could honestly remember discussing anything about the accident with William. So, it was good to have it out finally. In fact, William had seemed almost chipper this morning.

After one last run to the supermarket, he was at home putting the finishing touches on dinner when he heard Jerry and William come through the door. He was also acutely aware of another noise. He washed his hands, dried them on the tea towel, and headed toward the whimpering sound.

"David!" William ran forward with the little bundle of white fur held steadfast in his arms. "Look! Dad got me a puppy!"

"A puppy?" David didn't know whom to caress first. "A white Siberian husky." He chuckled, caught off-guard not only by the present, but also by William's intense focus on keeping the puppy in his arms. "Did your dad get you a bowl for the puppy too?" David laughed out loud this time as Jerry's arm came straight up in front of him, a bright yellow bag from a pet store dangling at the end of it. "How about a bed?"

"He's going to sleep with me," William announced as the puppy squirmed and licked so quickly that David could hardly keep it all in focus.

"I don't think so," David said, taking the puppy from William for a moment. "Okay, take the bag from your dad, and go fill the bowl while I explain some rules to... what's his name?"

"Her," William corrected over the sound of the tap running, his voice much brighter and fuller than it had been in days. "I haven't figured it out yet."

"There's a doggy bed in the back of the truck," Jerry said as he came over and stood beside David.

"She is *adorable*!" David whispered as he moved his head trying to get away from the puppy's tongue.

"He didn't want to get her at first," Jerry said as he reached out to tickle the puppy's belly. "When I told him I was going to get him a dog, he looked panicked at first. So, we went for an ice cream—wasn't

181

sure if you would want one, but got one for you anyway—and we had a nice talk." Jerry put an arm around his husband's shoulders. "He was afraid we might get one that was like Bob." Jerry smiled and let loose a one-note laugh. "You should have seen him in there; you would have thought he was buying a car, lifting this and checking that and feeling and poking."

"Poor baby," David cooed as he held the puppy up. "And poor William."

"We'll be as good as new in no time," Jerry announced as he exited through the door to retrieve the puppy's bed.

David walked, with the puppy still in his arms, back into the kitchen. "Maybe you and Opa Niels can talk about some possible names. He should be here any minute now."

"It has to be the perfect name," William said as he took the squirming puppy from David's arms and set her down in front of her brand new bowl. David smiled as he watched William standing guard over her while she lapped energetically at the water. "It has to be a really good name for when she's bigger too."

"You have lots of time." David washed his hands in the sink and then turned at the sound of the front door.

"Look who I found wandering around outside!" Jerry's voice caused William to look up.

"Opa!" William ran toward David's father. Despite the fact that David had seen the two of them together dozens of times over the past year, it never failed to cause a lump in his throat. "Dad got me a puppy! Come and see her!"

Niels greeted Jerry with a nod and a handshake and then hugged David quickly as William pulled him toward the far end of the kitchen. "What's her name?" David heard his father ask just one question, and then William was regaling his grandfather with a detailed account of the trip to the store and the reasons behind it. David was intent on pretending not to eavesdrop and didn't hear Jerry come up from behind.

"So?" Jerry wrapped his arms around David's waist. "Did I do good?"

"God, Jerry," David sighed as he leaned back against the muscular chest. "I was so worried about him after you told me about William sitting in the closet." David turned around to face Jerry. "And yes, you did a very good thing today."

"Good enough for a kiss?"

David smiled and leaned up to kiss Jerry, his exaggerated pout making David shake his head. They swayed for a moment, lips touching and teasing a little, and listened to William's giggles and Niels's deep baritone laugh. It seemed that everything would slowly get back to normal now. The only thing that would make this evening even better is if Cory had somehow managed to make his way back to the ranch sooner than expected. And, as if the higher powers were hearing his thoughts, David disentangled himself from Jerry when he heard the doorbell.

"I'll get it," he said as he headed to the door. "See if you can get those two to wash up and come to the table." David grinned at Jerry's salute and pulled open the door. It was a FedEx delivery person with a package addressed to David—from Switzerland.

There were no coherent thoughts—or more precisely, there were plenty of thoughts, but David couldn't seem to get his mind to settle on any one in particular. Frau Zimmerman had not yet replied to William's latest e-mail, the package was from Switzerland, and David was quite certain that the return address was a law office. He'd never had much cause to use the word, but he was quite certain that *Rechtsanwalt* was the German word for lawyer. And if this package was from a lawyer in Switzerland, it would probably mean—

"Hey, baby, you've got three starving—" David looked up and knew he must have scared Jerry into silence. "What's wrong, David?"

"I know I should open this, but I don't want to know what's inside. If I don't open it, then it won't be true. Not now, not again." He knew he was rambling, but he was more interested in not opening the package than making any sense.

"Whatever it is, baby, we'll get through it." Jerry took the package from David and opened it. He reached inside and found bubble wrap over a plastic bag over a beautifully-framed needlepoint sampler. "It's in German." David took the sampler and held it out so that he could read it.

"It reads: *A happy family is but an earlier heaven.*" David felt the tears stinging his eyes as he looked up at Jerry. "Frau Zimmerman had this hanging beside the fireplace. I remember…." David wiped at his eyes and watched as Jerry pulled out a letter and a sealed envelope. Jerry held the letter out to David, and he took it, getting only a few lines in before he heard the sharp intake of his own breath. "Frau Zimmerman had a stroke during this past weekend." He looked down at the letter and then back up into Jerry's patient eyes. "She didn't make it."

David heard the catch in his voice and leaned against Jerry, their arms going around each other. Neither of them asked how they would possibly tell William. As he regained control of himself, David wondered whether that old saying about bad news coming in groups of three was true; if it was, then they'd had their three already, and it was time for some good news.

Chapter 21

JERRY was lying on his back, listening to the soft, rhythmic breathing of the little boy next to him. Or was that the puppy curled up by the boy's tummy? William had cried himself to sleep almost two hours ago, but Jerry was still awake, replaying the evening over and over again in his mind. He'd passed through anger and denial and found himself—just after midnight—staring at the ceiling, trying to deal with one question at a time. It seemed that no matter what decision he made, he felt as if he was sitting down to write a test in another language. It didn't seem to matter that he recognized a few words; the questions didn't seem to make any sense to him. And just like that imaginary test, he found himself doubting his every action.

He'd carried William to bed for the second night in a row and found himself sitting beside his son, wondering what to do. Should he leave William alone and come back if he called out? Should he stay beside him all through the night? Should he try to keep explaining to William about death and dying and growing and maturing? And most importantly, was Jerry the best person to do any of this?

He and David had decided to let William have dinner with Niels and then play with the puppy for a few hours before they finally sat him down in the living room and explained the package that they'd received. At first Jerry had tried to tell William, but the words would not come. There was only anger. Jerry had found himself unable to put aside the many questions that seemed to accost him. *How much more is this poor boy expected to deal with? How many more lessons will he have to learn before he finally feels safe again?*

With his anger barely in check, he'd finally looked over at David and Niels. Jerry had been at a loss to explain something that even he didn't seem to understand. He let the other two men do the explaining, while he could only sit there and try not to cry himself at how unfair it all seemed. And he was glad—once again—that David had been there to help. And here he was, son and puppy fast asleep by his side. It was only Jerry who was awake at this hour, the uncertainty of it all making him feel as useless as he'd felt when William first showed up on his doorstep.

Jerry heard the gentle creak of the door and looked over to find David standing there, a small smile on his beautiful face. He tried to muster one himself, but found he couldn't. He watched as David moved slowly toward him, his hand extended. He took hold of Jerry's hand and pulled gently, beckoning Jerry to follow him. Jerry looked at William, his beautiful son still fast asleep, and raised himself from the bed and followed his husband.

"I couldn't sleep, either." David put his arm around Jerry's waist and they walked to the stairs and went to the kitchen. "I thought you could use some coffee."

"I feel so useless," Jerry sighed as he fell into his usual chair at the harvest table.

"Nonsense," David said, his tone soft but chiding. "You're doing exactly what he needs you to do."

"Nothing?"

"Jerrod McKenzie, you are a great father to William, an incredible husband to me, and the only reason both William and I are happy." David finished filling the kettle, plugged it in, and then took a seat beside his husband.

"I think the puppy will give me some serious competition," Jerry said, his muted chuckle seeming thin and pathetic. "But thank you. For helping me."

"That's what families do, isn't it?"

"And what about your old man?" Jerry raised himself off the chair and walked to the patio door, unlocking it and opening it. He felt the cool air caress his face. "He sat there with William on his lap and cried right along with him. He didn't even mention anything about death or dying." Jerry shook his head at the memory. "He told William about love... and when he started telling that story...." Jerry closed his eyes and brought his hand to his face, surprised at how quickly David was there, arms wrapped around him.

"It's okay, Jerry. We all feel a little overwhelmed by this." David led Jerry back to his chair. "I think it will be good for all of us to let go a little."

Jerry swiped at his cheeks. "I remember my dad always telling me that it was a sign of weakness to show emotion." He looked up quickly and then back down at his hands. "I didn't realize until I was much older that he was talking about business. But by then, I'd convinced myself that crying was only for girls... or fags."

"Irony," David said with a small flourish, and Jerry couldn't help but let the laughter escape.

"I don't...." Jerry finally looked up at David and began again. "I don't know how to fix this."

"Can I ask you a question you once asked me?"

Jerry nodded.

"Before I told you that I couldn't bring myself to sign the petition that Bennet and his brigade had presented me, you asked me, *Why them?*"

Jerry looked down at his hands, expecting more, but his eyes bounced back to his husband's face just as quickly when he heard no further words. "I don't understand."

"*Them* in your case isn't a group of people, but all of these thoughts you're having about fixing things or feeling useless or thinking you're not a good father to William." David reached over and held Jerry's hands in his, giving them a little squeeze. "Why are you letting these thoughts win?"

"I'm not... I don't think... I, uh...." Jerry closed his mouth as he saw David's eyebrows, and he realized what he was really being asked. "I asked that?" Jerry found himself smiling a little as David nodded. "Who knew I was that smart?"

"Everyone," David said as he stood and moved to Jerry's lap. "Everyone but you, that is."

"I love you, David."

"And I love you." David pulled Jerry's hand to his lips and kissed it gently. "And we both love William and will make sure that he gets through this." David got off Jerry's lap before the kettle's whistle grew too loud, unplugged it, and then turned back to face Jerry. "And if we have to, we'll buy him another twenty puppies."

DAVID and Jerry had made the decision to keep William home on Friday, thinking that a day spent with his dad and his new puppy would do wonders for his sagging spirits. At least, David had gone to work on that last day before spring break thinking that plan had the potential to work; it wouldn't work miracles, but it would certainly help William, or so they thought. But when he arrived home, he found that the day had been one filled with surprises, most of them good.

David parked his car in the driveway, pulled his briefcase out of the car, and headed to the house. When he opened the door, he wasn't sure—at first—if it was crying or laughing he was hearing. Fearing the worst, he deposited his briefcase on the bench, pried off his shoes, and headed toward the sound. When he descended the few steps to the living room, he found Jerry and William on the floor playing with one excited puppy.

"Hey, fellas, what's going on here?"

"I was teaching William how to train the dog." David turned at the voice behind him and wasn't sure at first if he was tired enough to be seeing things or if it was really Cory standing in front of him. "We still need to do some work on the whole fetch thing," Cory said as he held up a yellow tennis ball. "Hi," Cory said awkwardly, taking another step toward David.

"What... how... I thought...." He turned back to look at Jerry, who shrugged and showed a smile that told David that he knew more than the shrug seemed to indicate.

"I can explain later," Cory said as he held out his hand to David. "Is the offer still open? To live here, I mean?"

"Of course," David said as he pushed Cory's hand away and pulled him into a tight embrace. "Of course it is." David let go of Cory and turned back to Jerry. "Good day?"

"Finally," Jerry whispered as he pushed himself off the floor and took a hug for himself. "Okay, men, David and I are going upstairs for a minute. I don't want to see any pee stains on the floor when I get back. And I don't want the puppy peeing in here either."

William and Cory groaned in unison at the bad joke, while the puppy seemed frantic to try and lick both of their faces at the same time. Jerry put his arm around David's waist and led him upstairs.

Once they were in the bedroom, Jerry grabbed David over to the bed and pulled him down on top of him. "I guess right from the get-go, Cory's aunt was a force of nature. She wouldn't allow computers or cell phones or any contact with the *sodomites*." David laughed at Jerry's air quotes. "She even enrolled him at some military or prep-type school and had arranged for him to do custodial work as a way to help pay his tuition. I guess she told the headmaster that Cory was a recovering drug addict." Jerry was shaking his head slowly in disbelief. "The end came this afternoon, apparently. Cory's father is out on bail, finally, and showed up at his sister's place. Cory got home from school, found his father there, and took off in a cab." Jerry kissed David softly at first and then a little more deeply. "Do you have any idea how much a taxi ride from south Calgary to our house is?"

David saw the tilt of his head and the lopsided grin. "It was quite a reunion between the two of them, William and Cory, I mean. William was so excited and forgot to put down the puppy when he went to hug Cory, and then the puppy was all excited and was even more so when William made the official introductions—"

"Did he choose a name, yet?"

"No," Jerry said, shaking his head, his smile still bright, "it's just Puppy for now." Jerry looked down at his hands and then over at David. "William helped Cory unpack all of his stuff and then showed him the needlepoint we helped William hang over his bed. He was really great with William, helped him a lot by telling him about how he eventually got through losing his own mother. Cory told him how much Frau Zimmerman must have loved him to want him to have that, that she must have considered William to be like family, that what makes someone family is what's in here," Jerry said as he put his hand over his chest. "So, we all had a good cry because of that." Jerry kissed David gently on the lips. "I think William's going to be fine."

"I'm glad," David said, his voice almost a whisper. "Did you call Sara?"

"I did, and she called the police," Jerry said as he nodded. "She said something about D.E.C.A.—that's Drug-endangered Child Act of 2006 for the uninformed, like me—and Cory was officially free of that environment, and he'd done the right thing in running away, and now, hold on to your hats, he's free to live with us if he wants. There will be no more contact with either the father or the aunt." Jerry punctuated the explanation with a gentle kiss and rolled them both on to their sides.

"Looks like things are turning around for our boys."

"Our boys," Jerry echoed. "You know," Jerry said as he propped his head up on one hand, "that reminds me of a conversation we had at Christmas."

"Yeah," David sighed, stealing another kiss, "which conversation would that be?"

"The one where you told me that you'd adopt William—officially—after we got married." Jerry pulled his head back to look at David. "Is that still something you think about?"

"Ah, only every day," David said as he swatted playfully at Jerry's chest.

"So… then…."

"I didn't want you to feel like I was intruding," David said as he felt his face flush. "But, now, actually, it would be rather appropriate for me to adopt him—or at least get the paperwork going—on the one-year anniversary of his finding you."

"Of his finding us," Jerry corrected. "And the one-year anniversary of his bringing the two of us together—indirectly, of course."

David laughed at the memory that at once seemed so far removed from their lives and yet so recent in his memory that he could still smell the cologne, feel Jerry kiss him for the first time. "I thought you were an uncivilized redneck when I first met you, you know?"

"I remember." Jerry laughed and took one of David's hands in his. "And I thought you were the most beautiful man I'd ever seen."

David brought Jerry's hand up to his lips and kissed it softly. "You were ruthless in your flirting that first night."

"I kept making these moves, and I'd see you blush, and I was hoping that you were attracted to me… even just a little."

"I will admit to a lukewarm attraction at first."

"Lukewarm?" Jerry laughed heartily and pulled David's head toward him for a scorching kiss. "So somewhere between lukewarm and the end of the evening, I must have really gotten to you."

"I have no idea what you're talking about," David said as he pulled his hand away, the smile on his face betraying any real sense of indignation.

"I still think about that night sometimes, you know."

"You must have me confused with one of your twenty-somethings."

"No," Jerry said as he let himself fall back on the bed. "And do you know why I'm not confused?"

David raised his eyebrows in curiosity.

"Because no twenty-something... no *man* has ever—and I do mean *ever*—made me feel the way you do." Jerry pulled on David's shoulders, bringing their chests together again, and kissed him deeply. Their hands caressed shoulders and heads and faces. Finally, they separated and Jerry looked into David's eyes. "I think about my life before meeting you sometimes, and it makes me so sad to think that I could have just as easily gone on with what I thought was a happy life."

David watched as Jerry closed his eyes. He reached out and caressed his husband's cheeks. "I know." He leaned down and kissed Jerry's lips. "I know. I love you too."

"Do you know when I first knew that I loved you?" David shook his head. "It's my best memory, ever." Jerry raised himself on one elbow again. "After our first night together, I woke up in the middle of the night and just watched you sleep until I couldn't keep my own eyes open anymore. You were so peaceful." Jerry shook his head slowly. "So peaceful when you slept, but so... haunted when you were awake, trying to help William and me even though what's-his-face had broken your heart." Jerry took hold of one of David's hands and kissed it. "And when William came home from school, day after day, telling me how much all the other kids looked up to you, how patient you were with all of them, how you tried to make each one feel so special... and I found myself thinking, *And not one of them knows how much he's hurting.*"

"You are such a romantic," David said and smiled. "I think I fell in love with you that night by the fire. You held William as he slept. I knew there would never be anyone else for me." David pushed against Jerry's shoulder and then put his right hand under his head, caressing and kneading just the right way to make Jerry purr like a kitten. He looked into those beautiful blue eyes for a moment and then brought his lips to Jerry's, sealing their mouths together in a kiss that seemed to reassure both of them that their lives, Jerry's and David's and those of the two boys who completed their family, would be filled with everything that life had to offer.

Their lips parted, and as if reading David's mind, Jerry offered a sly smile and winked. "We can handle anything as long as we stick together."

Chapter 22

"I'M COMING already!"

David looked up as his husband got to his feet, Jerry's apprehension clear to everyone within a five-mile radius. "You did promise you'd teach him," he said as he accepted a quick kiss on the lips.

"I know, I know," Jerry sighed heavily and then turned to look at Niels who had Puppy in his lap. "Hey, Niels, I can't interest you in an hour of driving lessons, can I?" David knew that Jerry was only joking, but he looked over at his father to see the smooth and practiced reaction of a man who'd made millions of dollars dealing with this kind of pressure.

"And deprive you of one of the most exciting moments of being a father?"

David's eyes shifted back and forth between his husband and his father, the grin barely contained. He made a mental note to thank Jerry later this evening—in a way that only David could—for giving Niels a second chance to prove he wasn't going to hurt anyone. David smiled as Jerry only shrugged and headed toward the old pickup, mumbling something about Niels not knowing what he was missing.

"Do you remember when you were sixteen and I taught you how to drive?" Niels had his hand on his son's shoulder. "Some nights I wasn't sure I'd make it back alive."

"I wasn't that bad, was I?" David nudged his shoulder against his father's chest.

"No," Niels said as he brought his hand up to David's neck and gave it a quick squeeze. "No, you weren't bad at all." David reveled in the affectionate gesture, their eyes meeting only briefly before David looked out to see Jerry instructing Cory on how to check the tires for proper pressure. A quick snort of laughter escaped before he could censor it; William was trailing behind Jerry and Cory, being sure to mimic every command and suggestion that Jerry offered.

"He's something, isn't he?" David turned to look at his father. "William, I mean." David found himself looking out at the little guy who'd been through so much lately. David couldn't help but marvel at how resilient and earnest their little boy was.

"He's you."

David turned to look at his father again, the words not so much a shock as a surprise.

"He cares about everyone, wants to do everything just right, and when he loves someone, it's with a gigantic and loyal heart."

He smiled warmly and draped his arm around his father's shoulders. "Thanks, Dad."

"You're welcome, Davey."

He removed his arm from around his father's shoulders and said, "Although, I must say that I look at him sometimes and I swear I can see Jerry." David looked down at Puppy as she clambered onto his lap, and he stroked her soft fur lazily.

"That's only normal, I think." Niels leaned forward, his elbows perched on his thighs. "It's been almost a year now since the three of you became a family, so you'll all continue to… *absorb* some of each other."

"As long as they get Jerry's artistic talent and my—"

"Heart?"

David laughed as he looked over at his father. "I was going to say *math skills*, but I like yours better."

"Listen, Davey, I know Jerry doesn't like me very much—"

195

"*Didn't*," David interrupted. "He wasn't really sure of you at first, thought you would end up hurting me and William, but he's a really good man, Dad, and he's more than willing to admit that he was wrong to doubt you."

Niels smiled, his blue eyes twinkling. "I'm glad I didn't disappoint your husband." When he said nothing further, David turned back to see Jerry stepping down from the truck and finding a position behind it. He was about to instruct Cory how to parallel park. David figured this should be good for a few jibes later on tonight. "I'm glad I didn't disappoint him because there's something I need to ask you. A favor."

"Anything, you know you can ask me anything, Dad."

"Well, it's not you I'm worried about."

"Dad," David said as he turned to face his father. "What is it? You're scaring me."

"Diana has been asking about you." Niels offered a shrug and then added, "Well, it started with Diana, but now Kelley seems to be coming around as well."

David sat stock still, unable to move a muscle. He hadn't heard much about his sisters for almost ten years. It had been an unspoken understanding when he'd reconnected with his father that neither of them would dwell on questions and updates about the other members of the family; Niels's time—precious as it was—would not be wasted pontificating and wondering when the other members of the family would come around.

"Diana asked me a couple of weeks ago how my visits were going." To David, his father's glances between the ground and his son's face seemed incongruous; Niels was never nervous, for any reason. "I guess your mother told them that I was spending time with you and your new family, and well... Diana asked me to ask you if you would consider letting her visit."

"I... I'll have to talk to Jerry, but...." David's mind was racing. He thought of William and how he'd have three cousins in addition to a new brother and a grandfather. But then he also thought of how hurt he'd been when the sister he'd practically raised turned her back on him after saying all those awful things to his face. "What about that husband of hers?"

"They're divorcing."

"Oh, I'm sorry… for Diana, I mean."

"She feels terrible about what she said to you all those years ago."

"I don't know if I can talk about that right now, Dad. I—"

"I know we all hurt you… very much, but I told you last year that the rest of the family would come around in time." Niels put his arm around his son. "I think Diana realizes now how much she let her decisions be influenced by that… by Clarence, and she told me she misses you, misses not having you be an uncle to her children."

David felt the sting of unshed tears and closed his eyes, opening them slowly as the thought occurred to him. "They understand it's a package deal, right? Jerry is the man I love, he's my husband, and I'm not going to exclude him or William or Cory or tell them that they can't—"

"They understand," Niels said as he smoothed the hair off of David's forehead. "No one is interested in telling you how to live your life anymore, son."

David looked down as his hands, continued to stroke the puppy, and was surprised to see that he was shaking. He looked back up into his father's eyes. David had not yet heard the one name he hoped to hear. "And Mom?"

"I'm sorry, son."

David looked out at his family, the flurry of activity in the cab signaling that perhaps he should go over and give Jerry a break.

"She'll come around, I promise."

"You can't know that." David glanced at his father. "She let Oma die all alone."

"That's not fair, David," Niels said as he closed his eyes and shook his head. "Your mother and Oma had a very difficult relationship."

"That seems to be Mom's specialty." David regretted the words right away. For all of her faults, his mother had always been attentive to her children, encouraging them to do their very best at whatever they chose to do. She had not been a perfect mother, by any means, but she certainly didn't deserve to be summed up with those words. "I'm sorry," David said quickly. "I didn't mean that."

"I know, Davey. I know." Niels seemed pensive for a moment. "At the risk of giving you and Jerry far too much to discuss tonight, I was hoping that when Cory has his permanent driver's license—you and Jerry might let me get him his own vehicle?"

David shot a glance between his father and the flurry of activity out by the corral fence. All of David's men were out of the truck, and William was running back toward the house. "I think Jerry was planning on giving him the pickup, but I'll discuss your offer with him."

"Opa, David, did you see me?"

Both David and his father turned to see William running toward them, his eyes wide and his short legs carrying him toward them at a brisk pace.

"Dad let me sit on his lap and steer." William landed on his opa's lap, his eyes glinting in the dying sunlight, and his cheeks flushed from all of the excitement. As he panted, Puppy made her way onto William's lap.

"I did see you, William, and you're a natural." Niels wrapped his arms around his grandson and looked over at his son. "David and I were just talking about what a great driver you'll be."

"Cory's going to be a great driver too." William pointed out to where Jerry and Cory were obviously deep in some discussion or debriefing. "He only hit the corral fence once!"

"And maybe tomorrow he won't hit it at all," David said as he reached out to tickle William. "You know what might help him, sport? If you stay here with me on the steps, so he can concentrate better."

"Yeah," William said through his giggles. "Dad kept telling me to stop asking so many questions, said I was distracting Cory, so maybe you're right."

"And besides," David said as he reached out to tickle his son some more. "If you stay here on the veranda with me, you and I can eat cookies and play with Puppy." David reached down and picked up the puppy.

"Homemade?"

"Of course."

William turned and looked Niels in the eyes. "David makes the best oatmeal raisin cookies, Opa."

JERRY lay back on the bed, his hands going to cradle his head. He watched as David's hands worked to undo first his own clothing and then his. If there was ever a sight that aroused him faster than a completely naked David undressing him and kissing each exposed piece of skin, he honestly couldn't remember what it was. He closed his eyes as he felt the cool night air from the open window waft over his naked torso. David's hands worked quickly to free him from his jeans and underwear, and then Jerry felt the familiar caress of the strong, slender hands over his chest.

"Come here, baby." Jerry reached for his husband and pulled him up for a deep kiss. He was gentle at first, the passion building as it always did as their tongues found each other and their hands explored familiar territory, eliciting the hypnotic moans of pleasure. He felt David pull away slowly. "What's wrong?"

"Absolutely nothing, cowboy." David gave his lover a quick peck and then looked down, his hand still caressing Jerry's scalp. "I have some news for our family."

"Please tell me it's good news." Jerry pushed himself over on top of David and settled himself so that their bodies were aligned perfectly, like two pieces of a jigsaw puzzle.

"My dad was telling me that my sisters have been asking about me, wanting to reconnect."

Jerry felt David's heartbeat increase slightly, so he chose his words very carefully. It was one of the many things that had helped Jerry fall in love with him, this desire for everyone and everything to be perfect, like a Norman Rockwell painting or something out of a 1950s family sitcom. Before Jerry could find the right words, he felt David's hands move up his back and begin to caress his scalp again.

"I was thinking that I'll maybe go and visit a few times... just to make sure that William and Cory won't be forced into the middle of anything we don't want for them."

Jerry's smile was automatic, involuntary. "Sounds perfect then." He lowered his head until their lips made contact in a soft, gentle kiss.

"I wanted to thank you, Jerry, for giving my dad a chance." Jerry opened his mouth to offer some automatic, expected reaction, but David interrupted him. "Even he's noticed that you're much more open and welcoming."

Jerry stole a quick kiss and then cocked his head to one side. "I didn't like the idea of him hurting you again at first, but now... guess I finally realized I was just being overprotective."

David brought both of his hands to the handsome face and brought their lips together one more time. "You're a good man, Jerrod McKenzie." Another kiss. "And a great father." Another kiss. "And I'm the luckiest old fag on the planet."

"Don't know about the luckiest," Jerry said as he lowered his head for yet another kiss. "But you're definitely the sexiest." Jerry pushed his hips against his husband's, delighting in the sharp intake of air from David as their cocks were pressed together. "Now," he whispered into his husband's sensitive ear, "are we done with talking?"

"Oh... God... Jerry... yes... done."

"Can never get enough of you, baby," Jerry sighed against David's ear. He felt his lover's hands flex and release against his back and reached down to hook first one leg over a forearm and then the other. "You're the best thing that's ever happened to me."

"Oh, please, Jerry, please." David was writhing underneath Jerry, his hands caressing and exploring, pinching and kneading. Jerry placed his hands on the backs of his lover's thighs and pushed so that David's ass was raised in the air. His tongue found its way to the pink hole, darting in and out playfully at first until he could feel the slight tremors in David's thighs.

"Hang on, baby, wanna get you ready." Jerry returned his attention to preparing his lover, his tongue licking and poking and laving. He'd discovered, quite by accident one night, that if he hummed while he had his lips against David's hole, the smaller man fairly leaped out of his skin from the combined sensations. He didn't do it all the time, preferring instead to save it for nights like tonight. William and Cory were in bed, safe and happy, and mainly due to the beautiful and caring man beneath Jerry at this moment. Tonight would be one of those nights when Jerry would show David how much he loved him and how glad he was that he'd opened up his heart to David; he had a family now.

When Jerry felt the fevered grappling of David's hands against his and heard the inane ramblings of a man on the edge of ecstasy, he lowered his lover's ass and lined himself up, pushing in slowly, tantalizingly. There was nothing sexier than watching David's face as he opened himself up and took him in all the way. Jerry had always known he was bigger than most men, so he'd had to learn how not to push in all the way all the time; he'd had to learn how to find the other man's prostate, how to move and adjust so that he could hear those sounds he loved to hear. He leaned forward, letting his tongue find its way to David's ears, first one and then the other.

Jerry moaned softly when he felt those strong, slender hands find his scalp and begin to caress and explore. "The way you touch me, David," he sighed into one ear and felt the contraction of his husband's muscle around his dick. "So sensual, so sexy, so beautiful to watch." Jerry pulled out partially and heard the familiar gasp; he'd known exactly where to find David's prostate. "Right there, yeah, love to hear that sound." Jerry pulled out slowly and then pegged the gland again, and again, and again, enjoying David's gasps more and more each time. He felt his blood burning through his veins, felt the tender—yet firm—caresses over his scalp, and felt the telltale contraction around his cock.

"Need to come, baby," David grunted against Jerry's neck. "Oh, God, I'm gonna come soon."

"I've got you, baby, I've got you," Jerry sighed against one ear as he slowly lowered his torso onto David's, putting himself at an angle that allowed him to hit his lover's gland over and over again. With each thrust, he could feel David's granite-hard dick move against his abdomen; he knew it would only take three or four more thrusts for David to climax. He breathed heavily into first one ear and then the other, pulling back finally after the fourth thrust to look at his husband's flushed face. "Come for me, mountain lion, come for me."

"Oh, Jerry, oh, baby," David panted against Jerry's chest.

"Oh, God, so tight."

Jerry felt the contractions around his dick and threw his head back, amazed every time at how hot and tight David's hole was. He felt himself let go, felt the fire climb up his spine before settling in his belly. Jerry thrust forward with each of his own contractions, spilling his seed deep inside of his lover. David had finished with his own orgasm, but continued to contract his muscles in that special way that made Jerry feel as if he would be completely consumed and lost forever. And at moments like this, he didn't really care if it happened, as long as David was with him.

Chapter 23

CORY FLETT woke up late, or what his aunt and father would have considered to be late; it was almost eight in the morning on Saturday. Cory stretched and yawned and smiled, for the first time in a long time it seemed. He was in no hurry to get out of bed today. He was safe in a big bed, with clean sheets, and only the smell of breakfast; there was no lingering, stale odor of pot and alcohol. And best of all, Cory wouldn't need to get up this morning to go and wash the vomit off the toilet or his father's clothes.

He couldn't help but wonder about the weirdness of life, about how meeting just one person could change your entire outlook. As he stretched and threw the fluffy duvet off of his body, he tried to remember that word from English class, the one that meant lucky and fortuitous. He knew it began with sara-something, but couldn't remember the rest of it. He only remembered the first two syllables since it reminded him of Tara.

As he jammed his feet into his slippers, he found himself wondering what she was doing right now. He wondered if she missed him as much as he missed her. He'd flirted with the idea so many times of asking her out, but there was no possible way that he would have ever been able to bring her back to his place. Plus, there was the common knowledge that his father was a drug dealer and those annoying rumors that he was as well. Maybe now that he was with Jerry and David and William, he might be able to ask her out sometime. The thought that he wasn't at the school anymore didn't really bother him. This morning, anything seemed possible.

He walked down the hall to William's room to find the door open and the bed made. He quickly ran back to his room to make sure his own room was neat and tidy, then made his way to the kitchen, toward the smell of breakfast and William's contagious giggle and the yipping of that cute puppy.

"Finally!"

Cory laughed and tousled William's hair. "You could have come and woken me up, Billiam."

"I wanted to, but they wouldn't let me," William said as he pointed across the table at Jerry and David, who were already dressed in T-shirts and jeans.

"Sorry, buddy," Cory said as he sat beside William.

"No need to apologize," Jerry said as he stood and fetched a plate from the microwave. "William can wait; it won't do him any harm."

"How'd you sleep?" Jerry deposited a plate full of waffles and bacon and eggs in front of him, and David poured a glass of orange juice for him.

"Great," Cory said as he picked up his fork and knife. He looked around and wondered if he would sound stupid if he asked them to join hands with him while he thought of the things for which he was most thankful. He closed his eyes and bowed his head and said his own thanks.

"Will you help me pick out a name for Puppy?" Cory watched William look down at the puppy on the floor, finally reaching down to pick her up.

"Not at the table, William. If you want to play with Puppy, you can leave the table and go play with her.

"Sorry, I forgot." William hopped off his chair and sat cross-legged near the entrance to the kitchen. Cory watched, amused, as William picked up the puppy and placed it inside the small space created by his folded legs. As he tasted the bacon and eggs, he smiled and continued to observe the excited little puppy try to escape. "Hey,"

Cory said suddenly, his eyes darting between the adults and William, "what was Frau Zimmerman's first name? Do you know?"

"Wilhelmina, I think," David said after thinking for a few seconds. "Why?"

"You can use that to make a name for the dog." Cory turned in his chair and looked at William. "She loved you and so does the puppy, so...." He shrugged and tapped the side of his head. "It makes perfect sense."

"Hey, cowboy, that's a great idea." Jerry looked from Cory to William. "You could call her Mina, or... Willy?"

Cory looked over at David and couldn't help but notice the frown, or was that a look of disgust, or alarm? He wasn't sure about Willy; Mina might be a nice name for the puppy, though. "Or," Cory said, getting down on the floor beside William, "you could name her Billie."

"You know," David said, "Wilhelmina is the female equivalent of William."

Cory noticed William's little blond head pop up at last and regard David. "We had the same name?"

"Almost," David said with a smile. "What do you think of Billie, William?"

"I like it," William said and looked down again at his dog. "What about you, Billie? Do you like that name too?" The dog yipped and tried to lick William's face.

"Well, that's settled, then." Jerry stood and walked toward William. "You want to give Cory the good news?"

"Dad," William groaned, "he's the one who named her."

"Not that news, cowboy." Jerry squatted beside his son and brushed his hand over the short, blond locks. "About the classes we're going to after lunch."

"Oh, right!" William turned his head, still trying to avoid Billie's tongue. "Jerry's neighbor gives lessons on training dogs, and we're going to some classes. Do you want to come with us?"

"Sure, sounds like fun."

"WHAT'S taking him so long?"

Cory laughed as William struggled to hold the wiggling Billie in his arms. "Can I hold her?" William leaned over and let him take Billie.

"Don't squish her," William said as he surveyed Cory's puppy-holding technique.

"I promise I won't hurt her." Cory looked up at David, each of them smirking at how serious William was about Billie. Cory had a brief flash thought of the future and laughed as he saw how nervous and obsessed William might be when he started having children of his own.

Cory, William, and David sat on the front steps waiting for Jerry. "Do you know what's taking him so long?" Cory petted Billie, quieting her a little, and turned to David, who shrugged. "So, is this a business for your neighbor, or does he do it as a favor, or what?" Cory felt Billie begin to squirm again and pulled her closer to his chest, and she let out a little yelp.

"You're squishing her," William said, indignant. He reached over and took her back from Cory.

"Was not. She was just trying to get my attention."

"Paulie's a friend of Jerry's," David said, looking at his watch again. "I don't know what's keeping him, but if he doesn't hurry up, we're going without him."

"Couldn't he just meet us there?" Cory stood and stretched his back.

"Good idea," David said and patted Cory on the shoulder. "William, go inside and tell your dad that we're leaving and he can meet us there."

"Sorry, sorry, sorry," Jerry chanted as he stepped onto the veranda and turned to lock the door. "Kitty's fault."

"She's weird," William said and turned to Cory. "That's Dad's agent, and she's really weird."

"William," David sighed, "she is not weird; she's just different."

"Anyway," Jerry interrupted, rubbing his hands together. "Remind me to tell you about it later."

"Tell us now!" William jumped up and down, and Cory saw Billie get all riled up again, paws trying for purchase as she tried to reach William's face with her tongue.

"Later," Jerry repeated and took Billie from William while the little guy climbed up into the truck cab. "Okay, we're off to Paulie's, and then I was thinking we'd go out for dinner and celebrate."

"Celebrate what?" William was practically vibrating with anticipation. "Celebrate what, Dad?"

"Later," Jerry said a third time.

"If you have no intention of telling us, quit throwing out bait," David said as he reached for Billie. "Hi, there, you beautiful girl, you. I haven't gotten to hold you much, have I? No, I haven't."

"Keys, wallet, puppy, kids, husband," Jerry muttered to himself as he looked around the cab. "Okay, off we go." Jerry turned the ignition, pulled the car into gear, and did a U-turn out of the driveway. "When I talked to Paulie the other day, he told me that his grandkids are visiting, so there should be some other young'uns your ages to socialize with this afternoon." Jerry looked in the rearview mirror. Cory nodded and gave a thumbs up.

Cory leaned back in his leather bucket seat and settled in for a long drive, not really sure how far apart these ranches were. He was also enjoying the sounds of other people. Not necessarily the talking and the joking, but the sounds of people who seemed comfortable with each other. William hummed softly, Jerry and David were deep in conversation about other family activities they could plan for the rest of spring break, and Billie? Cory smiled as he saw that she'd finally fallen asleep in David's lap. Cory wondered if David had that effect on everyone or if it was just the lost and lonely.

Within what seemed mere minutes, Cory heard Jerry announce that they'd arrived. He didn't know why he'd thought that people living out in the country would live hours away from each other, but he knew that there were probably a lot of things he was going to learn about while he stayed with Jerry and David. And in a way, that thought filled him with dread. It wasn't that he didn't like to learn, but rather Cory would have to admit that he didn't know how to drive, had never asked a girl out, or even danced. He knew that they wouldn't tease him or ridicule him like his father had done, but it would still be embarrassing for him to have to admit these things. And what made it worse? He'd probably have to admit these things one at a time as each issue came up.

There were already a few other cars parked here and there along the driveway up to the main house, so they had to walk a little before meeting some of the other people. He made sure to wipe his suddenly sweaty palms on his jeans before shaking hands with everyone he was introduced to. There were about ten people in all so far, and Cory wondered how good this dog trainer, Paulie, would have to be to be able to work with so many people and their dogs.

"Hey, Jer, nice to see you." A large, very tall, gray-haired man came up to them. "Hey, William, is this your new pup?"

"Yessir, we're calling her Billie," William announced as he stood beside David, who still had the dog in his arms. Billie had woken up a couple of seconds ago and wasn't quite as energetic as she usually was. Cory figured that would change as soon as she looked around and saw all the people, not to mention all the other dogs.

"Well, Tara'll help you learn how to take real good care of her," Paulie said as he stepped aside and pointed behind him, then turned toward Jerry and David. "I don't think you two were together the last time Tara was visiting with me."

"Almost a year," Jerry said with a grin as he turned to look at David.

Cory, along with the rest of his family, looked up when the screen door opened, and he suddenly felt lightheaded, as if he'd ridden the roller-coaster one time too many. *It's Tara. It's her.* Cory didn't know whether to run and hide or try and act cool and suave.

He heard noises, saw Tara shaking hands with everyone and knew that he was supposed to say something, but he couldn't seem to get his mind to focus nor his mouth to work.

JERRY caught David's eye as Cory fumbled for a few simple words.

"Hi, Cory, I was wondering what happened to you at school." Jerry couldn't help noticing that both Cory and Tara were blushing a deep crimson, and Tara kept brushing her hair behind her ears. Jerry wondered if she knew that all of her hair was already behind her ears. "I was sorry to hear about your father." Cory nodded and offered his thanks. Finally, Jerry couldn't take it anymore and started to feel embarrassed for the poor kid.

"Hey, listen, Tara," Jerry began as he stepped up beside Cory. "We were thinking of getting another dog, a bigger dog, so David and I will be over here learning about them. You don't mind working with Cory and William by yourself, do you?"

"Not at all," Tara said with a smile as a young boy, a little taller than William, came up to stand beside her. "William, this is my brother Wayde." Jerry watched, his heart threatening to burst out of his chest, as William extended his hand to Wayde and the two young boys shook hands.

As William and Cory moved off to follow Tara and Wayde, Jerry could hear Tara begin to explain about some of the differences between training puppies and mature dogs. When Paulie moved off to welcome the last of his class for the day, David came up beside Jerry and touched his elbow. "Was that what I think it was?"

"Oh, you bet," Jerry said with a chuckle. "I'll have to give him some tips on how to be irresistible." He looked quickly at David, prepared for some scathing retort. Jerry wasn't sure, at first, if David had heard him; David was staring off into the distance, his eyes following the foursome and Billie.

"I think that would be great, cowboy." David turned back to look at him, his eyes bright, his smile as full and happy as Jerry hadn't seen in a long time. "But be careful, will you?" David pretended to brush something off Jerry's T-shirt. "Just teach him the basics for now. I don't think the world is ready for two of you."

"Are you flirting with me?" Jerry moved in close and felt David's hand on his chest. "I feel it only fair to warn you that I can't resist good-looking men with kids and pets."

"Neither can I!" David chuckled and then stopped. "Wait, what? Pets? As in another one? You were serious?"

"You're the one who suggested it," Jerry said, his shoulders hunched and his tone incredulous.

"I did not," David argued, "I said that we would have to buy William however many puppies... never mind. Besides, it looks like William and Wayde will become fast friends." He moved so that the sun wasn't in his eyes. "Should we get another husky, or...?"

"Why don't we let Cory decide?"

"Fair enough." David turned, his arms now crossed over his chest. "So, are you going to tell me what we'll be celebrating, or will you be the one following Billie around with a plastic bag for the next six months?"

"Please," Jerry harrumphed, "I shovel horseshit a couple of times a week. You think I'd be scared of a little puppy poop?" Jerry wrapped his arm around David's shoulders and leaned in to whisper in his ear. "Remember how I told you I applied for that artist-in-residence position a few months ago, and that if I got it, we'd be living in Europe for six months?" Jerry smiled as he saw the comprehension cross over David's face. "We've got a couple of months to get ourselves organized for six months in Italy!"

"Oh my God, Jerry!" David grabbed onto his forearms. "Oh my God, the boys are gonna go crazy!"

"Maybe William will even find someone to speak German with, so he can make sure he doesn't lose his German. And I, uh, made arrangements—with Kitty's help—to have Cory be my... uh... assistant during the afternoon sessions. He'll be able to experience some other art forms as well as work—"

"Wait," David said suddenly. "What am I going to be doing? I hadn't thought about that."

"Whatever you want to do, baby. That's the best part." Jerry led David over to the veranda where they both sat down. "You can be in charge of their schooling, and all of Europe will be your classroom."

"You know," David said as he narrowed his eyes, an idea clearly forming in his mind. "I should take off the entire year, and when we return, I can home school the boys." David smiled at the idea, but shook his head, as if he'd just realized what it would actually mean. "A whole year away from teaching my kids at school?"

Jerry heard the disappointment in his husband's voice. "Listen, baby, it's a great opportunity, but even if we all stay on the ranch and don't go, I'll be just as happy." Jerry leaned over and kissed David's nose. "I don't care where I am as long as the three of you are with me." Jerry kissed him again on the nose. And waited.

"Something tells me you know that I'm not going to let you turn this down."

"What can I say?" Jerry puffed out his chest and winked. "You are powerless before my charisma."

Epilogue

HE PUT the truck in park, turned the ignition off, and turned to look at Jerry. Jerry was smiling, so Cory assumed he hadn't made too many mistakes. "So?"

"Not bad, kid," Jerry said as he nodded slowly. "If you drive like that at your test next week, I think you'll be getting a driver's license."

"Really? You think so?"

"Sure do, Cory." Jerry pulled on the handle and opened the passenger side door. "Oh, and by the way, if you do get your license, you'll be happy to know that this truck will become yours. That is, after we get back from Europe. Even if you get your license, you won't be doing any driving in Europe. Too dangerous."

Cory saw Jerry wink and bring his hand to his hat; Cory had come to recognize this as Jerry's way of making promises. *My very own truck*, Cory thought as his hand came out to caress the dashboard. "I'm going to Europe," Cory said to himself. It was only for six months, and when they returned, David would be home schooling him and William until the following September.

Cory had thought about it long and hard, and he wanted to go with them. When he'd first heard about Jerry's new job in Italy, Cory wondered what would happen to him, and to him and Tara. He still woke up some mornings and couldn't believe that she really liked him, even after he'd told her about his father; of course, she'd heard the rumors at school, but it hadn't mattered to her. He'd told Jerry as they were working in the studio one day about his feelings and how he feared that Tara would reject him because his father was a criminal. But

Jerry had told him to take the chance, to take the risk. He did, and two months later, he still felt like he was floating some days. What made it all even better was that Tara thought *she* was the lucky one.

He'd be off in Italy for six months with David teaching him and William in the morning, and then he'd be with Jerry all afternoon, working as an assistant. He wasn't sure how he could assist a real artist like Jerry, but he couldn't wait to learn more about art. Jerry even promised to help teach him about painting and sculpture. Cory would be living in a villa, learning some Italian, and spending weekends traveling to some of the oldest cities in Europe. After Jerry and David had made the announcement, Cory had used his new laptop, the one they'd bought just for him, to go on the Internet. He'd been amazed at all of the architecture and paintings and culture he would be seeing.

CORY closed the book he and William had made after checking through it one last time. His aunt had thrown away the first one that they'd made. He felt the familiar sting of bile in his throat; she'd done it when he was at that awful military academy. He'd come home to find the ashes in the fireplace. She'd also taken some of his other projects and burned them as well. He'd told himself over and over again of the plan he'd made with Sara, Jerry, and David. He'd stay for two weeks at the most and then run away. There was no way his aunt or his father would be able to make him come back. Sara had confirmed that. But then his aunt had gone and said all those things about Jerry and David, and Cory knew he had to leave before the two weeks were up. If he hadn't, he was sure he probably would have done something really bad.

But here, with Jerry and David and William, Cory was happy. It wasn't the same thing as his own family, and he still missed his mother, but it was the next best thing. Jerry and David weren't at all what he'd thought gay guys would be like. He wasn't sure what he'd really expected, but it wasn't two men who rode horses and baled hay and dug fence post holes. And Cory would never admit it in front of anyone other than Tara, but he really liked it when they teased each other and hugged and sat watching movies with their arms around each other. It reminded him of his parents before his mom had died.

He'd talked to Sara a couple of times in the past few months, and she'd really helped him to understand what was happening to him and his father. He knew that he didn't have to see his father if he didn't want, and it helped to know that he actually had a say in what happened to him. Cory didn't know if his father would ever forgive him, but there would be plenty of time to see if there was any chance of a reconciliation. Cory was just beginning to realize that anything was possible now. Thanks to William, Cory was remembering what it felt like to be part of a family.

Cory grabbed the book, placed it in the gift box, and headed down the hall. "Hey, Billiam, you ready?"

"Do you think they figured it out yet?" William shut down his computer with a few clicks of the mouse and ran to join Cory.

"I doubt it," Cory said with a sly smile. "You're too good at keeping secrets."

"It was hard," William said with a heavy sigh, as if keeping the secret had winded him.

"You did good, buddy." Cory held up his fist as they approached the stairs and William bumped it with his own. "I can't wait to see the looks on their faces."

"Me too!"

"Hey, I was just going to come up and get you for dinner." David removed the oven mitts and tossed them on the counter. "Can one of you go to the office and get Jerry, please?"

"Sure." Cory placed the box on the counter beside the microwave and headed to get Jerry for dinner. He knocked on the door and announced dinner. Jerry, who was on the phone again, waved and started saying his goodbyes, holding up two fingers. Since he'd agreed to take the position in Italy, Cory noticed that it required Jerry and David spending a lot of time making arrangements.

"What's this?" Jerry came into the kitchen and saw the box on the counter. Cory saw him look at William, who looked like he was ready to explode if he had to keep the secret one moment longer.

"Go ahead," Cory said as he tapped William on the shoulder.

"It's for you and David," William announced proudly. "Cory and I made it for you. Happy Father's Day!"

"Happy Father's Day," Cory echoed as Jerry handed the box to David. Cory watched as David and Jerry exchanged looks, both of them seeming at a loss for words.

"You didn't have to get us anything," David said finally as he lifted the top off the box.

"We started working on it a couple of months ago," William announced as he left his chair and stood beside David.

Cory held his breath as he watched David take the book out of the box. He heard the sharp intake of breath as David saw the cover and the title.

"*The Adventures of Cowboy and Mountain Lion*," David said as he brushed his hand over the colorful cover. "Cory, William, this is amazing." David opened the book. "I don't know what to say."

"How long did it take you to do this?" Jerry asked as he took the book in his hands. Cory's smile grew as he listened to the awe and appreciation that was evident in both Jerry's and David's voices.

"We worked on it *forever*," William said, his eyes rolling in his head. "And we had to do it all over again when—"

Cory reached out and put his hand on William's shoulder. "It was a lot of fun doing it. William made up the story, and I did the drawings to go along with it."

"You did this twice?" Jerry asked, handing the book back to David.

"It's nothing," Cory said trying to avoid mentioning his aunt; he really didn't want to spoil this moment. "William was so excited to do something like this, just for the two of you. And I can't think of two people who deserve it more."

"I'm just speechless," David said, pulling William into a tight hug. "You two…." Cory watched as David kissed the top of William's head and then stood, moving toward him. He stood and hugged David, feeling a little embarrassed at the tight hug and the way David stroked the back of his head, but was amazed at how quickly that feeling vanished.

"I'm glad you like it," Cory said when David released him.

"Like it?" Jerry came over and put an arm around Cory's shoulder, giving a quick squeeze. It hadn't taken Cory long to figure out that David was the hugger in the family, while it took Jerry a little longer to show that kind of affection. It was another personality trait he shared with Jerry. "We love it. It was incredibly thoughtful."

"Billie helped too!" William was standing beside Jerry and holding up the puppy, who wasn't really a puppy anymore; she'd grown quite a few inches in the last couple of months and had also developed a fondness for Cory's running shoes.

"And what did you do, you beautiful girl?" David kneeled down beside William and began scratching behind Billie's ears, her favorite spot.

"She gave us the idea for chapter three," William answered as he handed the dog to David.

"We're going to read it tonight, for sure, to find out what's in that chapter," David stated as he stood. Cory saw Jerry make his way toward William and pick him up effortlessly.

"And we thank you and Cory and Billie. All of you are very special to us." Jerry said. Cory chuckled as he saw Jerry form his hand into a claw and place it on William's head. "But I hope you didn't write about the claw. You know how upset he'll be."

"That's chapter two." William giggled as the claw came down on his head. "We *had* to write about the claw, Dad."

216

"It's actually a really funny part of the story," Cory commented as he pretended to wrestle the claw off William's head. "I think he secretly likes the claw," he said to Jerry as William was returned to the ground. "Even he couldn't stop giggling when we were working on that chapter."

David had moved back to sit in front of the book and, Cory observed, was studying the title page. Cory watched him shake his head in disbelief as he opened it. "To David and Jerry," he said as he began to read, "the best fathers, whose story has been an inspiration to us. Love, William and Cory."

Cory leaned back in his chair and smiled. He was pretty certain that whatever he did with his art during his lifetime, no moment would ever equal this feeling, and—regardless of where he ended up—these three people sitting at the kitchen table with him would always be part of his family.

WILLIAM finished loading the dishwasher with Cory and then scooped Billie up and headed into the living room to see where David and Jerry had gotten in the book. He still couldn't believe how much they'd liked it. They must have hugged and kissed him and Cory a hundred times today; they liked their present that much. He perched himself on the arm of the sectional and waited for his dad to look up. *I'll have two official dads, soon,* he reminded himself. David was waiting for the official papers that meant William belonged to both of them now. When he'd arrived here last year, William didn't know where he would be living or if anyone would want him. But only a year later, both Jerry and David wanted him. And Cory wanted him. And they all wanted Cory.

That was the best part. William had gone from being alone at a boarding school in Switzerland to having two dads and a brother on a ranch in Canada. He still missed some things, though, and still felt sad sometimes that he would never get to see Frau Zimmerman again, but he would do what Cory told him and close his eyes and picture her big smile and her warm hands. It's one of the reasons that he thought Cory's idea of naming the dog Wilhelmina was so great. It was like part of her was still with him, that part that made him happy and made his tummy feel like it did when he would go on the roller coaster.

He knew that nothing stayed the same forever, but having Wilhelmina helped him never to forget that—before he found a home with Jerry, David, and Cory—he'd had someone else who thought he was special and loved him very much. Now, he could give that love back to her. He knew that Billie was a dog and that Frau Zimmerman had been a person and that they weren't the same, but thinking of it all this way made sense to him. It was like the time David was trying to explain fractions, and William just didn't get it. Finally, he told David how he did all the work with fractions, and it turned out that his way was just as good as David's.

Frau Zimmerman was gone and William knew he would never see her again, but having Billie helped him to focus on something other than losing her. At least that's the way David had explained it to him. He hadn't wanted to get the puppy at first. Why would anyone? He'd watched that show with his dads that showed the poor seal being killed because he had something weird growing in his mouth. And before that, Cory had had to go away, and William knew he would miss him so much. And then Frau Zimmerman had died; Opa Niels had tried to explain to him about how people needed to die and go somewhere else so that they could be with loved ones and be there to welcome the rest of us when it was our turn to die. It all helped, but William still remembered being sad, remembered feeling like nothing would be fun ever again.

But then Cory came back and wanted to stay. And it had been a lot of fun, the last couple of months. Cory had learned how to drive, had been taking some lessons on how to paint from Dad, and even tried to help David cook in the kitchen. Dad had teased Cory one day that he should stick to painting; David had been upset at that and told everyone that Cory would get better, but that he needed encouragement. Dad apologized right away. And now, Cory was getting just as good as David at making mac and cheese.

The only thing William didn't understand was Tara. Why would Cory want to spend so much time with her and not him? Tara didn't like practicing driving since she already had her license, didn't like to go swimming in the lake, didn't really like camping, and she sure wasn't as good a rider as Cory had become over the past several months. No, William just didn't get it.

Dad had told him one day that he would get it soon enough and that he would want to spend a lot of time with girls, but William had just shaken his head. *No*, he'd announced proudly, *girls are icky; I'm going to marry someone like David. He likes to have fun, he knows how to ride and he likes dogs, and he never complains about getting dirty or about how terrible his nails look after mucking stalls.* They'd all laughed, but William knew he was right. He'd find someone like David and live happily ever after.

William heard the doorbell and saw David get up off the sectional, so he plopped down beside his dad, Billie still in his arms.

"Cory was right, partner, this is very funny," Jerry said as he put his arm around his son. "I think you should consider being a writer."

"Nah, veterinarian," William announced and squirmed as Billie tried to lick his face. The phone rang once and then William heard Cory calling for Jerry.

"You can be both, chief. How about that?" Jerry put the book on the coffee table and ran to his study. William shrugged as he watched one of his dads leave and the other return.

"Good news, William!" David said as he came back into the living room and held out a small pile of papers. "That was the vet and all of the papers have been verified and it looks like Billie will be able to come with us to Italy." He watched David put the papers back in the big brown envelope. "We'll have to make sure we keep her safe, though, and watch out that she doesn't run away or get hurt."

As he watched David go to the kitchen to finish preparing dinner, William held Billie out at eye level and then pulled her back to nuzzle the soft fur at her neck, giggling when she yipped and started to lick his cheek. "Did you hear that, Wilhelmina?" He only called her that when no one else was around. "You get to come with us." He held her out in front of him and looked into her light blue eyes. "And I promise to take very good care of you. You're part of my family now, and that's what family is supposed to do."

Read the beginning of the story in

http://www.dreamspinnerpress.com

When D.W. MARCHWELL is not teaching future generations the wonders of science, he can usually be found hiking, writing, riding horses, trying new recipes, or searching for and lovingly restoring discarded antique furniture. A goofy and incurable romantic, D.W. admits that his stories are inspired by actual events and that he has a soft spot for those where boy not only meets boy but also turns out to be boy's soul mate. After almost fifteen years of working his way across Canada, D.W. has finally found the perfect place to live at the foot of the Canadian Rockies. He still can't believe how lucky he is, and, as his grandmother taught him, counts his blessings every day.

Visit his web site at http://www.marchwellbooks.ca/.

LaVergne, TN USA
20 December 2010
209464LV00004B/61/P